NEW WAVES

KEVIN NGUYEN

WHEELER PUBLISHING
A part of Gale, a Cengage Company

LIBRARY OF CONGRESS CIP DATA ON FILE.
CATALOGUING IN PUBLICATION FOR THIS BOOK
IS AVAILABLE FROM THE LIBRARY OF CONGRESS.

ISBN-13: 978-1-4328-8390-4 (hardcover alk. paper)

Published in 2020 by arrangement with Ballantine Books, an imprint of Random House, a division of Penguin Random House LLC.

Printed in Mexico
Print Number: 01   Print Year: 2020

For Andrew

For Andrew

"It is dangerous to go alone.
Take this!"
— THE LEGEND OF ZELDA

I
NEW YORK 2009

I never considered it stealing. If it was stealing, it would *feel* like stealing — illicit, dangerous, maybe even a little bit thrilling. Instead, it felt like exactly what it was: sitting in a dark room, watching a loading bar creep across a computer screen.

Thieves were supposed to have the grace of a pickpocket, or the patience to plan a real heist. We'd just gotten a little drunk at McManus's, the bar around the corner, and decided that this would be the best way to get back at our employer. Well, Margo had decided. And technically, she didn't work at Nimbus anymore.

She had texted me from the bar earlier in the afternoon to tell me she'd quit. Margo had needed someone to drink with, and I always obliged. I snuck out of the office when no one was looking, though really, no one was ever looking for me. When I arrived at the bar, she was already three beers deep

— the bottles lined up neatly in front of her, their labels meticulously peeled off, not a trace of paper or glue. She didn't say anything, just signaled to the bartender for two more.

I sat down next to Margo and her whole body clenched. I'd known her for a while and she was often angry, but it was the good kind: usually a vivid, infectious sort of fury — smart, spirited, just the right amount of snarky — aimed at institutions, structures, oppressors. She was unintimidated by people in power. In fact, she was energized by them, since they were targets worthy of her wrath. That is, unless she'd had too much to drink, in which case her marks were more haphazard. Two more beers and she admitted that she hadn't exactly quit.

"Are you kidding me?" I said. "You're the only remotely competent engineer at the company!"

"According to HR, I wasn't a good 'culture fit.' I wasn't 'getting along with the rest of the team.' " Margo began picking at the label on her fresh beer. "But that's bullshit. I know what that means."

Even from my desk on the other side of the office, I could hear Margo arguing with her colleagues. She didn't believe in collaboration if it meant compromising the

10

best idea. She was a brilliant programmer, and still no one wanted to listen to her.

Margo went on: "uncooperative," "opinionated," "not a team player." It was laughable how their reasons were couched in the tired clichés of a high school football coach. To her, and I guess to me, it underscored the kind of laziness that had been bred by capitalism — an attitude that claimed to respect competition above all, but was completely conflict averse.

"Did they at least offer you severance?"

"I quit before they could fire me," she said. "I told them, politely, to fuck off."

I was curious how polite Margo was capable of being in such a situation.

"I don't want their fucking money anyway. I've got plenty to live on. I'm a talented engineer and I can work wherever I want. Maybe I'll just take a year off, get away from all this."

She often talked about money this brazenly. It bothered me, since she knew I always had less than her. But at least Margo usually paid for drinks. I would motion toward my wallet as a courtesy and she would shrug it off, usually saying something like "I got this" or "Don't you fucking dare." Once, just once, when she was really toasted, she joked that I would be allowed to pay for beers the day she didn't make twice as much as me. (It was closer to five times, but I didn't correct her.)

Today, she wasn't paying. Today, she only wanted retribution. Margo had been stewing on ways to get back at Nimbus during her first three drinks. She already had a plan.

"What is any company's most valuable asset?" she asked.

"Its . . . money?"

"No, Lucas, what's more valuable than money?"

This sounded like a trick question.

"Code?"

"No, its information," Margo said. "And that's what we're going to take."

"Isn't that stealing?"

Margo pointed her beer at me. "What about copying it?"

This was her proposal: Nimbus was a messaging service with millions of users. We would take their user database. Margo could easily access, duplicate, and download it. The whole thing would only take a few minutes. We would just take emails. No passwords, no personal information.

"Why would anyone want a list of email addresses?"

"Millions of email addresses," Margo

clarified. "Any company would kill for a list of people using a competitor's product."

"Why?"

"For marketing, or whatever." Margo gestured at nothing in particular, like she'd just performed the world's saddest magic trick. She casually mentioned that she knew someone who worked at Phantom, Nimbus's biggest competitor. It was their CEO. Maybe they'd be interested in it.

"It's a bad idea," I said. "It's immoral. It's wrong."

"In what way is this immoral or wrong?"

"Because we're taking something that doesn't belong to us."

"Lucas, listen to me." Margo looked me straight in the eye. "Nothing belongs to us."

It was the way she said "us." Did she mean as employees of Nimbus? As suckers in a world that advantaged the wealthy? As two people who weren't white in America? Just me and her?

It didn't matter. The truth was that Margo had already decided, and I was three beers behind and playing catchup. But I had logistical questions, ones that she had anticipated and spent those three beers considering.

There would be some very light encryption on the user data, but every engineer

13

had access to it. This was a common problem at startups. When you start with a small team of engineers, none of them are dedicated to security. The goal is to build something as quickly as possible, so nobody gets hired to protect user privacy. Even as a startup grows large and stable enough to support a security team, it's already been deprioritized from the start.

I was still skeptical. "And there's no way for them to trace it back to us?"

"There might be a log of it. But if they pursue us, they would be admitting that there was a breach."

Margo had a mind for systems. And to her, every system was vulnerable if you understood the incentives of the people who built it. She could disassemble and reassemble anything, including the hubris of men. A security breach would be a publicity nightmare for Nimbus, and for the people who ran the company. Margo knew she could exploit their greatest fear: embarrassment.

It was strange that a company's reputation for security was more important than its actual security. But having worked at Nimbus for the past year — my first job in any kind of real workplace, much less a tech company — it didn't surprise me. No person should ever trust that their personal information is going to be protected by a company. The place was managed by a mixture of twentysomethings with little work experience and a handful of computer-illiterate adults brought in to babysit them.

The office space was generic, but it had been dolled up with brightly colored furniture and some tacky movie posters, all for the sake of reinforcing the "fun" work environment. The kitchen had free snacks and a beer tap. Action figures and Nerf guns were scattered across people's desks. There was a conference room dedicated to video games. Apparently investors loved these things. They'd tour the office every few months and take stock of the ways Nimbus physically embodied the tired notion that everyone could work hard and play hard, even if that meant the office looked like an eight-year-old's playroom.

All of the tasteless interior decorating choices were, at least, harmless and easy to ignore. But the office centered on the foosball table. People would play in the middle of the workday, and the sounds carried throughout the floor — four sweaty men grunting and hollering. Margo joked that, from a distance, foosball looked like four men jerking off into a box. No one ever asked Margo and me to play foosball. Not that we would've said yes.

"We'll find new jobs somewhere better," Margo said. "Somewhere less fucked."

"What tech company is less fucked?"

"I don't know. Maybe I just . . . move to Tokyo. Start over on the other side of the world."

"Why Tokyo? You don't even like leaving New York City . . ."

"Lucas, the point is that we should do something different," she said, "that we *can* do something different."

I didn't actively hate our workplace the way Margo did. It was a job, after all. But in a place where I had no love for my coworkers and no love for the office, Margo's vigor was contagious.

"Nobody at Nimbus cares about you," she said. "Except me."

Because I didn't know a lick about code, in this world I was worth nothing to places like Nimbus. I had moved to New York after barely finishing community college. I'd struggled for months to find a full-time job, and technically I never even found one. My position was in customer service. I was paid minimum wage to answer an unending onslaught of support emails, limited to thirty-five hours a week so the company

16

wouldn't have to offer me any benefits. I could barely afford rent.

And then, to my surprise, Margo said, "I'll only do this if you do this with me."

I thought she'd already made up her mind. But she needed me. I felt a swell of deep satisfaction rising from my gut as I imagined walking out of Nimbus for the last time. I'd thought that getting away from my old life and moving to New York would mean something, feel like anything. But the free snacks, the foosball table, the promise of working toward a greater good — these were all decorative things to disguise the fact that I could've been back at home, being paid the same, if not more. The office happy hours and the posture that this wasn't a workplace, but a family — just ways the company could trick me into thinking I was valuable, instead of actually treating me like a person with any worth. I'd known these things to be true, but when Margo laid it out like this, she was undeniably convincing.

"Okay, let's do it," I said. "Fuck Nimbus."

"Fuck every single person that's disrespected us. Like, fuck every man that did not take my opinion seriously because I'm a woman. And especially fuck every white dude who has tried to talk to me about hip-hop."

"Fuck everyone that assumed I was an engineer because I'm Asian. But really, fuck all the Asian engineers who treated me like I was worth less than garbage because I'm *not* an engineer, like that's all we're supposed to be."

Margo had more. "Fuck every person who came to me to ask if something was racist, as if my job was to be the racism barometer."

("Plus, I'm sure it usually was racist.")

("Oh, I mean, of course.")

"Fuck every person that told me I was being 'aggressive' and 'hostile' just because I was a black person expressing an opinion."

"Fuck every time I was ignored in a meeting, and then later told that I should 'speak up' and 'be more assertive.' Fuck their condescending tone every time they talk to me. Fuck their even more condescending, passive-aggressive emails."

"Oh, and fuck that racist-as-hell office manager who is always asking me to organize diversity events, like I don't already have shit to do."

("Isn't she, like, Puerto Rican?")

("Dominican, I think. But she still sucks.")

I laughed. "But truly, fuck every single

18

person that works there."

Margo clinked her beer bottle against mine and it was a done deal. We would have to go back to the office late at night when we were sure no one else would be there. So we sat at the bar killing time for another six hours, adding to the collection of unlabeled bottles in front of us, shouting out more people that could go fuck themselves.

By most accounts, Margo was accomplished. She'd been raised by a single mother in a poor but stable household. She'd never gotten in any sort of trouble, had done well in school, and went to college on an almost-full scholarship. After graduation, she landed a good job with a great salary as a server engineer. Everything she was supposed to do, she did, and then some. But it didn't matter how successful she was, even though she had carved out a space for herself in a field with virtually zero people that looked like her. Existentially, she would always feel like an outsider.

"How do you solve for that?" she asked later that night, the alcohol slowing her words.

I'd heard this rant many times before, especially when Margo was a certain kind of drunk — a dark and ponderous sort that led to slurry soliloquies.

19

"You know, Lucas, being black in America means constantly being aware of who you are," she said, as if she'd never told me this before. She went on: "People remind you all the time that you're black. And if they don't, you'd best remind yourself."

Her mind couldn't escape this conversation when she was drunk, and neither could I.

"Being black means you are merely a body — a fragile body," she said. "To be black is the most terrestrial form of being, the lowest level of Earthling in the eyes of other people."

It was almost funny how many times I'd heard her repeat this exact phrase, talking about the black experience as if she were an alien. Margo always did love her science fiction.

I knew the best thing to do was to let her keep going. But tonight, perhaps also under the influence, I pushed back.

"At least you're American," I said. Maybe it was a weak attempt to get her to change direction. Maybe I just wanted her to see me as equal. "You see black people on TV, in music, in politics, in some form every day. Asians are foreign, alien, otherworldly. We might as well be invisible."

Her reaction to this surprised me. She

could talk circles around me — she knew this. But Margo listened — and, in fact, envied.

"Imagine that: the ability to disappear," she said. "I'd give anything for a day where I don't have to be reminded of who I am." Margo grabbed my shoulders, shook me a little. "If there was a machine that could do it, I'd change places with you right now, Lucas."

As we paid the tab and got ready to leave, I knew what was coming next.

"I would be an Asian man and I would move through the world unnoticed and nobody would bother me."

True friendship was drunken body-swapping.

People talk about algorithms like they're magic. It's easy to see why. They govern how the internet is shown to us, conjured from spells. Their methods are opaque, and yet we put our trust in them. Algorithms to answer search queries; algorithms to tell us what to buy; algorithms to show us what news matters. Even when the behavior of a service can't be explained — an errant search result, a miscalculated recommendation — we blame the algorithm. We like to point the finger at computers because they are incapable of feeling shame.

But an algorithm is not that complicated. It's just a set of rules, a series of yes-or-no questions that a computer asks — really simple logic that could be represented by a very long flow chart. What's impressive about an algorithm isn't its intelligence, but its speed. A search query will go through thousands — hell, maybe tens of thousands — of questions in a matter of seconds. Because what do we value more: a thing done quickly, or a thing done well?

At the end of the day, though, we never ask about the person who wrote the algorithm. We never ask who they are, or what perspective they bring to it, because we want to believe technology is neutral. No biases or fallibility should be allowed to infiltrate it, even if the authors themselves are biased and fallible (and they always are). An algorithm is just a set of rules that works in a system. A system that works quickly and without prejudice. Thousands of processes in a matter of seconds because it has to work fast. No room for bias there. Not enough time for it.

Margo had often explained that a sloppy algorithm could easily fall into a pattern of reinforcing small mistakes. A system eating itself. Bad decisions at scale.

But when the stakes don't feel real, no bad decision feels that consequential at the time. In fact, it might even feel fun, like a high school prank. This certainly did.

When we finally arrived at the office, I insisted we keep the lights off, even though Margo pointed out that we would look more suspicious if someone came in and discovered us literally under the cover of darkness. I nodded in agreement, then ripped a drunken burp. Margo started cackling and soon we were snickering so much we forgot to turn on the lights, even though we'd just agreed we should. I bumped into just about every chair and table during the short journey to Margo's desk, each bit of fumbling progress punctuated by the sounds of trying to hold in our laughter.

Since I was a contract worker, I was supposed to be scarce after seven hours of work. I'd never seen the office at night. In the dark, the dimensions seemed different — deeper, even. During the workday it was polluted with fluorescent light and the clamor of people talking over one another. Now it was silent, save for the hypnotic drone of high-powered desktop computers that hummed even while they slept. I should have been nervous, but no one was around, and I felt bolder than I ever had before in this place. It would be so easy.

Margo guided us to her desk. Her personal effects were gone, but thankfully no one had removed her computer yet. She booted it up.

It only took her a few minutes to write a script that would duplicate the company's entire user database, but much longer for it to finish copying to a flash drive. And so we waited, staring at the monitor. Margo kept checking her phone and I kept my eye on the entrance.

"So this is what you do all day, huh?" I said, gesturing to her phone, where she had Facebook open.

"Coding is a lot of waiting around," she said. "And long stretches of contemplation."

"Is that true?"

"No, it's just a lot of busywork. This is why I am better suited to a life of crime."

"I'm starting to see why you got fired."

Minutes stretched into tens of minutes, then nearly an hour. Suddenly it had been nearly two hours, and we were starting to get a little sick of each other.

"Never have I ever . . . downloaded the email database from the place where I work," I said.

"That's not how this game works."

"Fine. Never have I ever . . . stolen anything."

"I told you, it's not stealing."

"I didn't say this was. I'm just saying I've never stolen anything."

Margo lowered a finger, signaling as part of the game of Never Have I Ever that she had stolen something before.

"What did you steal?"

"In college, the virginity of at least two white boys."

Margo laughed. I don't know if I understood the joke, but I laughed alongside her, realizing that my voice was starting to sound more anxious. My confidence was beginning to fade as my drunk did. I'd thought the process would be faster, that we would be in and out in a matter of minutes. Margo was strangely cool about the whole endeavor. She told me to calm down and went back to reading something on her phone.

"Apparently 'grand larceny' is stealing anything worth over a thousand dollars," she said.

"How much do you think this user data is worth?" I asked.

Margo laughed and made an exaggerated shrug. This did not make me feel better.

"Do you even know who you are going to sell this to?"

"Sell it? We're not gonna sell it."

"Then what are we going to do with this information?"

"It's, like, insurance. Against Nimbus. So they can't fuck with me."

I began to panic. "Margo, by doing this you're begging them to fuck with you."

"I'd like to think I'm daring them."

"You haven't thought through any of this —"

"Just trust me," Margo said. She grabbed my hand and squeezed it tightly. Her fingers were soft, cold, but slowly warmed as they became entangled in mine. Margo and I were as close as friends could be, but never would we have held hands like this. The feeling was comforting and intimate and I didn't understand what it meant — if anything — and we just remained silent, not verbally acknowledging that we were touching. All I knew was that I didn't want to let go.

There was no way to know then that, in a matter of months, Margo would be dead — struck by a car, meaninglessly — and I would carry both the weight of her loss and of what we had taken. And later, I'd fully realize it didn't matter that the act itself felt trivial: it was stealing, plain and simple.

In the year to come, I'd be lost without

Margo. And when I had no idea what to do with myself, I'd think about the night we made off with Nimbus's data: the two of us sitting in silence, hand in hand, our eyes locked on the loading bar, waiting for something we couldn't fully reckon with, watching it crawl slowly to the finish.

THE_LAST_ONES.WAV

The world ends and there are only two survivors: a man and a woman. They escape on a spaceship that exits the Earth's atmosphere just moments before the planet explodes. As the rocket hurtles through space, the man looks back and sees his home crumbling. Fire consumes the globe until there's nothing left to devour, and the planet disintegrates into an infinite number of little pieces, shooting out in all directions toward the unknown reaches of the universe. The man weeps for the billions lost. The woman is looking forward, her eyes taking in the vastness of space.

At faster-than-light speed, the ship hurtles through the galaxy. Days go by, even though the concept of a day is long gone. The woman prays that they land on a habitable planet. The man continues to cry.

Finally, the craft gets caught in a new planet's orbit. It slings them around in a violent loop. The ship's navigation is fucked by the new trajectory, and the vessel plummets toward the planet. As the ship spins out of control, the passengers are sure that this is their end. But miraculously, they hit water. The engines are destroyed by the impact, but the man and woman are safe.

The ship has landed in a ceaseless ocean. There is no land in sight. With no propulsion system left, they float aimlessly, guided only by the mercy of this strange sea.

A second miracle: after six days, the ship eventually beaches safely. The man insists on getting out first. He looks around. The island is tropical. Beyond the beach is a deep, intimidating jungle.

The man takes charge. First, they need to secure food and shelter if they're going to build their life together. Second, they —

Life together? This is news to the woman.

It is their duty, he says, to have a family, to continue the existence of the human race. They have a responsibility. Father and mother to a new generation.

The woman laughs. Duty? Responsibility? This is what people believed on the old planet. This, here, is a new planet. This is an opportunity, not a do-over.

The man doesn't understand. And the woman leaves the man behind. She sets off toward the jungle to live her own damn life.

II
M4v15B34c0n

Q: What will happen to my account if I pass away?

A: You can tell us in advance whether you'd like to have your account memorialized or permanently deleted from Facebook.

Memorialized or deleted. The only two states for a dead person's Facebook account. A single click to decide whether someone would be remembered or forgotten.

"Memorialization" was a bizarre concept. Aside from updating the user's profile picture, no other changes could be made to the deceased's Facebook account. Old posts and photos could not be edited or scrubbed. Private messages were locked and remained inaccessible. A memorialized Facebook account was preserved in stasis, frozen in time like a caveman in ice. Deletion was, on the other hand, a complete erasure.

So I asked myself: Would Margo rather be memorialized or deleted?

I couldn't decide, and I was stumbling around the support section of the Facebook site. Which didn't help because it was bullshit. I'd written plenty of similar Frequently Asked Questions copy for Nimbus, and had begun doing the same in the six months I'd been at Phantom. But an FAQ just looks like a website having a conversation with itself.

Q: What is a legacy contact?
A: A legacy contact is someone you choose to look after your account if it's memorialized.

I imagined the hundreds of hours of meetings that the copywriters at Facebook must've spent coming up with the term "legacy contact." I had to admire the cleverness of the title, even if it did seem manipulative. They might provide the option for account deletion, but it was never in Facebook's interest to delete anything. The company wanted to be a part of your life, even after you had left it. A dead person's account helped expand the empire.

31

Q: What can a legacy contact do?

A: Once your account is memorialized, your legacy contact will have the option to do things like respond to new friend requests (ex: old friends or family members who weren't yet on Facebook).

In the cemetery of the internet, the legacy contact was the groundskeeper.

Q: How do I request the removal of a deceased family member's account?

A: We're very sorry for your loss.

A strange touch of humanity on a largely functional page of technical documentation. It was the only answer that didn't immediately address the question. But I wondered: Who is the "we" in this case? The collective global corporate entity, Facebook? The answer continued:

> To help us remove your loved one's account from Facebook, we'll need you to provide documentation to confirm you're an immediate family member or executor of the account holder.

The only way a non–family member could be a legacy contact was to have been as-

32

signed before the person had died. Margo had not assigned a legacy contact before she died because, at age twenty-five, few people do.

The fastest way for us to process your request is for you to provide a scan or photo of your loved one's death certificate.

I didn't have Margo's death certificate, so I'd have to find another way.

I only had one white shirt — my only dress shirt. I'd bought it, along with a blazer, shortly after I moved to New York. It wasn't expensive but it was certainly out of my budget. It was my interview outfit; I thought I'd have more job interviews than I did. The only time I had worn it was when I went into the Nimbus office for the first time. I was told I was overdressed, but they liked the effort I was putting in. For a customer service job, you could never try too hard.

I realized the night before Margo's funeral that the light-brown sweat stains around the armpits and the collar hadn't come out in the wash. I brought the shirt to the laundry, sat in front of it for two hours and $1.75 worth of quarters while it washed and dried, but the stain persisted. Frustrated, I searched the internet with the phrase "how to remove collar stain" and stayed up late, mixing a careful concoction of hydrogen peroxide, baking soda, and dish soap. I scrubbed at the stains with a toothbrush. First the armpits, then the collar. If I brushed vigorously enough, I could make the shirt look new.

The funeral was at a cemetery in Crown Heights I'd never noticed before, the ceremony an hour in direct sunlight. I could feel myself sweating through my shirt all over again. New York usually smelled like lukewarm garbage, but the cemetery was fresh. It was quiet, too. A haven of manicured greenspace sectioned off for the dead. The service was sad and short. The casket remained closed.

I had expected to see Margo's mother cry. But that never happened. Somehow, she looked strong and stable. I admired it. If she could keep it together, I could handle myself too. When the service was over, I found my way to her. I'd been sitting in the back, in an attempt to remain inconspicuous. I navigated between a sea of black dresses and suits and an array of white folding chairs to get to the front, where Margo's mother was tending to an orderly swarm of people offering their condolences. I got in line, waited my turn. When my moment came, she identified me before I could introduce myself.

"You must be Lucas." She told me to call her Louise.

"I stick out a bit here, don't I?" I said. The funeral was mostly family, from what I gathered, and that made me one of the few people who wasn't black. A couple of co-workers showed up, though our interactions were limited to acknowledging each other with a nod. My boss, Brandon, was there, though it felt like he was trying to go un-noticed. At one point I looked over at him, and he pretended that we'd never made eye contact.

I asked Louise who were relatives and who were friends. She confirmed it was mostly family, plus a few neighborhood kids.

"Margo never needed many friends," Louise said. "She preferred talking to computers than to people."

"Maybe she was talking to other people on the computer," I said.

Louise didn't respond to that. Instead, she linked arms with me and we slowly strolled across the wet grass, mostly in silence.

"Come by the house sometime," she said. "I have a favor to ask you."

I was reluctant, but you don't turn down

an invitation from someone who just lost their daughter. I told her I'd be more than happy to.

It felt strange to take the subway home. Couldn't I, just for once, be entitled to a quiet, clean space, alone? On the platform, in the distance, I could hear the horrible screech of grinding metal. A century of black grime had crusted over the subway tracks. I watched a rat of mutant proportions casually wander the space between the rails like he owned the damn place. In a way, I guess he did.

I saw other people from the funeral, family members or people from a life Margo had never shared with me. Occasionally I would make eye contact with someone to share a moment of recognition — of sorrow, of grief, but mostly of having just come from the same place.

A week later, as promised, I arrived at Margo's house. She'd lived in the same three-bedroom apartment in Crown Heights her entire life, but not once invited me over. It always struck me as odd that we'd eat and drink in her neighborhood and she never showed me her home, even when I'd asked. Margo would explain it away with "the house is messy" or "my mom is crazy."

Neither turned out to be true. Her home was inside a gorgeous brownstone, the sort of building that becomes more beautiful the more lived-in it feels. Louise kept a tidy home, but everything looked as if it had been there for centuries, unmoved, permanent in its placement. Dust covered the glass of the cabinet containing fancy china, which clearly hadn't been used in years. The leather couch, situated in front of an ancient TV set, had deep, deep creases — imprints from decades of asses.

Louise was warm and, this time, very talkative. The conversation was a bit one-sided, but I didn't mind. She had stories of living in Haiti, growing up under dictators, eventually fleeing and seeking political asylum. Louise talked until my tea went cold, at which point she asked if I wanted more. So I finally asked the obvious question.

"Why did you want me to come over?"

Louise set a kettle on the stove, then guided me to Margo's room.

Walking down the dim hallway, I remembered a guest couple that had stayed at my parents' bed-and-breakfast a few years back who had also lost a child, their son, at a young age. They got very drunk at dinner, and the only way I could keep them speaking at a volume that wouldn't disturb the other guests was to talk to them. The couple said they traveled frequently now, just to get away. It was hard to be at home. They had left their son's room untouched for years, but they would occasionally step into it to remind themselves of him.

Margo's mom would have no such thing.

"I dearly miss my daughter, but I don't want a tomb in my home," she said as we approached the open door.

Margo's room looked like the bedroom of a teenager. Maybe this was why I'd never been invited over. We only ever met at work and at bars — neutral spaces, never private ones. She'd been keeping me away from something. But what?

She slept on a twin bed and the walls were plastered with band posters — remnants from high school. There was very little space to navigate because the floor was covered with piles of old science fiction novels. The stacks were imposing, especially stuffed in a room as small as this one. Margo would buy these paperbacks by the dozen at second-hand bookstores, less interested in what the text contained than in the aesthetics of the cover — always a painted starship rocketing past a Technicolor palette of planets and moons and stars. "Science fiction makes me nostalgic for the future," Margo used to say, cryptically, but here the evidence was everywhere. Her futures were informed by the past.

Louise said I could take any books I wanted. But it felt wrong to take anything. It felt wrong to even touch anything. I had the horrifying realization that Margo would never sleep in that bed again, sit at the desk, never rearrange these stacks of books. Her mother was right: it was a tomb.

"How come you never wanted Margo to move out?" I asked.

"Is that what she told you? That I kept her at home?" Louise looked incredulous. "Margo got a full ride to college on the West Coast, but she couldn't bear the thought of leaving home."

"So she never talked about, like, moving to Japan?"

"Sometimes I wondered if she was even my own daughter. I left Haiti in the '80s and never even thought about returning home. My son, who was born here before Margo, couldn't wait to get out of this house. He lives in Oakland now. But Margo — she wouldn't leave even after I insisted she find her own place." Louise laughed. It was nice to hear her laugh. "Japan? Forget it. She'd never leave the neighborhood if she didn't have to. She's like her father. He chose to stay in Haiti rather than leave with his family."

We walked back to the kitchen. She poured more hot tea into my mug, which I had almost forgotten I had been holding.

"Where is your family from, Lucas?"

"My dad's from Vietnam. Mom is Chinese, but her family has been here for a bit."

"And your father left after the war?"

"Right at the end of it. I think that makes me second generation, though I'm not sure how the definition applies to someone like me."

"Don't worry," Louise said. "It's all just a lot of . . . terminology. It means something, but it doesn't mean much."

Then came the reason she'd invited me over: "So I have to ask you a favor. Can you turn off Margo's Facebook? I check Facebook on my phone all the time but I have no idea how to make her profile . . ."

She set the kettle back on the stove.

"It would be better if my dead daughter's Facebook was not always showing up when I'm harvesting my crops and trying to not think about her."

I'd never seen the game before myself, but Margo had always complained that her mother was completely addicted to a popu-

40

lar farming game. Hours a day lost to it. When she was annoyed with her mother, Margo used to say, "You know who used to work the fields, right?"

The aroma of the tea was comforting. I took a sip. It was too hot.

"I don't know how I would do that," I said. "Could I take Margo's laptop?"

"What? Why?"

"Maybe her password is saved there."

This was true. But there were other things I was curious about, things I wouldn't be able to explain to Louise.

She thought about it for a moment. "I don't know, Lucas, that feels a little bit . . . personal." She went on: "You're an engineer, right? I am sure you can figure it out."

It just seemed easier to agree than to explain that no, I was not an engineer, and no, there would be no way for me to break into the world's largest social network. Louise kissed me on the forehead and thanked me.

"Oh, I think I left something in Margo's room," I said. "My phone." Which was a lie.

Louise gestured toward the hallway, indicating it was fine. I quickly made my way to Margo's room. Her laptop was resting on her desk. I grabbed it, tucked it uncomfortably under my jacket, and headed out the door. Louise had no clue what I'd taken.

On the train back to Queens, I thought about what I'd done and immediately regretted it. I had lingering questions about Margo, and maybe the laptop would have the answers. But it would be too weird to use the computer of your dead best friend. Looking at the same screen. Typing on the same keys. I imagined how guilty I would feel watching porn on the same laptop where she, well, also probably watched porn. At home, I struggled to decide on a place to put it and ended up leaving it tilting precariously on top of a pile of mail on my desk, hoping it would disappear by morning.

Thinking about Margo, I couldn't sleep. I still didn't understand why she had died. I'd been told she was hit by a car, late at night, after wandering out of a bar. A random, senseless death. That couldn't be it. I'd been drunk with Margo hundreds of times before. She wouldn't just stumble into the street. She wouldn't have died in such a meaningless way. She wouldn't.

There had to be more. I had no proof, but I suspected there must be a connection to Nimbus. She'd spited the company, and maybe they'd gotten back at her. It had been months since we stole their user data.

After we'd taken it, we both promised to delete the file, to never speak of it again. But I had a suspicion that Margo had not. The only way to find out was to see if it was on her computer. There must be answers there.

I was still awake when my roommate strolled in drunk at 2 a.m. and turned on his music, indicating he was coming down from a club drug (who knew which one). As the bass drops reverberated through the wall that divided us, my eyes kept catching sight of Margo's laptop across the room.

At 3 a.m., as the music still blared on, I stumbled to my desk and opened the laptop. I was anxious, unusually sweaty. I was afraid of what I needed to do, but also desperate to find an answer, something that might help explain why Margo was no longer here. I turned on the computer and waited as the loading screen bathed the room in startling, bright blue light. I had been drowsy, but now I was wide awake.

When the laptop was done booting up, I hit a log-in screen. It asked for a password, of course.

I had no idea what Margo's password was. Sleep-deprived and lacking imagination, I tried her first name. Then her last. Then them together, as if anyone — let alone

Margo — would be stupid enough to use their own name as a password.

In a moment of insane wishful thinking, I typed in my own name, as if I would be the key to unlocking every mystery of her life. Also no good.

Margo and I met at Nimbus. But it wasn't until a few months in that we discovered we had previously been in touch for years. In the early 2000s, we'd both been members of an exclusive online community dedicated to the distribution of pirated materials. Sure, that doesn't sound particularly cool, but at the time, PORK meant everything to me. You had to be invited, and even then, there was a weeklong screening process to ensure you weren't a narc.

If you got in, you discovered that PORK was nothing more than a message board. But it had a stringent set of community rules, active moderators who policed behavior, and a sense of elitism and purpose. As a teenager, I felt more welcome there than I ever had anywhere in my real life. There, you were identified solely by an unconventional username and usually an even more obtuse avatar. Your worth in the PORK community was determined by what you said and how you acted, not how you appeared to your peers. Online, I was not the chubby, acne-covered Chinese Vietnamese kid who moved through the halls unnoticed, invisible. On PORK, I had a voice.

I'd been allowed in because I was able to rip a few albums from my father's CD collection — most of them were compilations of Vietnamese ballads, a prospect so unexpected that the administrators were immediately interested. The music wasn't good, but it had a higher currency: obscurity.

You quickly learned the ropes or you were toast. It turns out all communities — whether in real life or on the internet — function mostly the same. There were rules and hierarchies. I joined as lucas_pollution, a name I thought was cool because I was fourteen. My avatar was a picture of a Japanese actor from a '60s gangster movie, chosen so I would appear culturally invested in something virtually unknown. Margo went by the name afronaut3000. At the time, that was all I knew about her. Her avatar was a photograph of some Brazilian author who was also a model. The photo was intriguing, but I knew it didn't tell me shit about who afronaut3000 was in real life.

What I did know: afronaut3000 was an intimidating and revered figure in the

PORK community. Her area of expertise was called "city pop," an era of Japanese music from the late '70s and early '80s.

I'll never forget the way she described it:

City pop is a mutant genre — funk, disco, soft jazz — driven by cultural assimilation of Western music. It was fueled by Japan's economic euphoria in the '80s, a celebration of capitalism. Everything about this era of art has detestable roots.

And yet, I can't stop listening to it. Its rhythms and tones evoke night-time cityscapes. Singers — mostly soft and soulful women — conjure the ecstasy of youth. Warm new-wave synths signal the promise of technology, basked in Technicolor. City pop embraces an optimism toward the future.

Simply put, the music is undeniable.

— AFRONAUT3000

One day, years later, at Nimbus, Margo accidentally sent me an email from her personal email instead of her work address. The from line read "afronaut3000@gmail.com," and when I immediately recognized the name, I quietly freaked out at my desk. For months, I'd been sitting mere feet away from afronaut3000. By this point, we were both nearly a decade removed from the heyday of PORK. Maybe she wouldn't remember me. But I definitely remembered her.

Margo was a server engineer, and her team rarely interacted with the customer service people. (Well, no one did, really.) But I saw her later that day in the kitchen. She was reading one of her sci-fi paperbacks and crunching on a bag of plantain chips. I had a whole plan to be cool and subtle, but instead I just blurted out, "I know you!"

"Excuse me?"

"Sorry, this is weird. But I've known you for years."

Margo put down her book and swallowed.

"From PORK." I was anxious, excited. "I know you from PORK. You're afronaut-3000."

Margo's face softened and she looked surprised, maybe even a little delighted.

"I have not thought about that in years. That is a real throwback. How did you know I was on PORK?"

I didn't really answer her question. "You were afronaut3000, right? You probably don't remember me, but I was on PORK around the same time."

"What was your name?"

"lucas_pollution," I replied sheepishly, realizing this might be the first time I'd ever said my PORK handle out loud.

"Oh my god. Of course I remember you. You helped me find so many city pop records. And you were always requesting Brazilian music." After a moment more of consideration, she said, "And uploading all those Chinese ballads."

"They were Vietnamese, but yeah."

"Those were good."

"No . . . they weren't."

Margo began to laugh. "No, they were really bad."

It was strange, to remember each other without ever having met. I had spent so many years of my life reading things Margo had written, messaging her, admiring her as one of PORK's heroes. We'd worked on projects together — she'd sent me to various libraries to find obscure recordings to rip and upload to PORK, since I'd lived nearish to a couple large universities in eastern Oregon with Japanese music in their archives. Margo had, in turn, dedicated a lot of time helping me track down rare bossa nova records, even though she wasn't a fan of it herself, the music too nostalgic for her taste.

In those days we mostly talked about music, but sometimes we'd talk about movies. Margo watched science fiction almost exclusively — and a specific, old, retrofuturistic kind. It was all consistent with her obsession with art that looked forward. I had a clear idea of who Margo was before I'd even met her, cobbled together from hundreds, maybe thousands of hours of interactions. And until that moment, I'd never known afronaut3000's face, let alone her real name.

At first, the perspective of afronaut3000 seemed incongruous with the Margo I knew in the office. On PORK, she'd embraced all art with optimism, with openness. At Nimbus, she was a cynic, the office skeptic who challenged every new idea. But over time, the two identities reconciled themselves to me. Sure, a lot of people used anonymity on the internet to be assholes. For Margo, it was the opposite: the opportunity not to be burdened by the real-life things that weighed her down.

We talked in the break room for the rest of the afternoon, not bothering to go back to our desks. She probably wouldn't get in trouble, since she had flexibility and status in the office. But I would most certainly get scolded for not answering enough customer service requests that day. I didn't care. Since I had moved to New York, this was the closest thing I'd had to finding a real friend, let alone rediscovering one.

The morning after we copied the Nimbus database, I woke up with a hangover, but was still desperate to see exactly what we had taken. Margo had made two copies of the Nimbus database: one for each of us. She'd named the file the-take.csv, and I was surprised to find that it was essentially one large spreadsheet. I suppose that's all databases are: cells of information, organized into rows and columns. So much of the world's information — from bank accounts to Social Security numbers, all the ways we define people's lives — is collected in two-dimensional grids that can be opened by the free spreadsheet software that comes with your college computer.

The file was bigger than I expected. It took a minute to load and, as it did, the columns appearing one by one, I realized we had made a horrible mistake. There was more here than we had wanted. Column after column after column.

We hadn't just pulled a list of email addresses. Margo's script had pulled everything. Names, locations, profile photos, everything sensitive from Nimbus's database that should remain private. Worst of all, we had passwords. Millions and millions of passwords. It was as though we'd botched an art heist and instead of stealing one painting had somehow cleared out an entire museum.

I texted Margo, asking her if she was going to work. I waited anxiously for her to reply. She didn't respond.

People sometimes call the subway system the arteries of New York, but that would presume the city had a heart. There is, instead, a mutual callousness among New Yorkers. Sometimes we see that hardened self in others, and we mistake that recognition for compassion.

On my subway commute from Astoria into Manhattan, I usually read a sci-fi book Margo had lent me. If it was too crowded to even hold a paperback in front of my face, I'd listen to bossa nova. But that morning I was too tense to do either. I was starting to feel like Margo's redemption was going to get us in a world of trouble. I still felt a little drunk from the night before. I tried to concentrate on the subway ads — this one promised to "tighten skin without surgery." I looked around at the people in the car. How many of their passwords did we have?

51

I'd debated whether I should show up for work at all, but thought it might be suspicious if I didn't, so I arrived and pretended that nothing had happened. Everything seemed normal. I received an email from my manager that expressed his displeasure that I had left the office early yesterday. I was surprised he'd even noticed, since we hardly spoke. I emailed him back and lied about being at a dentist appointment, ending it casually: "Teeth, you know?"

For the first few hours of the day, I worked very slowly, addressing the easiest customer service emails in my queue. Most questions could be answered by copy-and-pasting from a script we were supplied. We were encouraged to answer as many emails as we could as quickly as possible, but also to add "personal touches" to our communications wherever we could, to make the customer feel cared for. This meant pasting a robotic response from a script, then making it human by adding a ;) to the end. Basically, do things as efficiently as possible but also, please, have a heart about it.

Shortly after lunch, I finally received a text from Margo. She wanted me to meet her at McManus's again. I ducked out of the office, walked around the corner to the bar, and found Margo sitting on the exact same barstool as yesterday, peeling the label off an empty beer bottle. Déjà vu.

"Margo, have you looked at —"

She shushed me as the bartender approached. I ordered a beer.

Margo took a big slug from her bottle and said, "Yes, I've looked at it."

I waited for her to say more, but she didn't. I didn't understand why she wasn't freaking out like I was.

"We took way more than we were supposed to," I said.

"You're never 'supposed to' steal anything." Oh, *now* it was stealing.

"The file has everything in it. There's personal, private information. We're sitting on millions of stolen passwords and it's too much and it's a problem and I don't understand why you're so calm."

"And I don't understand why you're so" — she looked me up and down — "whatever this is."

"Margo . . ."

She put a hand on my shoulder. Her palm was cold and wet from her beer. "Everything is going to be fine. No one is going to find out. You just need to trust me."

I trusted Margo, but Margo also made a lot of decisions while drunk.

"Did you do this on purpose?"

"What? No, I just forgot a clause in the script that would filter to email addresses only."

This is how most technology is engineered. As servers became faster and storage less expensive, so grew the scope of what data you could keep around. This was thinking ahead. Track as much as you can and whittle it down to what you need later. Margo had forgotten the latter part.

"So did you talk to the guy you know at Phantom? Did he want the user data?"

"Yeah, I know him." A weird pause. She went on: "The CEO, I talked to him. I emailed him this morning, and we met up."

"It was that easy to get time with him? This quickly?"

"We're, uh, friends."

"You don't have friends," I said.

Margo, sensing my suspicion, deflected immediately: "I didn't tell him about the Nimbus data. And we're not going to tell anyone about it. Ever. What we did last night was very, very stupid and we will never do anything like that again."

Margo's raised voice drew the attention of the bartender.

"We're not talking about what you think we're talking about," she assured him, jokingly.

The bartender backed away.

Margo leaned in close. "We have to delete everything. And pretend it never happened. Got it?"

"Okay, but —"

"We're not talking about this anymore. That's that."

She pulled away and returned to her beer. And true to her word, that would be the last time she and I would ever acknowledge what we had done. I had a million more questions, but part of me was relieved, and I imagined Margo was too. In the sobriety of daylight, stealing data from Nimbus now felt horribly misguided. Dangerous for us both.

"Okay, now are you ready for the good news?"

"There's good news?"

Margo paused for dramatic effect.

"Phantom offered us both jobs."

"Us both? What do you mean?"

"Well, you have to go meet Brandon tomorrow morning."

"Who's Brandon?"

"Oh, the Phantom guy. The CEO. Brandon."

I was confused.

"When I went in, I told them I had just 'quit' Nimbus and they offered me a job.

And I said I would only work at Phantom if you could come along too." Margo started picking at the beer label. "Only if you want to."

She continued to sell me on it. The work might be the same, but Phantom had promised it would at least be a full-time role, meaning I wouldn't have to be a contract worker anymore. It was a much smaller company — just over a dozen people — so we wouldn't feel so isolated. And perhaps the best news: no foosball table.

"What happened to Tokyo?"

Margo laughed. "It's a nice idea I think about whenever I'm drunk."

"You think about it all the time then, huh?"

She looked away, hurt or insulted or annoyed, I couldn't tell. She took a big swig of her beer. "Take this job. For me. You're the only thing that keeps me sane at these places. So you're really doing me a favor, letting me drag you through all the same shit I have to be dragged through."

It was a weird way to say "you're welcome," but that's just how Margo was.

The next morning, I sat down with Brandon, Phantom's bright-eyed CEO. He couldn't have been much older than me.

Twenty-four at most. Conventionally hand-some: a tall, strong-chinned white guy with a smile most people deemed "winning." He wore a pastel green polo. He had a notice-able tan line around his eyes, the shape of ski goggles.

He said my name as he shook my hand and looked me straight in the eyes.

"Lucas Nguyen. Nguyen, that's a Viet-namese name?"

"Yes," I said, "my dad's Vietnamese, but my mom is Chinese."

"I was going to say, you look kind of Chinese."

White people often took pride in identify-ing which kind of Asian I was. On more than one occasion, people have tried to tell me I looked Korean, as if this was something I could be convinced of. When I told Margo how often this happened, she explained that white people spent an exorbitant amount of their energy saying racist things to prove they weren't racist.

Brandon continued to scan my résumé. It was clear he hadn't looked at it before now.

"So you did two years of college and dropped out?"

Before I could correct him and explain that community college was just two years, he continued, "I admire the bravery of

57

people who drop out of school."

He explained his vision for Phantom. All the ways we communicate digitally — email, text, instant message — were methods that left a permanent record. Since you could always go back and see an archive of past conversations, it affected the way we talk to each other. With Phantom, all messages disappeared after they'd been read. They were self-destructing. The ephemerality of Phantom was more like in-person conversation.

Brandon had been inspired by a particularly bad breakup, he went on. Afterward, he spent hours scrolling through text messages, looking at old pictures of them together — all the digital remains of the relationship. It made everything worse. If they had been communicating in something like Phantom, he wouldn't have been able to put himself through that. (Later, when I described this exchange to Margo, she would ask me why men were so inspired by their ex-girlfriends, the women they had treated like shit.)

There were more important applications for Phantom, he continued. Government or corporate whistleblowers could communicate in secret to journalists. (Margo, upon hearing this, mimicked the motion of a man jerking off.)

The language Brandon used was lofty, but I couldn't deny the idea's appeal. Compared to Nimbus's obsession with user growth and accumulating venture capital, Phantom sounded downright noble. (Margo pointed out that Phantom was also dependent on private funding.)

"You're aware of the conditions of Margo's employment?"

I wasn't sure what he meant.

"She said she won't work anyplace where you don't work," Brandon said. "Which I think speaks to her remarkable character."

A moment passed and Brandon further clarified: "Loyalty."

This wasn't an interview, I realized. Brandon clearly wanted Margo, and was just trying to figure out what the hell I could do at his company. He asked me what I currently did day-to-day, how I saw myself fitting in, where I thought I would be in five years. "I see you have some customer service experience at Nimbus."

"I answer a lot of support emails. Most of the questions we receive are redundant, so it's a lot of copy-and-pasting form responses," I said.

"This is what I'm thinking: We'll start you on email marketing, and then we'll move you around to whatever needs doing after that. You'll be a jack-of-all-trades guy. We're young and we're lean" — I couldn't tell if he meant the company or people like himself — "so everybody has a lot of different responsibilities. We're mostly engineers here, so having someone with a different perspective involved with everything is exactly what we need."

I knew this meant I'd be doing the work no one wanted to do, but I wasn't any worse off than I was before. Brandon looked at my résumé one more time.

"So when can you start?"

After the interview, I met up with Margo in Crown Heights, close to the house she grew up in. Because she'd lived there her whole life, she talked constantly about how much the neighborhood had changed, how nobody really knew about "the real Crown Heights."

It's true. When white people thought about Crown Heights, they mostly associated it with the street that made up its westernmost edge, where the past three years had seen nearly a dozen new bars and bougie restaurants open. A traditionally Caribbean neighborhood, it had become one of the many faces of gentrification in Brooklyn. In a decade, rents had skyrocketed faster than in any other neighborhood in the city, and the people walking along its streets had become progressively whiter too.

At a Trinidadian bakery, she suggested that we order doubles, a fried flatbread sandwich filled with curried chickpeas. It was salty and sticky and sweet. They were a dollar each, so I ate four. We washed them down with drinks at a bar nearby and I told her about my meeting with Brandon. I was impressed with his vision for the company, and Margo was skeptical of me, of how easily I was charmed. We toasted our new job prospects anyway. Here's to something not quite as bad as before.

My phone started ringing.

"My mom's calling."

"Do you want to answer it?" Margo asked.

The ringtone kept jingling while I thought about it. The vibration of the phone rattled violently against the bar.

"I'll call her back later," I decided, knowing I would probably forget to.

I let the phone keep ringing until it stopped. It felt somehow less definitive if I let it finish instead of cutting it off.

"Do you often screen your mom's calls?"

"Sometimes."

"I talk to my mom every day."

"Yeah, but my folks live across the country.

61

You live with your mom. That's not fair."

Margo laughed. "I am a grown-ass adult who lives with her mom. So: no, it's not fair."

We went for more food. Just a few blocks away, we each got a plate of saltfish — salted cod cooked with a Ghanaian fruit called ackee, served with rice and beans and a side of fried plantains. We sat on a bench facing Eastern Parkway.

"This is how I prefer to dine," she said. "Outside, not being waited on. Restaurants are so fussy."

"You know I used to work at my parents' bed-and-breakfast, right?" I said. "It's really not that bad."

"I just hate the idea of serving someone," she said. "Or someone serving me."

I watched Margo devour her entire plate. For someone so tiny and skinny, I'd never seen anyone put away food like Margo. She'd been blessed with the sort of super-human metabolism that is impervious to the caloric burden of beer and fatty, greasy foods. Margo joked that she had the dream body of a white girl — no ass, no tits, long legs like twigs.

It was summer, so the sun was still out at 8 p.m. The afterwork joggers were out in full force, running up and down the pedestrian alley of the parkway like some kind of disorganized infantry. The workout outfit was a uniform: dark athletic leisure-wear with neon accents, white headphones in ears. And then there was us, our asses parked on a bench, sweating from the spicy food we'd just eaten.

"Are we going to do this? Are we going to Phantom?" I asked.

"I don't see any reason not to," Margo said. "But let's decide over dessert."

I wasn't sure I could eat any more.

Margo and I started at Phantom the following week. Brandon introduced us to the rest of the company. Still, they were interested in who I was, where I had come from. I was flattered. Brandon constantly referred to the employees of Phantom as a "family," and I watched Margo roll her eyes every time.

We settled in quickly. And although most things were better than I'd found them at Nimbus — warmer, more efficient, friendlier — we'd traded in a foosball table for a ping pong table, and that was worse. The foosball table was noisy, but at least it was confined to a small area. The Phantom office was smaller, and now ping pong balls were often flying past my desk. I tried to remind myself it wasn't a big deal. Each time an errant ball bounced across my keyboard and onto the floor, I'd take a deep breath and chase it down, to show I was a good sport.

A few weeks later we'd settled into a routine at Phantom, which meant we'd found a new bar to drink at close to work. It was called Gainsbourg, an Irish pub with an inexplicably French name. Margo was playing a Pac-Man machine tucked in the back corner of the bar. She was usually the late one — always by ten or fifteen minutes, sometimes twenty. I'd give her a hard time about it and she'd tell me that everyone in New York is always late.

"Not me," I'd say.

"You're the only person I know that's punctual to a bar," she'd say.

"If you're someone who's on time, you're on time to everything." Margo would ignore me and march over to the Pac-Man machine.

But on this particular day, I was the late one. I'd been called into a meeting that went long, and clearly Margo was frustrated. She barely acknowledged me when I approached. I don't think she was mad because I was late, but that I'd chosen work over her.

The Pac-Man machine, which I never saw anyone use besides Margo, had a cup holder attached to the side of the cabinet. Margo picked her beer up out of the holder, lapped up the last few sips in one long chug, and handed me the empty glass.

"Next round is on you."

When I returned I carefully placed a full beer into the cup holder, making sure not to disturb Margo's intense concentration. She played her fair share of Pac-Man at Gainsbourg. Often she would order a beer and ask for the bartender to split a few dollars into quarters for the machine. The way she played was meditative. Concentrating deeply, she methodically planned her routes through the blue 8-bit labyrinth, looking up only to sip her beer.

I'd spent a number of hours watching Pac-Man over Margo's shoulder.

"Why do you love this game so much?"

Margo didn't respond immediately. I couldn't tell if she was thinking of an answer or if she was too focused on the game.

"The illusion of teamwork."

I pointed out that she was playing by herself.

"No, the ghosts," she clarified. "They're all programmed in a way that creates the illusion that they're cooperating."

I stared at the screen. The four ghosts appeared to be tailing Pac-Man. "Aren't they just following you?"

"Not exactly. Each ghost is controlled by a different simple logic. Blinky is always pursuing you; Pinky is always trying to occupy the space in front of you."

"The ghosts have names?"

"Clyde, the orange one, is a little more complicated."

"Clyde is a terrible name for a ghost."

"It bases its behavior on how close it is to Pac-Man, and flees if you get too close."

"Why does it run away?"

"I don't know. Every team needs a coward?"

Now I was staring intensely too, trying to make out the patterns. I didn't quite see them, but it wasn't the first time Margo saw something I didn't. Her brain understood the world through rules and reason — she could find patterns anywhere and exploit them.

She continued. "The trickiest ghost is Inky, though. Like Pinky, Inky tries to get ahead of you. But Inky's movement is relative not just to Pac-Man, but also Blinky. So Inky's movements appear random until it gets close, and then it looks like Inky is trying to trap you."

66

I watched Margo play for a few more minutes. Now that she had identified the personalities of the four ghosts, they seemed obvious: one is aggressive, one is conniving, one is cowardly, and one is volatile.

"The ghosts have two modes. All the behavior I just described was Chase Mode, which is how most of the game is played, with ghosts in pursuit of you. But when you eat the big pill" — Margo had timed it so as she said this, her Pac-Man swallowed up the power that made her invincible — "the ghosts go into Scatter Mode."

All four of the ghosts' paths suddenly changed and they began fleeing in different directions.

"And when they're in Scatter Mode, all the ghosts run to a different corner of the screen. When they're in danger, they completely abandon the logic of teamwork."

Margo beat the level, then turned away from the arcade machine, gesturing that I could take over.

"Anyway, I didn't answer your question really. Why do I like this game?" she said. "I like all arcade games. I enjoy how cynical these machines are. The incentive behind making them is to suck as many quarters out of a player as quickly as possible. So there's an adversarial relationship between the software and the user, but you have to design it in such a way that the player never notices."

A moment later, Margo said, "Maybe players just don't care?"

I was only half listening. By this point the ghosts had reverted from Scatter Mode to Chase Mode, and they were stalking me around the grid. My Pac-Man was twitchy and nervous and eventually the ghosts had me in a corner.

Margo continued. "Think about it this way: you don't spend much time designing the mechanics of Pac-Man. Players are always going to act unpredictably. They're both more clever and more stupid than you can plan for. So instead, you put all your energy toward what you can control. You work hard to engineer the ghosts."

The thought distracted me from the game. The ghosts eventually pinned me down in the bottom left corner of the screen, blocking all of my possible escape routes. They closed in on me and, on contact, Pac-Man's mouth opened up and folded in on itself. The game celebrated my death with an 8-bit chime. The arcade machine had earned itself another quarter.

"The orange ghost got me. Which one is that again?"

"Clyde." The coward.

"Fucking Clyde."

Margo had a phone with a shattered screen, a constellation of cracks that fractured the light of the display. She often dropped her phone, usually while drinking, and had done it so often she got tired of replacing it. She began to take a perverse pride in having a broken phone. Our new colleagues began to ask her why she wouldn't get it fixed, and at first she laughed it off but one day she let 'em have it. I'd seen Margo on this tirade before.

"Everyone has been seduced by the beauty of new technology. There's that fresh-out-of-the-package moment when every computer and phone is pure, uniform: smooth silver metal bodies, clean lines. And they feel good in your hands, like they haven't merely been built, but formed, like the word 'sleek' has only existed for hundreds of years to finally describe these devices.

"But what's beautiful in a store is often hugely impractical when it has to endure life outside. These are beautiful things made for impossible lives —"

Usually, here, Margo would have withdrawn her phone and started waving it around.

69

"This was designed by some men of some means who live in a specific part of California and believe technology should reflect their needs. Beauty can only be defined on their terms."

I remember, on one night, another Phantom engineer named Jared decided to challenge her.

"Okay, but is that wrong?" Jared asked. "These phones have sold enormously well because people want them."

And here's where Margo liked to deliver her point like it was a *Twilight Zone* plot twist, her voice raised, commanding the attention of everyone in the room.

"What does it mean that the world's most popular devices have been designed by and for the elite white men in Silicon Valley? Is this the new colonialism, a modern form of oppression that imposes the values and perspective of white men on the world?"

The room, as usual, went silent. It didn't matter if, by this point, the half a dozen drinks she'd had were causing her to slur. She wanted to blow everyone's minds with this revelation (which she often did). I didn't necessarily disagree with her perspective, but I'd seen Margo do this act enough times to find it funny. This particular time it was happy hour at the office, and she was going for it.

Margo and Jared continued to argue, to the point where most of us tuned out, myself included, and quietly retreated to gather around a game of ping pong. Likely as a means of defusing Margo and Jared's bickering, Brandon suggested we take the drinking to a nearby bar. Margo opted out.

"You want to grab some food in my neighborhood?" she asked me.

"I actually think I might go to the bar with the team," I said. Margo and I had gotten dinner in Crown Heights the night before. It was rare that I was invited to hang with anyone else. But I couldn't say this out loud, not with everyone around. It would sound pathetic. Maybe it was.

"Margo, come to the bar," Brandon said. I hadn't realized that he was listening. "Drinks are on me."

"I wouldn't want to intrude on boys' night." She wasn't wrong. The remaining crew was all dudes. Brandon seemed unfazed. I suddenly felt the gravity of my betrayal. Margo grabbed her coat and was out the door before anyone could say goodbye.

We went to a nearby cocktail bar, hidden in the back of an Italian restaurant. There was a rotary phone in the front, which

Brandon picked up to whisper the password ("clover"). A secret door opened to reveal a dim lounge and a handful of waiters in old-timey vests. There was no menu, just a short survey you filled out asking for your favorite spirits, and a personality quiz. I couldn't help thinking about how much Margo would have hated this place. She'd probably make a joke — something to do with Prohibition cosplay; I'd laugh. But the truth was that I kind of liked it.

The next day, Margo didn't answer my IMs, and when I caught her in person she brushed me off, said she was really busy. (The way our desks were positioned, I could see her computer monitor so I knew for a fact she wasn't.)

"It's weird, you liking this place so much," she messaged me eventually.

"I don't like it," I replied. "But it's better."

In the early afternoon she sent me a link, which I took as a peace offering after her standoffish behavior. We'd gotten into the habit of sending articles back and forth — a kind of "wow, look how fucked-up this is" rubbernecking at the world.

"This is some bullshit," her first message said. She followed up again a few minutes later, before I'd had a chance to answer.

"Did you read this yet?"

Sometimes I wished Margo understood that my day-to-day at work, though menial, had deadlines that I couldn't blow off. Still, I felt bad about the night before, so I closed my customer service emails and clicked her link. It was a news article surrounding the data released by an online dating site. The study had ranked the desirability of men and women by race, based on their user data. According to the numbers, the most desirable people were Caucasian men and Asian women. Least desirable: Asian men and black women. In the comments of the article, readers complained that the study was racist. But the author defended himself by saying that he wasn't projecting a value judgment. This was data. This is what the numbers said.

"Huh, yeah, that's dumb," I replied, not thinking much of it. Who was surprised by this information? Certainly not Margo. She didn't say anything after that, so I assumed she'd gotten busy or had moved on. Later, when I ran into her in the kitchen, she brought up the article again. She said that we finally had something in common: we were the ones no one wanted. She dubbed us "the Undesirables" and let out a sickly laugh.

I was unconvinced by the solidarity, even if I liked the idea that it bonded me with Margo. Just because black women and Asian men were at the bottom of the data set, it didn't mean our experiences were the same. But Margo kept pushing, drawing me back into the same conversation, trying to get a stronger reaction from me.

"Mostly, I can't believe people would state their dating preferences," I said. "Like, it's one thing to only date, like, Asian women. But it's another to click on a drop-down menu and select 'Asian women.' "

"Did you read the article?" Margo said. (Okay, so I'd read it quickly so I could get back to my emails.) "It's behavioral data. It's not what people said they were interested in. It's how they acted on the site. Like, dudes probably didn't admit they were only horny for Asian chicks, but those were the only girls they were messaging."

"I guess people assume that no one's surveilling their dating habits?"

"Maybe they don't care," Margo said.

She became even more annoyed when Brandon entered the kitchen. He seemed unsure of what to do, having just overheard Margo talking about men who "wanted to fuck Asian chicks." It looked like he was about to say something. Would he laugh

74

along? Or scold us for speaking inappropriately in the workplace? Neither, it turned out. He pretended not to hear us, and continued on his original mission, the pursuit of a granola bar. He grabbed one and quickly left the room.

"I've never seen him move so fast," Margo said.

In a low voice I said, "I bet Brandon only messages Asian women."

"Nah, he's secretly into black women. Trust me."

I laughed, but when I looked at Margo, she wasn't smiling. In fact, she looked pained. I'd rarely seen her like this. Hurt.

We went to Gainsbourg after work, and Margo drank at an even more alarming rate than usual. She wasn't in the mood for Pac-Man. Each beer came accompanied by a shot of well whiskey. I was trying to keep up. I thought we'd talked about it to death, but she was still going on about the dating article. I finally gathered that while the piece didn't reveal anything she didn't already know, Margo was an engineer, and having her experience reiterated and reinforced with data felt raw and personal.

"There's nothing new in that article," I offered, trying to find her some closure so we could both move on and talk about literally anything else. "You don't even do online dating. You don't even date. What's the big deal?"

"I don't want a boyfriend. I don't want a house. I don't want a family, not that anyone is asking. I don't want this job, but I also don't know what better job there would be. I don't want to live in New York, but I'll never leave. My entire life is just things I don't want," she said. "It's exhausting."

"I feel like you're mad I am not angrier about this article."

"No, I want you to get why *I'm* so mad."

"What about the article bothers you so much?"

Margo was immovable, but no clearer. "That kind of behavioral data — it's quantified desire."

"Is everything okay?"

"I don't know. I'm not sure why this is fucking me up so much. It all just feels very . . ." Margo searched for the right word. She was slurring again, and I couldn't tell if she said "empirical" or "imperial."

I thought we could reach an understanding if I explained where I was coming from: "I know Asian men aren't exactly anyone's ideal, for a bunch of messed-up reasons. We're seen as quiet. We're supposed to be meek." It made me a little sad to admit it

76

out loud. "That's just how people see us, and treat us. And this data is just proving a reality we already know."

I wasn't sure Margo was listening to me anymore. "Everybody wants to fuck a black girl, but nobody wants to fuck a black girl," she said, mostly to herself, and then downed her beer.

Clearly I wasn't getting it. There were gaps in our experiences. I knew that. Margo might be less frustrated with me if I acknowledged that.

"Maybe this information is less troubling to me because I'm a man?"

"True," Margo said. "Men are dumb as fuck."

I thought I could lighten the mood, at least. I repeated a joke I'd heard recently: that the scariest thing that can happen to a man is that his heart could be broken, but for a woman, her greatest fear was being murdered by a man. Margo didn't find it funny. She asked me what the joke even was, and I fumbled as I tried to explain that it had been funny when I heard a famous comedian say it.

Nothing I said made her less upset. In fact, it seemed like I was only making things worse. I was supposed to be the person that Margo could rely on for support. At the very least, she could sound off at me and I'd listen. But it was clear that today hearing her wouldn't be enough. She needed me to understand, and instead I was just making gross jokes. A second disappointment in as many days.

"I'm sorry," I said. "I'm trying to be helpful."

Margo looked up from her empty glass and met my eyes just long enough to register her confusion, and then disappointment. Then her face resolved back to the grimace she'd had throughout the evening, as if it was no longer even worth trying to figure out what was wrong with me. She ordered another round.

The day after Margo died, I went into the office. I walked by her desk, where all her things remained. Her computer was there, assorted papers, an overripe banana, a book she was reading. Everything still in its place, undisturbed.

As days went by, I walked by the halal cart we'd frequent for lunch, the café where we'd grab coffee, the bar we ended up at too often after work. Everything the same, just no Margo.

I never cried. I don't know why. I knew rationally that my best friend was dead, but my body wouldn't acknowledge it. I tried. I even set aside time in the shower, where my roommate wouldn't hear me. I thought about Margo. I thought about my parents, imagined their deaths. Summoned every sad thing I'd read in the news. Nothing. Instead I just felt dulled, like something was missing instead of gone.

The Monday after the funeral, though, someone cleared Margo's desk. Apparently the banana had gone bad, so someone had taken the initiative to get rid of everything. Occasionally mail would arrive for Margo, and the office manager stashed it in a conference room.

In the office, I am assumed to be industrious, efficient, quiet — like the engine of a Prius, humming along. The strangest part of being Asian in America is that you never have to prove how hardworking you are. People just assume you were born with a great work ethic, or that your stoic, disciplinarian parents beat it into you at a young age. But the truth was that I was quiet those weeks after Margo died because I was hungover at my desk. I answered emails slowly, only half paying attention to what I was writing, waiting for the day to end. On my way home I would pick up a six-pack from the bodega across the street from my apartment, and call it dinner. It was nearly enough calories to get me through.

The first few days, Brandon was unusually kind. He told me to take as much time off as I needed, and I explained I'd rather not take any, the office was a better place to keep myself occupied, which was something I said because it seemed like something to say. But I did very little. Afternoons dragged without Margo sending me things to read; workdays felt endless without someone giving me reasons to get angry.

It was dumb, but I missed Margo most during lunch because she always wanted to eat. We worked in a neighborhood that was filthy with startups, which also meant it was filthy with "fast casual" restaurants appropriating every variety of ethnic food into a similar format: a bowl of sorts.

"There's the Indian place, or the Greek place, or the Japanese place, or there are the three different Mexican places," Margo said. It had been a couple months since we started at Phantom, and she'd already explored all the lunch options. She loved them all. There was an efficiency to the formula. You picked a protein, some sides, some toppings, that kind of thing. And though there were always long lines, they moved rapidly. Your lunch was sent down a production line, its preparers dialed into a tightly designed system that would deliver your food quickly, packaged in a way that was easy to carry back to the office. Also, Margo didn't mind spending fifteen dollars every day on lunch.

"I brought lunch," I said, attempting to avoid using my lunch hour to spend more than an hour's wage. In reality, like most days, I'd planned to assemble a meal out of free snacks in the Phantom break room.

"Lunch is on me today," Margo said. "Let's do the Indian one."

At the restaurant, after a brief wait in line, Margo picked her format (biryani), her protein (chicken), and her sauce (tikka masala). I just followed her lead and ordered the same thing. On our walk back to the office, Margo popped open the lid of her food and took a bite.

"God, I'm starving," she said. "Did you know that chicken tikka masala is the national dish of England? But now its origins are up for debate. People aren't sure if it's from India or the United Kingdom." She took a bite. "Colonialism, man." She took another bite. "But it tastes so good."

"Are you going to feel this way when a Haitian fast-casual place opens?" I asked.

"Of course I'd complain about it at first," she said, "but I'd probably get over it once I realized I could have fried plantains for lunch every day."

"It's funny, I want people to take Vietnamese food more seriously. Like, stop thinking of it as a cheap meal and think of it as something worth paying for," I said. "But I also sneer at any bowl of pho' that costs more than, like, eight dollars."

I suggested we just eat outside, since Margo had already turned her attention to her orange bowl of food. It was nice out, so we found a bench on Twenty-third and Broadway, situated in front of the iconic triangular building for which the neighborhood had been named. At twenty stories tall, it had been a skyscraper when it was constructed at the beginning of the twentieth century. Now it was dwarfed by every other tower around it — all of them massive, devoid of any character.

Margo stopped and looked up at the building. "I read that its elevators used to be water-powered." She turned to me and I noticed a touch of bright orange tikka masala on her lip. "The building was always flooding."

As usual, she identified something by its biggest problem.

■ ■ ■

The Monday after the funeral, Brandon had briefly eulogized Margo at a morning stand-up meeting. He spoke about how talented she was, and how she would be missed, before immediately proceeding with the rest of the meeting, asking each engineer for an update on the status of whatever they were working on.

With Margo's death, the mood at the office was sullen. It largely went undiscussed, though a few coworkers did tell me they were "very sorry." As a means of raising morale, Brandon announced that there would be an office ping pong tournament that Thursday, starting at noon. Participation was optional but strongly encouraged. Brandon was obsessed with ping pong, and almost always won. I wondered if the tournament was supposed to raise the company morale or his own.

He sent me a reminder email the day before, telling me that I was the only one that had not opted in.

"I'm not very good at ping pong," I said, hoping the conversation would end there.

"I'm sure you're naturally gifted at ping pong. Plus we have sixteen employees, and it would make the numbers perfect for a tournament."

"It used to be seventeen," I said. Brandon was taken aback, and I immediately felt bad for snapping at him. It wasn't his fault Margo had died, and it wasn't fair that I was taking it out on him. "Is this ping pong tournament optional or not?"

"Of course it's optional," Brandon said, putting a hand on my shoulder. "But come on."

The next day it became abundantly clear to me, again, that I was not good at ping pong. It was also a relief when I was knocked out briskly in the first round by a lanky web developer named Josh who, toward the end of the match, began clearly taking pity on me in his serve.

Once I'd been knocked out, I tried to go back to my desk to get some work done — impossible with everyone still cheering and screaming. Every point was an exercise in life-or-death decision making.

It eventually narrowed down to the finals: Brandon squared off against a server engineer named Emil. Their styles were very different. Brandon was constantly on the attack, slamming the ball with a vicious forehand to the open corner. Emil played several feet back, waiting patiently for each slam and finding ways to return them. It was sort of mystical, the way Emil played — low and steady, never striking, and waiting for Brandon to make mistakes. After enough back-and-forth, Brandon would overshoot and Emil would win the point, each of these moments punctuated by Brandon screaming, "Fuck!"

"He's a chopper," said Tom, another engineer, to me, pointing in Emil's direction. "Chopper" referred to Emil's style of play, a strong defensive backspin that slowed the game down. Brandon didn't relent, though. He took each opportunity to speed the game up, to play it on his terms. He eventually pulled away. Emil stopped being able to return Brandon's slams and he took the game.

I was not Margo. But thankfully, computers were stupid. They had no idea who Margo was. But I did.

A secure log-in is protected by a common feature called two-factor authentication. What this usually means is that a site requires a password, which then triggers a different, randomly generated passcode that is immediately sent to your phone. Since nearly all hacking happens remotely, the addition of second, physical verification prevents many accounts from being broken into. For two-factor authentication, one's identity is defined by two things: something you know and something you have. Perhaps that's how we define ourselves, in the end: by the stuff in our heads and the stuff we own.

It had been a week since Louise asked me to turn off her dead daughter's Facebook profile. I'd tried to find ways to become Margo's "legacy contact." I contacted Facebook's customer support and was told that I would need to summon a death certificate, which I was too sheepish to ask Louise for. I didn't need to ask her for proof her daughter was gone. But then I realized that I didn't need to become a legacy contact. I could just sign into her Facebook account. After all, I still had a giant file of stolen usernames and passwords from Nimbus — the-take.csv. We had promised each other that we would each destroy our copy of the database. But I never did. Getting rid of it would have felt like deleting the greatest secret we shared.

When I got home from work, I opened the file on my computer. The spreadsheet software chugged, stalled, and crashed. I restarted. This would take a few tries.

I was working under the assumption that

Margo used the same password for her Nimbus account as she did for her Facebook profile. Did she use the same password for everything? I certainly did. Variations on it. A lot of people did that. It seemed reasonable that Margo might as well. But I knew there was no middle ground for this. I either had access to all of Margo's things, or I had none.

On the fourth try, the spreadsheet finally loaded. I filtered by Margo's first name. There were thousands of Margos. I then filtered by her last name. Still several dozen accounts. I had forgotten that, as an engineer, Margo used a lot of test profiles. But the passwords for all her throwaway accounts were things like "test1234" and "dummyaccount22." I scanned the list until I found the real one: M4v15B34c0n.

I wrote it on a sticky note. Writing it down on a piece of paper seemed less of a violation; something was lost in the transfer from digital to analog. In the moment, I didn't feel like I was doing anything wrong. In fact, I felt the opposite. Giddy almost.

I grabbed Margo's computer off the stack of mail it had been resting on. When I opened the laptop, it confronted me with the same log-in screen I'd been stuck at before. I took a deep breath and entered the password slowly.

It worked. I was shocked by how quickly — so quickly that I didn't realize I was now looking at Margo's desktop. Her wallpaper was a beautiful nebula, its pinks and blues spiraling like spilled neon against the blackness of space.

It terrified me. I closed it and vowed never to look again.

Before I moved to New York, I lived with my parents. They ran a modest bed-and-breakfast in a small town. Most of the guests were parents of students at a local private liberal arts college, which I had applied to and been promptly rejected from. It hardly mattered anyway because there was no way I would've been able to afford four years of tuition. Since it was a bed-and-breakfast, cozy and local and homey, guests felt strangely compelled to talk to me. When I served dinner or came to their rooms to change the sheets on their beds, people asked if I was a student, like their son or daughter, at the local college. I used to explain that, no, I went to community college. But over time, I just started lying to make the conversation less embarrassing. I did go to the local school. I was studying English literature with a minor in economics, I was part of the debate team. Yes, I had heard of your son or daughter. I hadn't met them in person, but I heard they're great.

In the evenings, there was always plenty to prepare for the next morning's breakfast. My mother cut up fruit in the kitchen, while I cleaned the dining area and set the tables so they would be ready well ahead of our 9 a.m. serving time. Once the day's duties were finally done, I'd spend the rest of the evening on the family desktop computer in the basement, scouring the internet for jobs, applying, and never hearing back. I had turned down beds and set tables and vacuumed the hallways of this dusty house since I was old enough to walk. I was twenty-three and ready to move out.

My parents were also ready for me to move on. My older brother was in his second year of graduate school, studying to be a pharmacist, having earned numerous scholarships along the way. He had always been a much better student than me. In fact, he'd really been better at everything. Straight A's, a king of extracurriculars, even a decent athlete. He looked and lived the way Asians were supposed to: lean and charming and gifted in the classroom. I possessed none of those qualities. I was above average in height, but always on the heftier side. My mother said she was to blame, that she overfed me as a baby. But I didn't eat more than anyone else in my family. I was just bigger.

I wasn't a terrible student by any means, but there was little I could do to distinguish myself. There had always been an expectation at my high school that I would do well in the maths and sciences, even though I never showed an aptitude for either subject. The high school guidance counselor urged me to take advanced placement classes my senior year for calculus and chemistry — both of which I nearly failed out of. My GPA dropped so significantly that any hope of financial aid or a scholarship was out of reach. I told the guidance counselor that I shouldn't have been in those classes. He said he'd expected more of me. That made one of us.

I was finishing up two years at community college in eastern Oregon the spring after the housing market crash. Finding a job without a bachelor's degree was hard enough. I knew it would be damned near impossible in a faltering job market.

Since we were only a fifteen-minute drive from the private college, the week of graduation was always a busy month at the bed-and-breakfast. Once, as I was on my way out the door, I told Mom I was headed to school and was overheard by two guests, Helena and Paul, a white couple who were in town to visit their son Michael, a student at the college. I'd made the mistake of telling them, when I had served them breakfast, that I was also a student there. They offered me a ride.

"Oh, it's really fine," I said, trying not to get caught in my lie. "It's just thirty minutes on a bike."

"Nonsense, we'll take you there," Paul insisted. "Michael is an English major as well."

My mother shot me a confused look but said nothing as she collected Helena and Paul's plates.

I found myself in the back seat of their massive SUV, a rental, which reeked of lingering cigarettes and the stench of whatever chemical had been used to try and remove the cigarette smell. Helena talked about how proud they were of their son, that he had a wonderful job lined up back in Santa Fe, where they were from. She asked me what my plans were after graduation, and I said I was weighing my options.

When we arrived on campus, I thanked them and quickly wandered off. I could catch a bus back to town, which might only take forty-five minutes, and then I would just have missed a class and a half. But as I headed toward the student center, I caught a glimpse of a bulletin board with various flyers for jobs. So far, my job search had been fruitless.

I hadn't been to the campus since I'd applied there. I'd known then, as I walked across beautifully manicured quads and toured the various ivy-adorned brick buildings, that I had no chance of being accepted. Today, students were splayed out on picnic blankets eating lunch they'd brought from the cafeteria. There was a couple that had fallen asleep in a hammock together, textbooks shielding their faces from the sun. It was a gorgeous late spring day, and the campus looked like something out of a brochure — truth in advertising, after all. I didn't feel regret. It was a world I'd never earned.

I approached the bulletin board. There was a bright flyer urging students to visit the guidance counselors at the career center. Maybe there were job postings there. At this point, I had nothing to lose.

It took me a little while to find the career center. I was able to locate the building, but I meandered up and down several floors before realizing the career center was in the basement. There were some chairs and magazines and little else, like the waiting room of a dentist's office. By the door was a receptionist, clearly a student just doing her homework. She took off her headphones and asked if I had an appointment.

"No, I just, uh, wanted to . . . look at some of the materials," I said.

I walked over to a shelf of leaflets and printouts and pretended to be interested in them. I picked up a brochure titled "Getting Results from Your Résumé" and waved it at her. She didn't seem convinced, but she also looked like she couldn't give less of a fuck. The headphones went back on and I kept looking around the room, looking for another job board. No luck. I headed toward the exit.

"Are you my ten o'clock?"

I turned around. It was a white woman, likely in her early sixties. She wore a cardigan and cargo shorts, an outfit that reminded me of a first-grade teacher chaperoning a field trip.

"No, sorry, I was just looking around," I said.

"Well I guess that means my ten o'clock appointment isn't coming," she said. "Which means I'm free, if you'd like me to look over any résumés or cover letters."

I don't know why I went along with it. Maybe I was just flattered she believed I was a student there.

As she led me to her office, she barked at the woman behind the desk, "Laura, take off the headphones."

The office was what you might expect from a guidance counselor who gives career advice to wealthy students who had probably never had a real job before. Encouragement was key. Motivational posters with famous quotes covered most of the wall space — as if Martin Luther King Jr. had a dream to apply for an unpaid internship. Stacked on her desk were pamphlets, alongside what appeared to be a stack of résumés. There was very little light, just fluorescent bulbs casting a harsh shadow. She introduced herself as Riley, and, summoning all the wells of my imagination, I came up with a pseudonym for myself.

"John," I said, shaking her hand.

Riley asked me what I wanted to do in life, and I confessed that I would probably take any job, that I'd already applied for dozens and my response rate was dismal.

"It's a difficult time to find a job, but you'll always be rewarded if you're persistent. Many students think that just because they've earned a bachelor's degree they're entitled to a job."

Little did she know, I hadn't even earned the right to feel entitled.

She continued: "But the upside to a tough job market is that it forces young people like yourself to take bigger risks. Are you looking at things mostly in this area?"

I told Riley that my parents were here, but I would be willing to move somewhere else.

"Where have you always wanted to live?"

I paused. The idea of leaving Oregon had never crossed my mind — not because I loved where I'd grown up, but because it seemed so unlikely that I'd ever make it anywhere else. Even my brother, with all of his academic success, had stayed in the state. Like the patrons of my parents' bed-and-breakfast, Riley was another white stranger that I found myself not wanting to disappoint, or embarrass myself in front of.

"New York," I said. It wasn't an honest answer, but it was a believable one.

"And why do you want to move to New York?"

I knew nothing about New York. I'd certainly never been. I had no idea what it really looked like or the kinds of people who lived there. I had, however, years ago, imagined that all my friends from PORK

95

lived there. It was subtle, but sometimes people would reference specific neighborhoods — the Lower East Side, Williamsburg, Fort Greenpoint, I thought it was called. To me, it was the place where music existed.

"I have friends there," I finally said, "in New York."

"That's never a bad starting place. And careerwise, why do you want to be there?"

"There's so much music in New York. It's, like, a scene."

Riley laughed. "It's definitely a scene, that's for sure."

She told me she had lived there years ago. The city was so different, dangerous really. Disgusting, dingy. Her apartment had rats, and at night she heard them scurrying through the walls. She lived with half a dozen other people and they basically slept on top of each other. She was miserable, but never happier.

"That was so long ago, though," she said, leaning back in her chair.

"So I should or shouldn't move there?"

Riley began typing, then clicked a couple times. She turned her computer monitor around so I could see the screen.

"Here are some music jobs in New York."

We talked through "opportunities" for a

while. They were scant. Riley seemed surprised. For anything I did find, she promised she'd write me glowing recommendations, which was kind of her but would be an impossibility once she figured out I did not attend that college, that I didn't have a bachelor's degree.

She regaled me with more stories of her time in New York. She'd been there in the '70s. The blackout happened just a week after she'd moved there, caused by a lightning strike that tripped up a power station. It only lasted a day, but it threw the city into chaos — looting, arson, bedlam — and yet she still spoke about it fondly.

"It's funny. I'm nostalgic for everything that was bad about New York."

"I guess the hard things in our life are what define us," I said.

She laughed. "You're a hoot. I think you'll do great in New York."

Just before I left, she gave me one last piece of advice: "Success comes to those who are confident and organized." She handed me one of the pamphlets from her desk: "Be Confident, Not Cocky: Penning Your First Cover Letter."

I didn't know how to summon confidence, but the bit about being organized stuck. I could definitely be organized. Since I was in

97

middle school, I'd managed the accounting for my parents' bed-and-breakfast — a process that involved Mom reading out receipts and bills while I entered them into a spreadsheet. Later that evening, I opened the spreadsheet software. The computer fan whirred intensely as I created my first document that didn't involve my parents' business. I listed dates of when I had first sent in my applications, dates I had followed up, more dates of when I had followed up again. I could see that at first I had been picky about listings. But as days and weeks went by, I applied for anything that was available. I took Riley's advice and began looking at jobs in New York, but I still didn't hear back from anyone. I'd become more organized about my search, and all that had led to was an increase of pitying responses from employers thanking me for my interest.

I maintained the spreadsheet meticulously. It grew and grew until I realized I had applied for over a hundred jobs. On nights when I couldn't sleep, I would thumb through the spreadsheet row by row, column by column. A catalog of my failures.

At the time, journalists were still piecing together what had happened to the economy. New York banks, housing and greed and something or other. As the story unraveled, it did so through a string of nonsensical terms. High-risk subprime mortgages had been packaged as collateralized debt obligation, whatever the hell that meant. But as I read deeper into it, hoping to understand, to not feel like such a loser, I could see that all the obtuse language was just a disguise for relatively simple things. By pooling risky assets into larger batches, they could sell worthless loans for a small amount of money. Banks did this over and over, until it was no longer a small amount. Shuffling deck chairs for massive profits.

But what did it actually mean for a bank to sell debt to another bank? That was even simpler than I could ever have imagined. Individual debt was just a line item. Packaged together, such debts were represented by hundreds of rows in a spreadsheet. New York bankers were trading fucking spreadsheets, I realized. These spreadsheets were massive, but they listed all the pertinent information a debt collection agency might need: names, addresses, phone numbers, dates of delinquency. It reminded me of my awful job applications spreadsheet. The information was similarly organized, and it all added up to very little. I had several thousand dollars' worth of student loan debt from community college, which also lived in a cell, in a spreadsheet, somewhere.

I dragged my spreadsheet into the trash. I bought a plane ticket to New York. I didn't have a job yet, but I would figure it out when I arrived. Besides, if I was going to be jobless, I might as well be jobless somewhere else.

Eventually Margo's argumentative posturing in the Nimbus office caught up with her. Or so she suspected. A third-party firm had done a survey of Nimbus's user demographics, revealing that a disproportionately high number of the users were African American.

"You can say 'black,'" Margo said.

One of the two men from the consulting firm — both tall, blondish white men in their early thirties — said he was more comfortable referring to the demo as African American. It was how they had self-identified on the survey.

Margo pushed. "It's more inclusive to say 'black.'"

They ignored her. But the results of the survey had shocked the mostly white execs at Nimbus. The service they had created was being used primarily by people who did not look like them. It became clear that this was seen as a negative. It was a problem, and they were struggling to find the language to express why.

To Margo, the takeaway was obviously that Nimbus should start working on features that appealed more to black people. The company should start hiring more black product managers, black engineers, maybe even some black leadership. The room, mostly white, did not take kindly to Margo's suggestion, and instead saw it as an affront. The CFO, a British man in his fifties who had previously worked at a bank, informed Margo, with the kind of condescension that is only worsened by a British accent, that Nimbus was raising another round of funding, and that a product which appealed to African Americans — "just twelve percent of the U.S. population, mind you" — would never appeal to investors.

The CEO, another white man, attempting to soften the blow, harped that African Americans were, on average, poorer than the rest of the population, and therefore were a less valuable demographic than those with higher disposable incomes.

The second consultant clicked through his slides to land on his closing point. If Nimbus's user base grew only in the sector of African Americans, the business would become unsustainable within six months.

This was when Margo lost it. She stood

up at her seat, began shouting, her voice frustrated and incredulous and confrontational. It was one thing to say that black people were less valuable than everyone else. To her, it was another to declare that black people were unworthy of technology.

When Margo emerged from the meeting, she found me at my desk and asked me to follow her into the hallway outside the office. Once we were out of the view of other Nimbus employees, Margo embraced me and began to sob. I hadn't yet realized what was going on. She just kept saying "fuck this place" over and over. I awkwardly rubbed her arms and told her everything would be fine. Margo pressed her forehead into my shoulder, and we embraced more deeply. We'd never held each other this way, and I was surprised how natural it felt. Her crying didn't last long — the whole thing must've lasted a minute at most — and once she was done, she took a step back, said thank you, and headed to the bathroom to clean herself up. I remained there, stunned by how intimate that had felt, and confused by what had just happened.

Several HR complaints were filed against Margo for the outburst in the meeting. Some of them felt her tone was disrespectful and hostile; others declared her behavior aggressive, specifically toward white people in the office. When she was eventually let go, the event wasn't cited. Nothing was, except the general "fit" of Margo in the workplace.

"It was probably that," she said. "But I have no way to really know for sure."

That's what racism in the workplace looked like. You could feel it everywhere — in your brain, in your heart, in your bones — but you could never prove it. And that wasn't even the worst part. At the bar, just hours before we'd made off with Nimbus's user data, Margo conceded that she had played right into their hands. She was frustrated, chose to speak out about it, and had accidentally become the thing white men had always expected she was: an angry black woman.

"What was the alternative?" Margo asked. "Not saying anything at all?"

I wasn't sure why she was asking me. There was no universe where I would have the answer.

I often went to the movies alone. New York was a great place to be alone because there were so many people. You were alone but in a dark room for a couple hours, together with strangers. Plus, the longer I was in my apartment, the more tempted I was to open Margo's laptop.

Like many things in the city, the cineplexes of Manhattan are built vertically. The layout of a movie theater resembles a maze of escalators. It was easy to purchase one ticket and spend the rest of the day sneaking into showings of other movies. But it turns out that if you see three or four movies a weekend, you can watch nearly everything in the theaters, even in a city that screens every movie. So I just started seeing the same films again. They wouldn't even be ones I liked. But what was important was that I was watching a movie, which means I couldn't be thinking about anything else.

I had so little going on during the weekends that I started spending all day at the multiplex. One Saturday, after waking up early and being unable to fall back asleep, I headed straight to the theater. I was there at 9 a.m., an hour before the first showing. I just waited around outside, doing nothing until I could enter. The earliest movie was an animated kids' movie that I had no interest in, but I watched it anyway. An hour and a half later, I snuck into a period drama that I'd already seen twice, then a new action movie that I hadn't seen but missed the first half hour of. When it was over, I found the next screening of the same movie, watched those missing thirty minutes, and sat through the rest of it. Again, I bounced around from theater to theater until there were no more showings. I emerged from the building and it was dark out. I went home and, the next morning, repeated it all over again.

The first day of movies had kept me distracted enough. But the second day, I left the theater feeling a new kind of emptiness. But maybe I was just hungry from subsisting on popcorn. The subway ride home from Midtown to Astoria was long, and it was already past midnight. All the Greek restaurants were closed. I passed low-rise after low-rise. Most of Astoria's buildings were described as "prewar," a term I'd always found strange, as if things occurred before or after the only war that has ever happened.

As soon as I was home, I ordered Indian food, more than enough for two people, thinking it polite to offer some to my roommate. Sometime between the time I placed the order and when it arrived, he left the apartment. I was thankful to be alone, although I wasn't sure why, because I'd been alone. I hadn't really interacted with another person in days. And so I ate the entirety of the food by myself.

The reason you don't feast on Indian takeout late at night is because no one wants to wake up at 4 a.m. with the sensation that your bowels are about to empty themselves all over your bed. I rushed to the bathroom and thankfully made it in time. I didn't have time to lower the toilet seat, so I sat uncomfortably on the rim of the toilet bowl, trying not to think about how long it had been since I'd cleaned it.

I got back into bed but couldn't fall asleep. It was dark out, and would be for another couple hours. It was never a comfortable temperature in the apartment. It was always too hot, even in the winter. The heat was controlled by the building manager, who cranked it all the way up, turning the entire building into a sticky, humid sauna. But summers were even worse. I hadn't saved up enough money for an air-conditioner, so every night I lay on top of my bed, sweating. I tossed around. I looked at my phone. I tried pulling the covers over my head.

If I was going to be miserably warm and feeling as if every calorie had just emptied out of my body, I might as well do the miserable thing I had been putting off. In the dark, I searched for Margo's laptop. I felt its shape on my desk, its smooth, hard edges against my palms. I opened the screen and the blue light was almost cartoonish, an oyster opening its bivalve to reveal what had been growing there.

The computer asked me to log in again. Margo's password had been burned into my memory. I carefully typed out "M4v15B34c0n" and hit ENTER. In the weeks since, I'd felt bad for taking Margo's laptop against Louise's wishes. But she'd tasked me with one job — to deactivate Margo's profile — and at least I could do that for her. I opened the browser and began to type in Facebook, but as I keyed an *F* and then an *A,* the browser auto-completed the URL, suggesting instead a website called Fantastic Planet.

I course-corrected to Facebook, typed "M4v15B34c0n" again — it worked — and suddenly I was looking at her profile. She had over two dozen unread messages. I clicked into her inbox.

These weren't old, neglected messages. All of them had been sent in the past few weeks. I didn't recognize the names of the senders, but the messages were almost all the same. Things like "I miss you so much but I know the Lord is taking care of you now." Anecdotes about Margo. Some of the senders were family; others were people Margo had gone to college with. None of them had been at the funeral, as far as I could recognize.

I didn't understand why anyone would message Margo after she had died. It seemed strangely performative, only it was completely — as far as they knew — private. Each one left me with a hollow feeling, though it could also have been the place in my stomach that once contained two servings' worth of Indian food.

One message caught my eye. It was another name I didn't know. He was a fratty-looking white guy. I assumed he was someone Margo went to college with. His profile picture was him drinking a beer on a yacht, eyes hidden by sunglasses, his expression equal parts arrogance and smugness — a bad stereotype of a white guy, the kind of person Margo would never be friends with.

The message read: "You were always kind of a bitch, but I'll miss you."

What the hell? What comfort did this person get from calling Margo a bitch after she had died? I thought about replying and telling him that he was an asshole. That would be a wake-up call, having a ghost tell you to go fuck yourself. Maybe the message was some kind of inside joke. Was this person close enough to Margo to call her a bitch? I didn't want to think about it. I deleted the message.

I was stalling.

Once a Facebook account has been permanently deleted, there is no way to recover it. Are you sure you want to permanently delete your profile?

Facebook's language was grim. It was as if permanent deletion was a prospect greater than death. I clicked YES.

You know once you commit to this there is no going back. Please check the following box to acknowledge.

I checked the box.

You know what you're doing, right?

I did.

Are you really, really sure about this?

I wasn't, but I proceeded anyway.

Killer_Performance.Wav

The powers that be were midway through their quarterly metrics presentation when Daniel stumbled into the meeting, bleeding everywhere from a large hole in his chest.

"You're really getting blood all over the place," said the CTO.

"Ugh, there is blood all over my shit!" the CFO barked, trying to gather his printouts before they could be soiled by Daniel's bodily fluids.

The CEO stepped in. "This is quite inappropriate. Daniel, get yourself cleaned up," he said, before telling the CFO to continue with his slideshow.

The CFO tried not to be jarred by the interruption. He clicked his clicker thing, and the screen moved on to the next slide.

"As you can see, killings are up 11 percent year-over-year, which is just shy of our target of 13 percent," he said, worried that the room would be disappointed.

The CEO interrupted. "We set those targets to be ambitious. The fact that we're still seeing double-digit growth — in THIS economy — is nothing short of impressive."

The room clapped politely to acknowledge the feat. Then the CEO stood up, to further emphasize just how great these numbers were. The CTO, CMO, CPO, and CLMFAO followed suit, standing and clapping. Daniel continued to bleed all over the table.

"Did anyone call the medical team for Daniel?" the CTO asked.

The CMO pulled out his phone and summoned a medic, then gestured to the CTO that it had been taken care of. "They'll be here in, like, two minutes."

The CFO moved on to the next slide.

"We attribute this 11 percent year-over-year growth to two factors: one is an improvement of efficiency of killings, which obviously has a great deal to do with the progress that the CTO has made in both our technology and our processes." The CFO nodded to the CTO, who smiled back, appreciative of the callout. (The CFO knew this would come in handy later.)

"We're not just killing more, but we're killing smarter. That's what keeps us ahead of our competitors."

Next slide.

"The second reason we've been able to maintain such steady growth in killing is because we're improving the way we manage our killers. All killers are held to a rigorous set of standards, and measured against one another to foster a sense of competition among them. We incentivize better work with bonuses, and we punish — well, sorry, that's

111

not the right word."

The CFO gestured toward Daniel. "Let's just say we de-incentivize poor performance."

As if on cue, Daniel let out a groan, then a gurgle, then coughed up a small pool of blood on the glass conference table. The room erupted in laughter.

"I . . . was . . . There was an ambush," Daniel said, weakly.

"And this failure to kill will show up on Daniel's daily metrics report, which we send out by email each morning," the CFO said.

Finally, the medic arrived. He apologized for the interruption, grabbed Daniel by the feet, and dragged his limp body out the door. Just before exiting the room, the medic cautioned that people should be careful of the streak of blood that Daniel's body left behind, god forbid anyone slip on it and get seriously injured.

To close out the meeting, the CEO stood up to make one final statement. Y'know, rally the troops, really motivate them moving into Q4.

"It's easy for all of us to sit in this conference room and look at a slideshow and appreciate a chart that has a line sloping upwards. But I don't want anyone here to lose sight of what we have accomplished here. When I started this company, people said it was a crazy idea. But we showed them that — through hard work, hiring the right people, moving quickly but intelligently — we could change the world."

The CEO continued: "I mean, guys, we did it: murder at scale."

More polite clapping, just before happy hour.

Daniel got fixed up quickly, and the next morning he was back at his desk, ready to work again. The day before had gone badly — reinforced by the performance metrics email Daniel received that morning — but he felt motivated to improve, to climb back up to the top of the killing board, where he'd been just a month before.

The timing wasn't great, though. The following week brought Performance Reviews, and Daniel's had a lot of red flags on it: "hostile," "inappropriate," "not a team player." They were damning words to appear on a Performance Review, and Daniel suspected they'd come from his intrusion into the CFO's meeting. He hadn't intended to interrupt — it was just difficult to find the medic's station after losing so much blood.

But Daniel suspected that the CFO, always known to hold a grudge, had torpedoed the Performance Review. It didn't take much to sink someone at the company. You could always file an unsolicited evaluation of an employee, and it had to be acknowledged and assessed by HR. Combined with his slipping killing performance, Daniel was put on a Performance Improvement Plan, playfully called a PIP. The document laid out a long list of things that he would have to do in order to keep his job. Many of the instructions were vague and involved things like having a better attitude and showing more collaboration with team members. But you couldn't measure that. So, of course, there were numbers associated with it: increase shootings by 20 percent, stabbings by a whopping 50 percent — knifework was always Daniel's weakness.

Because it wasn't just a matter of showing improvement of soft skills, but proving that you were putting in the effort. As Daniel ate a sad-ass salad at his desk, he wondered if he was up for it. He could spend the rest of the day trying to kill a whole lot more people, or, instead, update his résumé.

III
PERSONAL EFFECTS

The only thing in my room that scared me more than Margo's laptop was the sticky note with her password. I should have thrown both away. I'd deleted Margo's Facebook account. What use did I have left for her laptop and password? I had never had trouble throwing things away. When I moved to New York, I'd only taken enough clothes to fit in a single suitcase because I couldn't afford to pay the sixty dollars the airline charged to check a second bag. Everything I owned could be replaced.

A week had passed since I'd disposed of the Facebook account. I'd decided that maybe it was time to cool my movie-watching habit, so I replaced those long hours on the weekend with . . . nothing. Just drinking beer in my room, imagining what Margo and I might be up to if she was still around: getting day-drunk and wandering around the park, eating until we could smell the spices in our sweat, more Pac-Man of course. My eyes kept returning to the laptop, which I still could not bring myself to throw away. I still had one lingering question: What the hell was Fantastic Planet?

"Fuck it," I said out loud to no one. I opened another beer and swiped Margo's laptop from the desk.

Again, when I typed in *F* and *A,* Fantastic Planet autopopulated in the web browser. I clicked through.

What appeared was a log-in screen. I looked at the note. *M4v15B34c0n.* It worked again, and Fantastic Planet revealed itself: an old-school message board, not terribly different from PORK. But outside of that, it was not immediately obvious what I was looking at. There was some activity, though not much. Unlike PORK, these threads weren't neatly organized. It was more of a mishmash of topics, ranging from discussions of specific books to news stories to collections of JPEGs of optical illusions. I didn't really get it.

I clicked around for a while. Though no clear overriding subject emerged, there did seem to be a few consistent themes. There was a love of science and technology, an almost outdated romanticism of it. Most messages involved a lot of ponderous writing about the mysterious wonders of space. In fact, many of the images posted were from the '50s and '60s. Preserved on Fantastic Planet was an appreciation for the space age — tomorrow, as imagined by the past.

I discovered from Margo's history that she'd been on Fantastic Planet almost every night. She contributed to certain threads regularly, particularly in conversations about science fiction authors. The strong-willed, no-bullshit Margo I'd known was nowhere to be found. This afronaut3000 was anything but combative. She was earnest and enthusiastic. Her presence on Fantastic Planet was oddly peaceful. It reminded me of the afronaut3000 of PORK.

There were a number of unread messages for Margo, almost all from the same user: mining_colony.

The subject lines were:

Hey
Hello
Haven't heard from you in a while
Everything ok?

All of the messages were time-stamped days after Margo's death. I scrolled through the inbox — the conversations between

Margo and mining_colony went back over three years. And it appeared that they had talked nearly every day since they'd begun. I had so many questions. Who was this person? How come I'd never heard of them? What had they been talking about every day for the past three years? My face was suddenly hot, so I took another long drink of my beer. Who was this person that Margo talked to more than me?

And then, in a strange moment of drunken clarity, the right question: Did I have to tell them what had happened to Margo?

Which was followed by a predictable kind of drunken frustration, as I closed Margo's laptop and tossed it in the garbage.

Why do you look so mad?

I'm not mad. I'm just frustrated. All product managers do is nag me about whether I'm going to make my deadlines.

Isn't that their job?

To annoy me all day long? Apparently. The worst one is Scott.

Which one is Scott?

Bald, has that weird thing on his face he calls a "beard."

Oh, he runs Board Game Night at the office.

Scott is constantly "following up," "nudg-

118

ing politely," always wants to "touch base," whatever the fuck that means. I know what I have to do at my job. I don't need some unremarkable white boy reminding me.

Well, are you going to make deadline?

Not if I have to keep doing these needless "check-ins." Like, if I am behind on my work, there's nothing a product manager like Scott can do about it. He doesn't know anything about code. He just knows how to talk around it so he can look nice in front of his boss.

My new plan is to just confuse him. Last check-in, I told him a story about this Japanese marathon runner who set a world record in the early twentieth century. He was so good they called him the "Father of Marathon."

Why not "Marathon Dad"?

Even though he was the best long-distance runner in the world, he's actually most famous for vanishing at the 1912 Olympics in Stockholm. Back then, it was strenuous to travel. So it takes him eighteen days to get from Japan to Sweden, first by boat, then by train. On top of that, his stomach just doesn't agree with the local food.

Too many Swedish Fish.

Come race day, he's in terrible shape, but he runs anyway. It's a disaster. He's slipping in and out of consciousness. Midway through the race, he stops in at a restaurant to ask for a glass of orange juice. It's there he realizes there's no point in continuing on with the marathon. So he stays at the restaurant for an hour, enjoying himself. Even orders more food he hates. And when he's good and ready to leave, he gets directly on the train, then on the boat, and is on his way back to Japan.

The thing is: he never tells any of the officials. So when he doesn't finish the race, they just assume he died somewhere along the way.

At this point, I'm sure Scott has no idea why you're talking about this.

He strokes his crap beard and says something like, "What does this have to do with your deadline?"

And what *does* it have to do with your deadline?

I tell the rest of the story. It's not until 1967 that a Swedish newspaper realizes the runner is alive and well. So as a lark, they invite him back to finish the race. Thankfully, more than fifty years later, the journey from Japan is not nearly as arduous. He finally completes the marathon: a time of 54 years, 8 months, 6 days, 5 hours, 32 minutes, and 20.3 seconds.

That's how long it's going to take you to finish your work?

Nah. I just tell Scott, "I'm going to stop coming to these check-ins. Assume I died."

And what did he say?

He doesn't say anything. He is so bewildered he just stands up, mumbles some stuff about "keeping up the good work," and walks out of the room.

Aren't you worried that you'll get in trouble for not making your deadlines, though?

Oh, I am actually way ahead of schedule. I've been shipping code early without telling Scott. I am on top of my work. But this makes Scott look like a shitty product manager because he can't keep up with me.

That's sinister.

Listen, I don't need someone to confirm I ran twenty-six miles. I'll just go the distance myself.

When I started at Phantom, I'd endured a lecture from Dennis, the marketing manager, who explained that user acquisition was a funnel. He drew a diagram on a whiteboard.

"This is the top of the funnel," he said, circling what was obviously the top of the funnel. He took the marker and drew a line down through the triangular shape, charting the progression of a user through the funnel. His explanation made the process look self-evident, like every person started at the top of his diagram and would inevitably end up at the bottom of it, making them an acquired customer.

He circled the bottom of the diagram. "It's quite simple, right?"

The lesson stuck with me, mostly because Dennis had accidentally used a permanent marker on the whiteboard, his freehand scribble forever preserved on the backside of a ruined whiteboard we now kept in a storage closet — physical evidence that Phantom was being run by idiots.

Every Friday, there was a company-wide meeting where Dennis would run through the acquisition numbers, usually cause for him to pat himself on the back. But when the news got less exciting and the graphs began sloping downward, he decided to cancel the weekly meetings. "I'm giving everyone back thirty minutes of their day," he wrote in an email, as if he were doing us all a favor.

I wasn't surprised when Dennis was fired shortly after. We were still a small enough company that Brandon had to explain why they'd decided to "part ways" with their head of marketing. Brandon was diplomatic. Dennis simply "wasn't a culture fit" anymore; he could "do better work elsewhere." I wondered if, when Brandon fired Dennis, he'd phrased it like that to him too, like he was doing him a favor.

Soon after, Brandon scheduled check-in meetings with everyone at the company. Apparently this was the first person that Phantom had ever let go, so Brandon wanted to make sure the firing didn't affect morale. I told him it wasn't necessary — I'd barely worked with Dennis anyway. But Brandon insisted.

At the café during our one-on-one meeting, Brandon offered to buy me a coffee.

"What do you want? My treat."

It was late in the afternoon, and I didn't want anything.

"Come on, let me get you a drink. Or do you want a pastry?"

I felt obliged to pick something out of the case, even though I was too hungover to eat something sweet. Which is how I ended up picking at a raspberry-almond scone that I had no interest in putting in my body. I watched it crumble all over a napkin as Brandon talked. He'd had the idea for Phantom for years. In college, he'd studied computer science at the country's top-ranked program, but his interest was always in the way technology could set people free. Democracy would spread through information; it was a moral imperative for Phantom to succeed. I'd heard this all before but it was different this time.

Things at Phantom were going well and he seemed excited, like he was pitching. As a means of showing me the company's humble beginnings, Brandon shared the original deck he had sent investors. (Naturally, he had brought his laptop to the café.) From what I knew of the venture capital world, getting funding seemed appallingly easy. I couldn't get a loan to pay for my community college classes, but at twenty-two years old, Brandon was able to secure a seed round of $200,000 to start Phantom, which at the time was just an idea. I couldn't help but notice that there were typos throughout the deck.

Still, I had to admire the story. He had used China as an example of an authoritarian regime, abusing over a billion people by limiting their internet access. Unimaginatively dubbed "the Great Firewall of China," the web in China had certain facets that were made off-limits by the Communist party. All access was closely monitored, to ensure no one was organizing to topple the government. With Phantom, Chinese users could at least communicate with people outside the Firewall. Since the messages in Phantom disappeared, it would protect them from the consequences of saying the wrong things. At the end, there was a rough estimate of what growth would look like if Phantom could crack the Chinese market. There wasn't a clear plan for how the company would do that, just the promise of potential. It was a mission, paired with a market opportunity. Investors could feel good about where they were putting their money, and feel good that they'd get it back too.

For Brandon, technology wasn't a mountain. It was the tectonic plates under the Earth, slowly moving and reshaping the landscape above it. When I asked him about that metaphor causing earthquakes, Brandon shook it off and explained that that was why we needed people in technology with a sense of responsibility. The way technology was right now — uncharted, unregulated — meant that it would cause havoc. I thought back on this conversation often that year as I watched the high-minded optimism of Brandon slowly erode as investor pressure mounted. If technology represented the landscape that people actually traversed in life, it was one that could be drastically shaped and reshaped by money — advertisers, investors, whoever had it. Even I knew that.

As far as I knew, Margo didn't have other friends. She wasn't supposed to have other friends. If she did, more of them would have turned up at the funeral. But there were hundreds, maybe thousands, of messages in her archive at Fantastic Planet. This person, whoever they were, would want to know what happened to Margo, right? Maybe they would also understand how it felt to lose her.

I woke up in the middle of the night, my body weak from dehydration, which was becoming a familiar feeling since I'd felt this way every day in the three weeks since the funeral. I stumbled to the dark bathroom and shoved my face under the faucet to drink. I turned on the light. My eyes were red, my face flushed, water dribbling from my chin. I looked like shit.

From the garbage, I retrieved Margo's computer.

By reading Margo's message history, I eventually figured out that the username mining_colony referred to a book titled *Min-*

ing Colony. The author had come to Fantastic Planet for help with her science fiction novel, and most of what Margo discussed with mining_colony was in reference to a manuscript. That must've been sent through Margo's personal email, which I hadn't accessed yet. I told myself I wasn't going to break into any more of Margo's accounts. Fantastic Planet was already too far.

Margo's notes for mining_colony, though, were detailed. As a lover of sci-fi, she had extremely specific ideas about how to evoke its pulpy bygone era. The two would joke often, and as I worked through their extensive message logs, their conversations veered toward the personal. I recognized some things. Margo made broad passing references to her job, her "asshole boss" (Brandon), and a boy she had been sleeping with (who? she'd never mentioned this). I admit some part of me expected her to reference me, though I never found anything. I tried not to be disappointed.

mining_colony had stories of their own, equally mundane: the maddening solitude of working from home, how days could go by without leaving one's apartment or interacting with anyone in person. mining_colony's last message was still the most recent one: "Everything ok?"

The sun was coming up.

"Hi mining_colony, this isn't Margo," I typed. "But I wish it was."

I passed out, and when I woke up again, there was a reply.

"Who's Margo?"

I'd combed through nearly three years' worth of messages and hadn't noticed that not once was Margo referred to by name. She'd kept the handle from her PORK days. It was funny: Margo had talked to this person every day, at length, for three years and they never exchanged any real, identifying information. It wasn't much different from the friendship that Margo and I had developed on PORK — anonymous, but not really anonymous.

I drafted several responses, but none of them seemed right. How do you tell your dead friend's online pen pal that she's died?

"This account belonged to Margo," I wrote, and attached a link to the obituary. In some ways, it seemed like a cheat. I realized that this was how I'd operated my entire life. My feelings and sentiments were represented through files, through things made by others on the internet: links, mp3s, JPEGs. Employing the work of others to get around having to convey it yourself was a huge crutch of communicating on the internet. From the obituary, I had ready-made language to use to tell a stranger that Margo had stumbled out of a bar, into the street, and been hit by a speeding cab.

mining_colony's reply was nearly instant. "Oh my god. This is terrible."

"I'm sorry for your loss," I typed.

I waited for another reply, but a few minutes passed. I was ready to be done with mining_colony. This would be the last time I opened Margo's laptop, the last moment before I would throw away the sticky note. But their next question sucked me in.

"So who are you?"

Hi
I'm glad we switched to email. This is a little less strange, yes?

RE: Hi
For sure. It felt wrong to be on Margo's account.
Okay, let's start with the basics: what is your name?

RE:RE: Hi
Oh right, I guess formal introductions got lost in the whole "hey this person you know isn't replying to your messages

129

because they . . . aren't around anymore"
thing.
Ugh, this is so weird. But I'm Jill. And you?

RE:RE:RE: Hi
Lucas.

RE:RE:RE:RE: Hi
Despite the truly awful circumstances, it is
nice to meet you, Lucas.

She confirmed what I'd deduced: she was
a novelist. It turns out I knew a lot about
her already, just from reading through her
messages with Margo. But I let her explain.

RE:RE:RE:RE:RE:RE:RE:RE:RE:RE:RE:
RE:RE:RE: Hi
For my second book, I knew I had a rough
idea for a science fiction story. But I had
no idea how to do it, to tell a story in a reality divorced from our own. So I signed
up for the Fantastic Planet message
boards. I was in conversation with Margo
(I'm gonna have to get used to calling her
that) and we got along really well and
started messaging each other every day
after that.

I told her Margo and I had worked together for the past two jobs. We were close friends.

RE:RE:RE:RE:RE:RE:RE:RE:RE:RE:RE:
RE:RE:RE:RE:RE:RE:RE:RE:RE:RE:RE:
RE:RE:RE:RE:RE:RE: Hi
You know what the craziest thing is? Until reading the obit, I never realized that Margo lived in Brooklyn. It says she lived in Crown Heights. I'm in Cobble Hill, which means that we've been talking for years and lived, at most, a mile or two apart. I wonder if I might have passed her on the street or sat next to her on the subway, not knowing that she was someone I talked to every day.

Jill had an unending stream of questions about Margo. Some were specific:

How tall was she?

5'4"? 5'3"?

Others harder to answer:

What did her voice sound like?

Firm.

I could sense a curiosity, but also a desire

131

to understand how much Margo matched the afronaut3000 she had been imagining for years.

Do you have a picture of her?

Margo wasn't really the type to take photos. I searched her hard drive for images. Very little surfaced. Eventually I found a picture of her, posed coolly outside of a bar, basking in the light of a neon sign advertising a cheap brand of beer, not smiling (of course). She had on a patterned head wrap and a solid mustard dress. If you squinted, you could make out the hints of a lit cigarette in her hand. The photo wasn't recent — dated five years back — from sometime in college. It was the best I could find, so I emailed it along.

Jill replied immediately: "She was beautiful."

"She really was," I said, realizing just as I hit ENTER how weird that must sound. I'd never thought of Margo as beautiful. Like, she was. But that wasn't what our friendship was. It was one of trust, a closeness that two people felt when they lived in a world that fundamentally did not understand them. It wasn't romantic. Besides, if I had truly —

Do you want to meet up?

I was surprised by the question. But I didn't want to show hesitation, so I didn't.

The instant messaging service Margo and I used kept an archive of every conversation we'd ever had. I searched our shared history for any reference to "Jill." Nothing came up, which made sense, since Margo had likely never learned Jill's real name. I tried a second search, for "author" or "novelist," which yielded a few results, but nothing relevant, just scraps of loose talk. Last, I tried looking for "mining colony."

About a year ago, Margo had recommended that I read something called *Mining Colony*. She had described it as "Raymond Carver in space," a campus novel on an asteroid. I added it to a list of other books Margo had told me to read. She read at a superhuman rate, and I was adding things to that list faster than I was crossing anything off. But I remembered distinctly the excitement with which she'd spoken about *Mining Colony:*

"Okay, so the story is set on an asteroid

cluster — two floating rocks in space. The first, the bigger of the two, is a mining colony called Excavator-IV. It is, like all things involving miners, very poor. The work is hard and dangerous. But not far away is Excavator-V, the other rock, where all of the mine owners live. It's also home to a university that specializes in higher education for fields related to space mining. So basically, it's a story about the tensions of inequality between the two asteroids."

I'd told Margo that it sounded great.

"I'm still in the middle of it," she'd said, "but it's already among the best things I've ever read."

At the time, Margo hadn't revealed that *Mining Colony* had a special connection to her, that she'd helped shape it.

Now was as good a time as any to read it. I left my apartment with the intention of buying a copy, and realized as soon as I was on the street that I had no idea where the closest bookstore was. At the bodega, I got a coffee and asked the cashier. He had no idea, gave me my change, and told me to have a nice day.

I remembered there was a big bookstore in Manhattan near Union Square, the kind you would find mostly situated in a mall, usually nestled between an electronics store and a department store, always a coffee counter somewhere near the bestsellers. When I arrived, I wandered around looking for Jill August's book. First I scanned the science fiction section. No luck. I checked the general fiction shelves. Not there either. I asked a bookseller, who attempted to summon *Mining Colony* on the computer. No records. What they found instead was another book by August. *Adult Contemporary.* The cover was sparse, just strong lettering over what looked like a stock photo of a family. I bought it.

I cracked the book open on the subway ride home. I walked from the train to my apartment turning pages, then continued back in bed in my apartment.

Adult Contemporary was completely different from what I was expecting. In the first scene, the two kids — a brother and sister — are sneakily checking the "casual encounters" section of Craigslist. They're young (middle school and high school), and reading each other the prurient details of men and women's fetishes. It's all laughs until they stumble across one ad that has a photo with a woman that looks suspiciously like their mother.

The children are unsure what to do; whether they should tell their parents or just pretend they never found out. The middle-school-aged son feels an allegiance to his father and wants to tell him. The daughter, who is in early high school, believes that it must all be a misunderstanding. She convinces her brother to stay quiet.

The daughter, though, begins spying on her mother. She keeps a diary of her mom's comings and goings. She begins paying close attention to the relationship between their parents — how often they talk to each other and show signs of affection; how often they argue or seem at odds. It's a great literary trick, and we see that the daughter's close observation of her parents' marriage parallels her own discovery of what love and intimacy really mean.

The book is divided into two parts, and toward the end of the first half the daughter, after much deliberation and amateur sleuthing, decides that their mother is definitely not cheating on their father with strangers on Craigslist. The mom's schedule checks out. Mom and Dad are clearly still in love. Everything is the way it's supposed to be.

But one day, the brother cuts class to smoke weed in the park with some friends. (There's an entire subplot about him being peer-pressured into drugs.) On his way there, he sees his mother's car parked at a local motel. He investigates and, to his horror, discovers her walking into a room with a stranger. He is so shocked he is nearly seen by his mother. Still, he is able to take a picture of the two of them with his Polaroid camera.

Later, he shows his sister. The photo is blurry and washed-out. They argue about whether it means anything. The sister becomes incredibly upset, and takes the Polaroid and marches downstairs to show her father the picture, to tell him that his wife is a horrible cheater. She finds both her parents at the kitchen table, laughing and drinking wine together. The daughter, feeling raw in the moment, decides that she will just confront both of them at the same time.

She yells. She shows the father the picture. She points at her mother and calls her a liar and a whore. The mother begins sobbing. The father looks heartbroken and stares at the picture. He doesn't say anything.

The daughter begins yelling directly at her mother, asking her why she would do something like this, why she would do this to her family, how could she be so selfish. The father finally speaks up. He tells his daughter to shut up. He tells her that he knows. He tells her that she knows that he knows. He tells her that this is an arrangement they have. The money is good. They need the money.

This is where the first act ends, with the revelation that the mother is a sex worker.

I looked out the window and realized the entire day had nearly passed.

Margo's death had put a damper on the office for a few weeks, but eventually the mood at Phantom was possessed by a new crisis: teenagers.

Brandon had lofty goals for Phantom, but he did not anticipate his technology would become the next big thing with kids whose communication habits were radically different from those of the adults the service was designed for. Teenagers were sending messages at a clip that seemed impossible. Was it possible that kids in middle school and high school sent a hundred times more messages than their parents? The increased usage caused major instability in the Phantom servers. For two weeks, backend engineers were pulling insane shifts at the office, attempting to keep all the servers online.

It was difficult to figure out who was the first individual user to spark Phantom's popularity, but the data scientists pinned the teen sweep to a small high school in

Central California. Gathered around one of the data scientists' computers, we watched in awe as the users spread from California, jumping to New York, and then spreading inward from the coasts. It was like watching a contagious virus infect the entire country.

Venture capitalists were never interested in revenue — they were interested in the *potential* of revenue. That's how investing works. User growth had slowed nearly to a halt, which threatened the next round of funding. So the sudden boom in new users was a small miracle. But with an entirely new demographic of users came an entirely new set of challenges, and we were wholly unprepared.

As Phantom's user base was growing, so were the number of support requests that had to be answered, and right now our customer support team consisted of me. They were going to hire, but Brandon hoped I wouldn't mind taking on more work in the interim.

"This is what we talked about, giving you greater responsibilities," he said.

"Well, if I'm doing more, can I have a raise?"

"What?" I'd caught Brandon off guard with my request. "Yeah, sure. Of course."

He offered a 10 percent bump so readily

139

that I was left wondering if I should have asked for more.

Growing up, a package would arrive in the mail for my father every three months. It was notable just as mail — he rarely received anything by post — and notable for its contents: always a pair of VHS tapes, bundled together, the packaging emblazoned with the soft photography and swirly type announcing *Paris by Night*.

The concept was relatively straightforward: it was a live variety show, mostly music with a few low-stakes comedy sketches. The entire thing was in Vietnamese — the singing, the monologues — filmed entirely in California. Besides sriracha, *Paris by Night* was the biggest cultural product of Vietnamese Americans. It was also the only thing my dad ever watched on our television.

We owned a DVD player, but *Paris by Night* kept arriving as a pair of chunky tapes. My dad claimed he didn't know how to change our mail-order subscription, but I think he liked the familiarity of VHS. Its size was so distinctive that you couldn't mistake it for anything else in the mailbox. Every time it arrived, it was assumed that me and my mom would watch it with him that evening. It didn't matter that neither of us spoke Vietnamese. Each *Paris by Night* was four hours long.

We'd been watching these quarterly since I was a child. Each new one had slightly stronger production values than the one that had preceded it. Watching *Paris by Night* was a bit like watching the Academy Awards, except there were no awards. If the Oscars used all the performances and jokes to pad the show's run time, then imagine *Paris by Night* as simply hours of filler. It was also the only time I ever saw my dad laugh — a real laugh, summoned deep from the belly. He cracked up so hard that sometimes he teared up. Someone onstage would, in Vietnamese, deliver a punchline, their face waiting for laughter and applause. It always came. My mom and I never had any idea what was going on.

Mom did laugh along, though. Once, I asked her why she was laughing when she couldn't possibly understand the joke.

"That doesn't mean it isn't funny," she said.

A couple months after I'd moved to New York, Dad called to tell me about the new *Paris by Night.* We were on the phone for a while as he gave me the play-by-play of each performance, and the sketches that fol-

141

lowed. He struggled to translate the hosts' banter, often saying that it was funnier in Vietnamese, and then laughing at the joke I still didn't understand.

He asked how my work was going. He'd hardly ever touched a computer — had only recently gotten a cell phone — so I'd always struggled explaining to him what exactly Phantom was. But at least now he understood the concept of text messages. Instead of talking, you sent written sentences back and forth. Simple.

What Phantom did, I explained, was made those messages disappear after they'd been read.

"Why would you want them to disappear?" he asked. "What if you want to see them later?"

I thought about my father's *Paris by Night* tapes. Usually when you finish a VHS tape, you rewind it for next time. My father would never bother rewinding his *Paris by Nights* because there would never be a next time. He'd store the videos on a shelf in a closet — single use, then cast away into an archive.

"Why don't you throw those away?"

"What if I want to watch them again?"

"You've never watched a *Paris by Night* twice."

"But what if, one day, I did want to."

"Wouldn't it be more useful to have all that closet space back?"

My father took a moment. It seemed never to occur to him that he didn't need to keep all the tapes he'd watched.

"It would be wasteful to throw them away."

I wasn't going to try and convince him.

"Text messages, they go away already," he said.

"What do you mean?"

"After some time, they disappear."

"They're probably still on your phone."

"No, you forget them. Time passes and you can't remember what you said to anyone, or what anyone said to you. They all disappear on their own."

I had no idea what my dad was going on about but I let him keep talking.

I arrived to work late. I'd cut down on my drinking significantly, but I'd gotten used to showing up sometime after 10 a.m. And, more importantly, so did everyone else. So really I was just showing up at my regular time.

Brandon and Emil were arguing in the conference room, and it was loud enough that everyone else in the office had stopped working, many of them turned around in their chairs just to observe the conflict.

"Privacy is one of the reasons I started this company," Brandon said. "If we give up on protecting the privacy of our users, then there's no point."

Emil's response was calmer and more measured. "That was before our service was being used by people under the age of eighteen. If we don't start monitoring what people are saying, we are going to get in serious legal trouble."

It took a moment for me to piece it together. The genius of Phantom was that messages were temporary. Once something had been seen, it disappeared. Emil reminded Brandon that one of the company's big sells was how "ephemeral messaging" would be a way for whistleblowers to message people without fear of leaving a paper trail. But of course, the majority of Phantom's users were not anonymous whistleblowers sending incriminating evidence of corporate transgressions and government corruption. They were not implicating white-collar criminals or toppling authoritarian regimes. As far as any of us knew, that had never happened. Our users were regular people, just making frivolous conversation with each other. And now, they were mostly very young.

There had been several cases of teenagers sending sexually explicit messages to each other.

> send me pics of your tits
> bitch suck me offffff
> i wanna cum on ur face lol

The screenshots had come through the customer support email. These were hard to investigate because it was merely one person's word against another's. In one case, a woman reported that she had received sexually explicit language from another user, insinuating that the man would like to have intercourse with her. The details were disturbing in nature. But since all messages self-deleted, I had no way to verify if the screenshots were real. On one hand, I knew the chances were very low that someone would go out of their way to make up a story like that. On the other, I didn't have any proof. I wrote back to the user and said she could simply block his account and she would no longer receive any messages from him — a recommendation that was unsatisfying to both of us.

Other cases were even more complicated, especially when it came to bullying.

talk to me again and i will end you
your dead faggot
i'm gonna throttle you so hard that you'll
    shit your teeth
don't make me rape your face

Now that Phantom was made up of teenagers, this became a growing concern. How
do you prevent users from harassing one
another? What is the line between teasing
and bullying? Did we have an obligation to
protect our users from one another? These
were all questions we'd put off confronting,
because they didn't have clear solutions.

Emil proposed that we start saving records
of all conversations between users. They
would appear to be deleted to the user, but
we would have them stored, to be summoned in case of customer service requests.
We could analyze messages in broad swaths.
Emil's example: All users that were flagged
for harassing another person could be
grouped together, their behaviors and patterns identified so future iterations of
Phantom could learn to automatically flag
inappropriate conduct. I was surprised by
how confident Emil was in this idea, considering it undermined everything that Brandon had set out to do with the company.

"Think about how much time that would

save out of Lucas's day," Emil said, pointing toward my desk. Another surprise: I had no idea Emil cared about my time.

Like everyone else in the office, I was pretending to work, headphones on but playing no music, listening to the argument but staying out of it. I could hear others in the office typing furiously. Everyone was messaging each other. I caught stray glances around the room. No one was messaging me, though. Instead, I thought about all the things I would be saying to Margo if she were here.

"If we give ourselves the power to read people's private messages, then we're just like every other company out there," Brandon said.

"We're not reading individual messages. We are writing software that allows us to comprehend huge amounts of messages. No human being has to violate a user's individual privacy."

"But a human writes that software." Brandon pointed to another engineer, Tom, who ducked behind his monitor. "This idea is insane. You're insane. You can't say that we're protecting user privacy if you have the ability to look at their private communications — even if it's just code that's crawling it. Emil, that's unethical."

"Ethical? You believe it's more morally justifiable to create a platform that doesn't protect its users from harm than it is to lightly moderate people's behavior."

"Not if we violate users' privacy!"

Like all arguments between angry men in a workplace, the disagreement became circular, then personal, then unresolvable. Neither was going to change his mind, and eventually Brandon pulled rank as CEO. His closing argument was that in the case of any future legal issues the company might have, it would be better to not have any evidence at all. The last thing Phantom would want is to have its data subpoenaed and used in litigation against itself. If no one had proof, it didn't happen. Both men marched away, pissed. They were steaming, like they'd each been robbed of the most precious thing in his life but couldn't do anything about it. I found the whole thing hilarious.

It didn't take long for Emil's concerns to expand outside of the company. The following weekend, a news story ran about a high school sophomore in the suburbs of Orlando who had been viciously bullied. The report, which ran on a local news station, had accused Phantom of enabling harassment. I suppose they weren't wrong.

The whole Phantom staff — all sixteen of us — crowded around Emil's computer to watch a clip of the segment. It opened with some low-quality B-roll of students in a computer lab and a voiceover from the reporter asking, "Do you know what kinds of messages your kids are sending? They could be harassing their classmates. Or worse yet: they could be the victim of bullying."

It only got worse from there. The reporter interviewed several parents to ask them if they knew what their children were doing when they used a computer. None of them had firm answers. The reporter wasn't subtle in her attempts to drum up parental fears about what their kids might be doing on the internet.

At the end of the segment, Brandon appeared on camera to defend Phantom. He was in rare form. Usually confident and well-spoken, he looked totally unprepared. He stumbled over his statements, leaning on vague responses and the occasional clumsy question-dodge. Finally the reporter asked, "What kind of commitment can you make to combating the bullying problem on your software?"

"At Phantom, we are wholly committed

149

to stopping bullying wherever we can," Brandon said.

"But what does that mean?"

Brandon appeared only to have canned non-answers. "We're going to do everything in our power to take this problem seriously."

The anchor pressed, the slightest hint of a grin forming at the corner of her mouth the moment she realized she could go in for the kill.

"You're not saying anything meaningful."

"No, we —"

"Tell us one concrete step you will take to ridding your software of bullying."

I was surprised when Brandon answered coolly and eloquently. He'd practiced the nuclear option. "We're dedicated to the safety of our users, which is why we're going to start monitoring Phantom for inappropriate messages."

As the video clip came to an end, we all knew exactly what it meant. Emil had won. We would start saving user messages. At Phantom, nothing would disappear anymore.

Jill was taller than I'd expected, though I didn't know what exactly I had expected from the tiny black-and-white author photo on the jacket of her book. It reminded me of an online avatar, a small square picture meant to represent an entire person.

But Jill was tall, nearly six feet. Her posture was slightly hunched in the way someone is when they're self-conscious of their height. She had shoulder-length dark brown hair; an array of light freckles; white, clear skin.

We made pleasantries. *It's nice to meet you. How is your day going? Let's do anything to circle around the fact that we're both here, at this bar, because our mutual friend is dead.*

"I'm going up to get a beer. Can I get you anything?"

"Just a water," Jill said. "I don't really drink."

I'd asked Jill if she wanted to meet at a bar, and, like an asshole, had not even entertained the possibility that the stranger I was meeting up with could possibly be a nondrinker.

"I should have asked. Honestly, I've been trying to cut back too. We can go to a place for coffee instead if you'd like."

"This is fine. Really. Also I don't know what café would be open at nine p.m. around here."

I ordered a beer and a water and returned to the table.

"I've actually never been to this bar

151

before," Jill said. "You can tell I don't go out a lot. I picked it because it's the closest one to my apartment. I didn't expect it to be so . . . grunge-y."

She waved her hand, ironically gesturing toward the bar's interior as if it were a game show prize. It was a fake dive bar, deliberately disheveled to make the upper-middle-class patrons of Brooklyn feel more casual or whatever. But the bar was dirty. The floor was sticky with filth, foam peeking out of cracked barstools, gum caked the underside of every table. Jill and I were the only patrons. Maybe it was just early.

She came out with it.

"When you sent me the photo of Margo, I admit, I was kind of stunned. I had no idea she was black."

"Well, my entire relationship with Margo was informed by how she saw the world as a black woman," I said. It was surprising how that came out, the almost self-righteous tone of it. Part of me felt the need to assert that I'd known Margo better.

"We talked about certain kinds of personal stuff often, but we never really talked about race," Jill said. "It didn't come up."

"So you just assumed she was white?"

"I did. Is that shitty?"

"It's not. It's just . . ."

Jill took a moment. Maybe she felt guilty. White people often did. She collected herself, then continued: "When you write a novel, you have this opportunity to describe your characters — physically describe them. So as you write, you make this conscious decision whether or not to define their race. Are they black? Asian? Latino? White?"

"I think if you don't tell people, readers will just assume the character is white."

"That's true. And that's something you have to reckon with. But also, when you don't define what a person looks like, you let the reader decide."

"So I could imagine the family in *Adult Contemporary* as Asian?"

"Oh, you read my book?"

"I did. Well, I'm halfway through. I started yesterday."

"That's so flattering."

"I like it a lot."

"Even more flattering."

"But I imagined the family was white."

"You don't have to, though. There's nothing in the book that says they're white. I didn't impose those rules on you. You're free to believe the family looks however you want."

"How did you imagine they looked when you wrote the book?"

153

"Well, white," Jill said.

She pressed on: "So you read some of the conversations Margo and I had?"

"Just some of them," I lied.

"Fuck, that's . . . that's weird."

"Sorry, I didn't —"

"No, it's okay."

I gave an unconvincing nod, followed by an even less convincing "uh-huh."

"Before Margo and I met in real life, we were friends on a music forum."

"Could you tell she was black?"

The question was uncomfortable, how bluntly she asked it. But to be fair, I was the one who'd started this conversation by using Margo's race as evidence that I was the closer friend.

"Well, on that message board she also went by afronaut3000, so I just sort of assumed. It would be pretty embarrassing for, like, a white dude to go by afronaut."

"I guess . . . I should have known from that."

"Was that not a sign?"

"You never know online. It's always a possibility. A lot of white guys like to represent themselves with avatars of anime girls."

"That's true. It's one thing for white dudes to be into Asian women. But why disguise yourself online as one?"

"Oh, it makes perfect sense to me," she said. "They love the stereotype of something small and cute and quiet."

Then suddenly: "Were you and Margo dating?"

"No —" I was mid-sip and nearly choked, caught off guard. "No, no, no, no. We were just friends."

"Defensive?"

"Not dating. Not at all."

"Hmm, even more defensive."

"I promise you, Margo and I were just friends."

"But you were, like, in love with her?"

"It wasn't like that. Not romantically, at least. Nothing ever happened."

"Nothing happened. You were just madly, deeply in love with her. You could never say it because you were afraid it would spoil the friendship. But in your heart —"

"JUST. FRIENDS."

I was shocked by how defensive I sounded. How could Jill understand the depth of the friendship Margo and I had? There was no way to explain to a stranger that the closeness we shared was something more meaningful than romantic intimacy. We'd first known each other as anonymous avatars. We'd connected as non-bodies. It almost

155

made the idea of being in love sound frivolous.

But now I was shouting — at a perfectly pleasant person, no less — and it just made me unconvincing. I felt unconvincing. Maybe I was just fooling myself. I thought about the conversation I'd had with Margo when the dating site report had deemed black women unfuckable, and how much that had hurt her. Yet here I was, in a conversation with a white person, explaining how I did not want to sleep with a black woman.

"Okay okay, I'm teasing. I believe you." Thankfully, Jill was not picking up on the levels of this. She was just having a good time. "It's funny you got so worked up."

"Thank you," I said, pissed. "I'm glad this is working for someone."

There was a pause, and I could tell Jill was building toward something. She took a long sip of water, then placed the glass back on the table. Then took another sip.

"Everything okay?"

"You mentioned in your message that she had been hit by a car, but I didn't know if there was more to it."

"It's not even a story. It wasn't dramatic so much as it was sudden. Margo was leaving a bar in Manhattan and a taxicab was speeding down the street and I'm pretty sure it was all in the obit I sent you . . ."

I trailed off, unable to finish the sentence, unable to make eye contact with Jill. I just stared down at my beer glass, which was nearly empty. All that was left was the last warm sip.

"Was she drunk?"

"Knowing Margo, almost definitely. But she'd been drunk many times before and not fucking died. So that just didn't have anything to do with it," I said. "There's no way. There has to be more. Something else."

I could feel a pain in my gut, a gut that was used to being furnished with more cheap beer than it had been recently. Jill looked uneasy.

"That is so fucking sad. So sudden. And she was, what, twenty-six?"

"Twenty-five."

"Twenty-five years old, Jesus."

Jill stood up and went to the bar. She returned with another beer for me and a shot of tequila for herself.

"I thought you didn't really drink," I said.

"I don't," she said, a second before emptying the contents of the shot glass down her throat, standing up, and ordering a second.

A few drinks later, we were playing an

arcade game that involved aiming an orange plastic shotgun at stiffly animated forest life — rabbit, deer, occasionally a moose. When they scurried by, you unloaded a digital blast of buckshot into them. Jill was having trouble coordinating the pump-action mechanics on the gun.

"Why can't I murder this stupid moose?"

She was yelling. Also, surprisingly, the bar was crowded now. People had started trickling in as the hours passed (what time was it?). The music had gotten louder too, a deafening fury of distorted guitars on a heavy metal soundtrack (who listened to this?).

"You have to pump the gun to reload."

"What?"

"Pump the gun to reload."

"I can't hear you."

"If you want to keep shooting, you have to reload the gun."

"This game sucks. I hate it."

"Yeah, it's really not fun."

"Do you have any more quarters? I want to play again."

I went up to the bar to get change. From my wallet, I fished out a twenty-dollar bill.

"Are you sure you want twenty dollars' worth of quarters?" the bartender asked. "That's, like, eighty quarters."

158

"We're going to play eighty more games of the stupid hunting game." I laughed. "Also two whiskeys please."

We did not play eighty more games. After a couple more attempts, Jill got frustrated. I gave the game a go, but found it hard to concentrate. It was overstimulating. There were animals everywhere, coming in from all angles of the screen. Every time I fired the gun, the game made a loud *pop* and the screen flashed, startling me. I had never gone hunting before, but wasn't it supposed to be a quiet, solitary activity? This game was like shooting fish in a barrel, except all the fish were deer and annoying as hell.

Jill took the orange gun out of my hands and placed another quarter in the machine. The game began and she started shooting.

"I know it's stupid to say this to someone who actually knew Margo in real life when I didn't." She sighed. "But I miss her."

"I don't think that's a stupid thing to say."

"It's a stupid thing to say." Jill shot at a rabbit and missed. "Margo and I spoke every day. She was by far the person I talked to the most for the past two years. And now she's gone." Jill shot at a buck. It didn't go down.

"I spend all day by myself, trying to write." She shot the buck again. The buck model flashed red, to illustrate that it had died. "And at least while I was alone in my apartment, I could talk to Margo."

At the end of each round, all of the creatures you missed were also displayed with your score, as an incentive for you to play again. The moose trotted across the screen, still alive, as if to taunt Jill.

"Fucking moose. One day I will slay you."

"You guys are very bad at this game."

A man had approached us from behind. He was tall, white, dressed in flannel, a full beard — a handsome kind of disheveled that toed the line between deliberate and effortless, kind of like this bar. He didn't look at me, only acknowledged Jill.

"I'll have you know, sir, that I am very good at this game. Look, I just killed a rabbit and a deer." Jill pointed at the screen, which still displayed her winnings.

"I'm not one to criticize a lady's form, but I believe you're holding the rifle wrong. You want the butt of the gun up against your shoulder. Here, let me show you."

He moved in close to Jill, put his arm under hers to position the rifle. I was surprised that she didn't immediately push him away.

"You seem like someone who's played a lot of this arcade game," Jill said.

160

"I've played all the *Big Buck Hunter* games," he said. "There's *Big Buck Hunter: Shooter's Challenge, Big Buck Hunter II: Sportsman's Paradise, Big Buck Hunter: Call of the Wild, Big Buck Hunter Pro,* and *Big Buck Hunter Safari.*"

"Is the idea here that you're going to impress me by being good at *Big Buck Hunter*?"

"I could impress you in a lot of ways."

Jill let out something between a groan and a cackle. "What's your name?"

"I'm Dave."

"Dave." Jill took a step back and laughed. "Get the fuck out of here."

Eventually, we retired to two seats at the bar. Jill never got that moose.

The bartender did not love that I was paying for our next drinks in quarters, partly because, by this point of drunkenness, it took me forever to count them. But she was patient, if annoyed, and I appreciated that. I tipped her twelve quarters.

"I don't think I've had this much to drink since college," Jill said.

"You mentioned that a few times already."

"Did I?" Jill laughed, amused by her own drunkenness. She was laughing a lot. So was I. I'd almost missed it.

"I'm not sure I've had this much fun since Margo died," I admitted.

"Me neither," Jill said. "Though I only found out she'd died, like, last week. And that her name is Margo."

"How come you never asked about her real name?"

"A couple of times, I suggested we talk on the phone. Sometimes she would give me complicated or confusing notes on my story, and I said it might be easier to talk it through on a call. But she just further clarified by text. I don't know. It seemed like she wanted our relationship to be where it was and how it was. And I had to respect that. Although . . ."

"What?"

"We'd never met, and, at least on a few occasions, she tried to convince me to visit Tokyo with her. Like, she seemed obsessed with going to Japan. Did she talk about that with you?"

"Yes, it came up," I said, which was partly true. Margo mentioned traveling to Tokyo, but never with me. I had other questions, though.

"Why was she helping you with your book?"

"I have no idea. I think about the hundreds of hours she spent helping me —

reading pages, giving notes, talking through minute details. She should've asked me to pay her, really."

"It's okay. Margo was always fine on money."

"Really? What did she do?"

"She was an engineer."

"Like a coder?"

"Yeah, like a coder. A kind of exceptional one too. A goddamn genius — good at the nitty-gritty and the big picture. There wasn't a thing she couldn't figure out. Not everyone in the office liked her, but they all respected and admired her. She had a way of seeing the world for its composite parts. Everything could be broken down into systems, each with their own rules and consequences. I think engineering data architecture was effortless for her. It was so self-contained. But when she'd look at the world more broadly you could see her trying to piece it all together, but it was just too much at times. Systems of sexism, systems of racism, systems of social class, all interlocking and tugging at each other in different directions. And the engineer part of her brain couldn't stop trying to understand and solve those things. Too much for one person."

"Margo carried the weight of the world."

"No one asked her to, though."

"Was she . . . Did she seem happy?"

"Margo was too brilliant to be happy."

"I know I only saw one small, narrow part of her, but the Margo I knew always seemed joyful."

"I know she could be. She often was. But so many of the conversations we had were about systems of oppression, and rebelling against them. How could we not talk about that stuff all the time? We were surrounded by it."

"I mean, I'd be at home alone, no one to talk to. And Margo was always there to give me feedback and encouragement. Every conversation we had was just brimming with energy and optimism. There were so many times when I thought about giving up on the stupid thing. I'd said as much to Margo, and she would always remind me that what I was doing was difficult but worthwhile."

"Sounds wonderful to have that in a friend."

"It was. Publishers hated the book. Nobody wanted it. It only exists as a file on my computer. But at least Margo liked it." Jill raised her drink. "To Margo."

I obliged. We clinked glasses.

As we were leaving the bar, we caught sight of Dave. We'd seen him use the same moves on other women playing *Big Buck Hunter*. He'd rejoined his party, half a dozen bearded, flannel-clad guys. They were all drunk, rowdy, overconfident. I thought we would escape without being noticed.

"You're leaving with this little guy?" he said. I was too drunk to recognize that he was trying to insult me.

Jill shot Dave a dirty look, turned around, and kissed me on the mouth.

There are days I hate New York, and then I go to a bodega and completely change my mind. They have everything — all the essential foods and goods — and they're everywhere and open all the time. Bodegas represent New York's sweet spot between chaos and convenience — dollar stores by way of foodstuffs. Sure, there are all your grocery staples, but the charm of bodegas comes from the surprises. The snacks can vary wildly: tightly condensed packages of ramen; off-brand cookies of unknown origin; ice-cream sandwiches of various forms; flavors of chips that haven't been available for decades (the bags are maybe that old, who can know?), all packed into tall, narrow shelves as if they were rations in a fallout bunker. And then there's the bodega grill, which offers delicious low-grade meat in any format you can dream up. At 2 a.m. you can order a "chopped cheese," a kind of mutant burger made of ground beef and onions and American cheese, grilled to greasy perfection and spatulaed onto a roll. Or a pita. Or a bagel. You can order anything from a bodega however you want it — extra mayo, no tomatoes, douse it in hot sauce — and no one will judge you. Once you have a corner bodega that can make you an egg sandwich on a roll in the wee hours of the morning, there's no going back.

I'd woken up while Jill was asleep and decided to make breakfast. Her fridge was mostly containers of leftovers and condiments. She had three things of ketchup but no eggs. I figured a scramble with some vegetables would be a safe bet. The bodega across the street from Jill's apartment was nicer than any of the ones close to me in Queens. It even had a small selection of produce. After I'd located a carton of eggs, I passed by an endcap of gummy bears. They were that German brand that everyone assumed was Japanese because of the cute illustrated bears on the label. In Brooklyn, even a run-down bodega could have expensive, gourmet candies. I grabbed a package.

By the time I returned to Jill's, she was

166

awake, doing dishes in the kitchen in her underwear.

"Oh, I thought you had left." She seemed startled. I'd snagged her keys on the way out, assuming she'd still be asleep when I returned.

I raised the plastic bag of groceries in my hand. "I just went out to get some stuff to make breakfast."

I was worried that maybe Jill wanted me to leave, had been hoping I'd already left. But she smiled as I laid the groceries out on her kitchen table.

"Okay, I'll make coffee," she offered.

Jill put some water on and disappeared back into her bedroom. She only owned one pan, which I retrieved from the drying rack and set on the stove. I rifled around the kitchen looking for a cutting board.

Jill reemerged in sweatpants and a T-shirt. "What are you making, Chef?"

"Just an egg scramble with onions, chives, mushrooms, and tomatoes." I dropped a dollop of butter into the pan.

"That sounds delicious. Don't take this the wrong way, but never in a million years would I have expected you could cook." Jill seated herself at the kitchen table, one of the dining chairs turned toward me. She discovered the package of gummy bears and

167

opened them.

"I don't think I'm a very good cook. But I used to make a few things at my parents' bed-and-breakfast. I learned every way to cook an egg." I'd finished washing the vegetables. "Do you have a knife?"

Jill pointed me to a drawer. She only had one chef's knife, fairly dull, but I could make do. I sliced the onion and tossed it into the pan.

"That's really sweet that you helped out at your parents' place. Did you do that through college?"

"No, I basically worked there full-time with them. And I did some classes at community college."

There is an expression people make when they realize you are less educated than them. It's not a disappointed or judgmental face — just surprise. They often think they have to realign the way they talk. They want to speak on your level (as if anyone who didn't go to a four-year college is on a different level), but they're also aware enough of how they sound that they don't want to come across as condescending. Which they inevitably do, because they just end up making small talk.

"What's your parents' bed-and-breakfast like?"

I moved on to the tomatoes. "It's small, sort of quaint. We only have three rooms for guests."

"And you make onion-chive-mushroom-tomato scrambles every morning?"

"It's funny. We used to make Vietnamese food. Phở in the mornings, which was easy because we'd make it the night before. Guests seemed to like it. But then we had a negative user review from a travel site that complained that we only served 'Asian food' instead of a traditional American breakfast. And as soon as that went up, the number of bookings dropped pretty dramatically."

"Who doesn't like phở?"

"At least one person. And one review nearly sank my parents' entire business."

"But everything is okay now?"

"We stopped making phở and started making eggs. The only way to get the review taken down was to make it inaccurate." I plated the scramble onto two dishes, and placed one in front of Jill. "Everybody likes eggs."

She thanked me meekly and looked at her plate.

"Sorry, that was a weird story to tell as I serve you eggs."

"No, I asked. And this scramble does smell great." Jill put away the gummy bears.

"You should make me phở sometime, though."

"You should only be so lucky."

"Then I'll leave you a negative review online about how it's not white people food."

I laughed. It was a good joke. At the bar, we'd connected over Margo. Then we were both drunk, and had hooked up in some part to spite a rude stranger. I wasn't sure why I had decided to stick around the next morning. Maybe it just felt good to make breakfast, to do something nice for someone else. Or maybe the impulse was more selfish. When was the last time I'd had someone to talk to at a meal?

But I think that's what made me feel okay around Jill. We were both mourning Margo, a selfish act we could do together.

"Do you have any salt?"

Jill checked the cabinet above the stove. "I think I'm all out, actually."

That wouldn't do. I ran out to the bodega to get salt. I was back in a minute.

In a strange way, Phantom's problems in the national spotlight were good for the company. After months of trying to fundraise, Brandon found himself able to get a quick influx of cash from existing investors.

His TV appearance had impressed them. Apparently he'd handled the press crisis well for a young CEO. It didn't matter that he'd fumbled a bit on the local segment; all the follow-up interviews he did — and there were many — made Phantom seem like it had identified an issue and already had a plan in motion for how to solve it. This is what investors loved: people who solve problems. It didn't matter what the problem was, or who might have created that problem in the first place. The basis of all technology was founded around the idea of solving for X, regardless of what X was.

The solution, it turned out, would be labor intensive. Phantom users had the ability to report or flag inappropriate behavior in the service. If someone said something that made you uncomfortable, you could go to a menu that would allow you to send your complaint to customer service, with the guarantee that it would be investigated within twenty-four hours. We received nearly two thousand of these requests a day. We predicted that number would balloon to upward of ten thousand by the end of the month. If I worked for twelve hours straight, without a break, I could get through maybe three hundred of them. To really address anything, it would take people. Lots and lots of people.

"Congratulations, you're going to be a manager," Brandon said to me, his hand forward, waiting to be shaken. This would mean another pay bump, but, more importantly, stock options. "You own a piece of this company now," he continued. I wasn't sure how I felt. They'd had no other choice.

At first, hiring was difficult. But as it became more and more difficult to get asses into seats — and as the monitoring requests continued to flood in — we started taking just about anyone. I wasn't much older than most of the applicants, many of whom who were recent college grads. But they all seemed so young, so eager to get in even though we paid close to nothing for tedious, repetitive work.

It was a Band-Aid when we needed stitches. Margo would've hated it: the shortsighted solution, the exploitation of cheap labor. Her concerns would have been voiced. Brandon might have listened, too.

The size of the office would double in two weeks' time, creating a fracture in the workplace dynamic. It wasn't just a divide of new and old people. Phantom used to be mostly engineers, and suddenly it would be just as many customer service people like me. We might not have had the power, but now we had the numbers.

Okay, I visited three different libraries, but I wasn't able to track down most of the records you were looking for. I did find a little Tatsumi Yamashita. They weren't even part of the library's collection. I just happened to run into an Asian Studies professor who had some CDs in his office.

You mean Tatsuro Yamashita.

Yeah, whatever.

Where are you based?

I'm in Oregon.

Like, Portland?

No, further east. It's a college town. Nowhere cool. Anyway, I've started uploading the files to PORK. By the way, where do you live?

Brooklyn.

Oh, cool.

In New York.

You'll be surprised to learn that most people know where Brooklyn is.

How many black people live in "eastern Oregon"?

Oh, there's a huge community.

Wait, really?

Are you kidding? No. There are barely

173

any other Asian people either.

Lots of Asians in Brooklyn.

Is that in New York?

Funny. By the way, I found a bunch of the bossa nova albums you were looking for. Mostly a lot of Antônio Carlos Jobim. Those soft guitar grooves are nice. I'm uploading it now.

Amazing.

Hey, lucas_pollution, I'm just looking at these files you just sent. They're MP3s. Would you mind re-ripping these in FLAC?

What is FLAC?

It's a lossless format.

And it's pronounced "flak"?

Yeah, it's basically the highest-fidelity audio file that exists.

Audio . . . fidelity . . . okay . . .

Ugh, so when you convert audio to a WAV or MP3 file, there's a compression algorithm that restructures the file. Basically, the trade-off for smaller file sizes is a loss in quality. For most people, it's hard to notice that difference.

Why does it matter, if no one notices?

Because we're building an archive at PORK. We want the best versions of this music as possible. The point is to collect as much perfect information as we can.

But if normal people don't care —

174

It's not up to "normal people." PORK is not a community of "normal people."

I'll say.

Don't get snarky with someone who is higher-ranked than you on PORK.

Okay afronaut3000, here's a question: How can something be totally lossless? Like, the idea of something being copied, and not losing anything?

. . .

. . .

. . .

. . .

Fine, I don't really have a good answer for that. But it's what we have to do here. If PORK is going to be the enduring archive of music we all hope it will be one day, then we have to go the extra mile to rip lossless audio. You feel?

To get lossless versions, I have to go back to the university to rip the CDs again, right?

Oh, definitely. Track down that professor again.

Such an amount of effort to get something "lossless."

A lack of loss!

No loss!

Zero losses!

We'll never lose anything ever again!

■ ■ ■ ■

Piracy existed before PORK. It would exist long after PORK. Piracy would be around until the sun exploded and there was nothing left of Earth.

For the music pirate, it was an immense amount of work. And yet, they did it for free. There was nothing to be gained. PORK didn't offer monetary rewards for uploading new music, but it did manifest one's efforts in the forum's social structure — the more of your files people downloaded, the more quickly you ascended the hierarchy.

It's still not clear to me why people would dedicate so much of their life to something that was both illegal and gained them nothing. Maybe for some, it was a love of music, an appreciation so deep that they felt they must do everything in their power to lower the barriers of entry to a much-loved record. Maybe, for others, it was an act of rebellion, a way to fight back at the behemoths that had appropriated and corporatized music. Maybe most people just did it because they could. Or maybe they were bored. It seemed like most of the internet was built by people either because they could or because they were bored.

Aside from a suitcase worth of clothing, the only things I brought with me to New York were my laptop and an external hard drive. It was a beast of a peripheral, so bulky and large that it required its own separate power supply. Every time I plugged it into a computer, you could hear the disk inside the black plastic enclosure whirring loudly. You could name hard drives. I named mine OZYMANDIAS.

It contained all the music I had ever downloaded. Every MP3 was neatly organized into folders by artist and album. The hard drive itself wasn't sentimental to me, but the files were. Which is a strange thing to say — that these MP3s, which could be duplicated within a matter of seconds with two keystrokes, had any value. But I'd spent so much time collecting and meticulously cataloging them. There were small albums I returned to often, but the vast majority of the bossa nova I'd accumulated over the years had gone unlistened-to since they'd first been downloaded. Sometimes I wondered if I hung on to my music library because it meant something to me, or if it was just because I'd put so much work into it.

After the first night we spent together, I

thought there was a good chance I might never see Jill again. I wasn't sure if I wanted to. But she texted me the next day and we more or less repeated the first night on a regular basis: have a couple drinks, hook up, eat eggs in the morning.

Sometimes I wasn't sure if I was into Jill, or if I just liked having someone to be around again. Our conversations didn't resemble the ones I'd had with Margo, but at least we could talk about Margo. I started coming to Jill's place after work. Her neighborhood in Brooklyn was a convenient commute from the office in Lower Manhattan, only a few stops on the F train. She was usually wrapping up a day of writing (or not writing), and we'd meet at that terrible bar near her apartment. Jill was never able to kill that moose.

Even though I was staying over at her place most days of the week, we never discussed whether we were a couple. Instead, we were filling the role Margo had played in each of our lives. I unloaded my anxiety about work and the craziness at the company. Jill would tell me how her writing was going, which, it turned out, was not very well at all. She'd been in a rut for months now, not sure how to snap herself out of it. Her second book, *Mining Colony,* the one Margo had told me all about, had failed to find a publisher, which is why I couldn't find it at the bookstore. Jill's confidence was totally shot after that, and she was trying to rework the novel.

Our weekday routine spilled over to the weekend. Jill looked confused — though she tried to hide it — on the Saturday morning I showed up at her apartment with an external hard drive. I'd just spent an hour and a half on a slow subway train from Queens. I unloaded the black box from my backpack, and began scanning her apartment for an open outlet. I was searching under her desk, had hardly acknowledged her, when she asked what the hell I was doing.

I explained that this was my most valued possession: my music library.

She still looked skeptical. "Boys really love their hard drives."

I explained further: it contained a lot of music that Margo had recommended to me. "As high school kids, as strangers, we spent hundreds of hours gathering music," I said. "Even though we worked at the same place when we met in real life, this was really the project we had collaborated on together."

She seemed to understand. I plugged the hard drive into the USB port of Jill's laptop.

"This is the first album that Margo ever recommended to me on PORK."

I hit PLAY. It was immediately clear that the sound quality of Jill's laptop speakers was horribly inadequate — tinny and weak at the high frequencies, garbled and muddy at the low ones. I pulled out a pair of headphones from my backpack and handed them to Jill.

"What is this?"

I just wanted her to listen. The name of the artist wouldn't mean anything to her anyway. But if she just experienced it, I thought maybe she could feel what I'd felt the first time I heard it. I remembered the moment distinctly. The '80s Japanese music Margo loved was bathed in synthesizers. It was a strange inflection point in music, where aesthetics became increasingly electronic, but the recordings were still recorded in analog studios. It represented a time of transition, and would inform the American sound for decades to come. Hearing it brought the warmth of familiarity, and the sudden realization that it was foundational to so much of the music I'd heard all my life.

All Jill could muster was: "This is pretty catchy."

I played her another song.

Headphones off. "What is this band?"

I explained that it was a group that was huge in Japan in the '80s, pioneers of synth pop. They'd earned the nickname "the Beatles of Japan" for a few years.

"Huh, I've never heard of them."

Pushing the headphones back over her ears, I thought about how a band could be one of the biggest bands in the world, even make it to the States, and inspire a generation of pop music, and in a matter of decades, it could disappear almost entirely from American consciousness. The group's music wasn't available anywhere in the United States, unless you scoured the rare remaining record shop that happened to sell import vinyl — and even then, you'd have to already know what you were looking for. Discovering this music was nearly impossible.

This was one of the draws of PORK. Music pirates are stereotyped as cheap — too cheap to pay for music. Sure, many are, but there were communities like PORK that served a greater purpose. The internet at the time was disparate and disorganized. There was order to PORK, ambition. It sought to be a definitive archive of music. PORK gave me a sense of purpose in the shapeless days of my adolescence: I was researching and ripping and downloading audio as a means of preservation. I maxed out the allowable number of CDs I could check out each time I visited the library. At home, I'd meticulously tag and ID each track I copied as an MP3. It was hours upon hours of busy, satisfying work.

"So why was Margo into this music, in particular?"

I tried to give a little context. "In the late '70s and '80s, funk and disco had swept up clubs in Tokyo, just as it had most of the world. The influence of American culture reflected the country's postwar hegemony; but inadvertently, it had spread the influence of black music around the world. Margo had always been drawn to Japan's fascination with American music. She joked that it was like seeing her reflection, as an American obsessed with Japanese culture."

"Did it bother her at all that Japan had appropriated black music?" Jill asked.

"You know, I asked her this too. It's true: Japanese musicians were imitating the soundscapes that defined decades of black culture," I said. "But to Margo, it was cool that the influence of black music could reach as far as Japan. Geographically, that's about as far as it could go."

"Plus," Jill added, "the music is really

damn good."

At first I'd been ranting breathlessly at her. But as I played her more, her enthusiasm spilled over into something genuine. She began asking more questions about the music itself, telling me which songs she liked, the ones she liked less.

"I'm glad you're into it. I wasted so much time researching and ripping things on PORK."

"It doesn't sound like you were wasting time," Jill said. "It sounds noble, almost."

"Well, it was all for naught."

"What do you mean?"

"PORK was shut down a decade ago."

PORK had been and still was illegal, even if it had higher, almost academic aspirations. I woke up one morning and went to log in, as I did every morning, and the site was gone.

"So all the friends you'd had on there —"

"Effectively gone. The site disappeared overnight. Years of work by dozens of people gone. The only thing left was a government takedown notice. It was like waking up and all your friends have been raptured."

"God, that's so sad. I can't even imagine losing all of your work and all of your friends with no warning."

"You know what's funny? Technically, that

was the first time I lost Margo."

Jill embraced me. We were seated on the floor of her bedroom, holding each other, our bodies positioned to avoid the clunky laptop and hard drive between us. It felt good. The only person who had known about this part of my life, the hundreds of hours of music, the amount of time I'd spent amassing it, had been Margo. There was a comfort in sharing that with someone new.

"So Margo's expertise was in '80s pop music —"

"— from Japan."

"And what was yours?"

I leaned over to the computer and navigated the cursor through several hierarchies of folders on my hard drive. There was a lot of music here that I hadn't listened to in years. I recalled some of it; other names seemed vaguely familiar. I picked the most obvious one. I could hear the faint, warm sound of intricately strummed nylon guitar strings from Jill's headphones. Then a low, soothing baritone.

"Is this Portuguese?"

I nodded. "How did you know?"

"I had an ex that spoke Portuguese."

It was the first time Jill had mentioned an ex.

"My specialty was bossa nova. It's Portuguese for 'new wave,' a kind of fusion of jazz and classical guitar from Brazil. It was big in the '50s and '60s."

"It's very . . . tropical," Jill said. "I like it. It reminds me of 'The Girl from Ipanema.' "

"So there's a story behind that song! One of Brazil's most beloved guitarists wrote 'Ipanema' with a saxophonist. When they needed a singer, the guitarist suggested his wife, even though she had no formal vocal training. Skeptically, the saxophonist is like, 'Sure.' That song became bossa nova's only international hit — and, most likely, the lasting legacy of the entire genre."

"It's the only one I've heard."

"Later, the guitarist's wife would split with him after having an affair with the saxophonist."

"Dramatic. And yet, the music is so calm."

I played more. We spent the afternoon flipping through my music collection. I went to the kitchen to make a couple of egg sandwiches, and Jill brought her laptop along, the external hard drive still plugged in, cradled in her arms. I turned on the stove, and Jill hunted for another power outlet. Butter sizzled in the pan as she picked songs at random, delighted by every new sound coming from the computer.

■ ■ ■ ■

The conversation about Japanese music eventually led to a discussion of Margo's obsession with going to Tokyo. She'd mentioned it to me only a few times in passing. She talked about it like Tokyo wasn't a city on the other side of the Earth. It was a different planet altogether, light-years away. But to Jill, Margo talked about it like it was a real possibility.

"We joked that we were going to take a girlfriends' vacation to Tokyo," Jill said. "Maybe she was serious about it. I'm sad I'll never get to do that with her."

"Margo never left New York, though," I said, puzzled by the idea she would propose such far-flung travel. "Never really, anyway. She rarely got any meaningful distance from home."

Jill pulled out her phone and opened the browser. She tapped around for a while, trying to summon the right combination of search keywords from her memory to direct her to the page she was looking for. Finally, she found it. A video. She hit PLAY.

The clip opened on a small temple, tucked in a quiet cranny of Tokyo's sprawl. From the outside, the building was both traditional (wooden hip-and-gable roof; large sliding doors) and somewhat modern (brutalist sheets of concrete). But as the doors slid open, the temple revealed a brilliant, otherworldly splash of colors. At first, it appeared to be some kind of light fixture attached to the wall, changing calmly from shades of purple to blue to green in naturalistic waves. But as the camera moved in closer, we could see the temple's beauty for its component parts: 2,045 little Buddha statues, each illuminated by an LED light, which changed hues in patterns that resembled a tranquil sea of color.

"Is this some kind of art installation?"

"No, it's a burial ground."

I took the phone from Jill's hand. There was an accompanying article with all the details. This was a high-tech cemetery, where people's physical remains were stored in small boxes and represented by tiny light-up Buddhas, each connected to a computer system storing their digital remains — a marriage of analog and digital in death. Graveyard technology. A necropolitical computer system.

"Margo joked that she wanted to have a tombstone here," Jill said.

But Margo already had a place in the ground.

■ ■ ■ ■

Later, post–egg sandwiches, we returned to the bedroom with the laptop/hard-drive setup. I put on more music and we started making out. Mid-kiss, Jill laughed and told me that it was very funny that I had a hard drive named Ozymandias.

"Kind of ironic for your music library."

"Wait, why?"

"My name is Ozymandias, king of kings. Look on my works, ye mighty, and despair!"

I didn't understand.

"Shelley?"

"Who is Shelley?"

"Percy Shelley, the great English Romantic poet?"

I didn't know who that was, or how to respond. Could I hide it? Should I?

"I was in middle school when I picked the name Ozymandias," I said, trying to explain it away, "but it was a character in a comic book that I liked."

Jill laughed. "What college did you go to that didn't make you read a Shelley poem?"

"I didn't go to 'college' college. I went to community college."

"Oh, I thought that was . . ."

Jill laughed again. I wasn't sure why she

was laughing. I guess she didn't know why either, so she stopped.

We were quiet for a moment, though music continued to play from Jill's computer.

"I recognize this song," Jill said. "Or at least the melody."

I was surprised. This was a pretty obscure song — one I could barely identify — by a Japanese musician who toyed with electric organs, a rare series of instruments called Electones. The piece had a solo keyboard part, noodling and meandering, melancholic. If you listened closely, you could hear a quiet, nearly invisible drumbeat, keeping time like a metronome.

"You definitely don't know this song," I said. "In our PORK days, it took Margo and me a colossal effort to dig up anything about this artist. Through sheer perseverance, we learned this guy's music was largely improvised explorations of mood and tone. He was a recluse who lived in Nara, a Japanese city famous for its wild deer. That was about as far as we got. Information on the internet was nonexistent; trips to the library were fruitless. This dude had put out four albums of extraordinary synth work that were hugely admired among Electone collectors, but no one knew a damn thing about him."

Jill couldn't figure out how she knew the song. We listened to it again. Then again, and Jill finally had her eureka moment. She took the laptop, closed my music library, and opened her own. She scrolled for a bit until she found the right track. She hit PLAY.

I should've seen it coming. The song Jill had been thinking about was a recent one, which sampled the melody that had been familiar to both of us. That electric organ — once so sparse and sad and winding — was now featured beneath the vocal track of a white guy singing about loneliness. This is how music persisted, sequestered and repurposed, a ghost of its original composition. I looked up the artist, and it confirmed everything I had suspected. His look could be described as "immaculate dirtbag," a perfect five o'clock shadow and a flannel befitting a hangover.

"You hate this song, huh?" Jill asked.

"It's fine."

" 'Fine' means you hate it."

"No, I just —"

"You can hate it."

Jill was smiling again. "I want to hear more of Margo's music."

"I think I've played all of it. At least, the files that I have."

"On Ozymandias," she teased.

"Yes, on my stupidly named hard drive."

"But you have Margo's computer, don't you?"

"I do."

"If you said you have Margo's laptop, does that mean you have all of her music?"

Did I? "I never thought to look. I mean, it's probably on there?"

"Instead of listening to the music Margo gave you, couldn't we listen to her actual library?"

"That's . . . a good point, actually."

"Let's go."

"Right now?"

She was already on her feet, reaching into the closet to find her coat.

When we arrived twenty minutes later by car, I could tell Jill was taking stock of my apartment. We'd been hanging out for a few weeks, but she had never come to my place. Compared to her apartment, which had the decor and cleanliness of an adult woman who lived by herself, mine must've come across like a college dorm. There was a sink full of dishes and a too-full garbage can — the attrition of two roommates who never quite divvied up responsibilities for the home — and a lack of furniture or wall art

191

that, for the first time, made me self-conscious. Jill withheld judgment, or at least withheld vocalizing it. I quickly pulled her into my bedroom, which wasn't any less of a disaster than the shared spaces of the apartment, but at least this mess was mine. Dirty clothes were scattered across the floor, and, more embarrassing, empty beer cans lined my bed.

Margo's laptop was at my desk. Jill sat on my bed as I booted up the computer. I logged in with the password, still represented in my handwriting as a sticky note applied to the screen: *M4v15B34c0n.*

"Is that Margo's password?"

Jill grabbed a pen from the desk and searched around until she could find loose paper. She settled on an unopened envelope for an unpaid bill. She scrawled out:

M4V15B34C0N

MAVISBEACON

"It's Mavis Beacon!"

"What's Mavis Bacon?"

"No, *Beacon.*"

"Okay what's Mavis Beacon?"

"You know, she does . . . the thing."

Fumbling with her words, Jill stuck her

hands out and began making a motion like she was playing piano.

"She's a pianist."

"No, what's the word?" Jill's hand motions became more exaggerated as she tried to summon the right word. Maybe she was casting a spell?

"She's . . . a witch. Mavis Beacon is a witch."

"No, on the computer. The typing game. With the car."

"I'm going with 'witch.' "

"*Mavis Beacon Teaches Typing!*" Jill lifted her arms in the air to celebrate her victory, a moment of victory only she understood.

"What is that?"

"It's *Mavis Beacon Teaches Typing.*"

"Repeating the name of the thing back to me doesn't explain what it is."

She laughed and hit me gently on the shoulder.

"Mavis Beacon was this software that taught people how to touch-type," Jill said. "We had to use it in computer class when I was in fifth grade. It had this game where you were racing another car, and you'd be able to speed by it if you typed enough words in a row quickly and accurately."

Jill pulled up the Wikipedia entry for *Mavis Beacon Teaches Typing.*

"Oh my god, Mavis Beacon is not a real person?" she said.

There was no Mavis Beacon. She was a fictional character designed for the software. But she had a real face.

Jill kept reading out loud from Wikipedia. The name Mavis was chosen after a favorite soul singer of one of the developers, while Beacon was picked because it sounded like a good name for a teacher — Ms. Beacon, someone who would, literally, guide you.

"Well, that's a bit on the nose," Jill said.

I wanted to know more. Why was this Margo's password? "Keep reading," I said.

The owner of the typing software had discovered the woman who would become the model for Mavis Beacon working behind the perfume counter at a Saks Fifth Avenue in Beverly Hills. She was born in Haiti and named Renée L'Espérance.

"That might be an even better name than Mavis Beacon."

I pulled the computer away from Jill. "You know, she looks a little bit like Margo," I said.

"She does?"

Aside from the Wikipedia entry, there was almost nothing out there on Renée L'Espérance. The only thing I learned is that while she had been the face of *Mavis*

Beacon Teaches Typing, she hadn't received any residuals on sales of the software. There was a rumor that she had returned to the Caribbean.

"Do you think there's some significance? Her password being Mavis Beacon?"

"For a lot of people, learning to type was the first introduction they had to computers," Jill said. "And Mavis Beacon was the face of that. Which means a black woman was a lot of kids' first association with technology."

"Imagine growing up, being introduced to computers, and expecting that world to be populated with other black women," I said. "Margo was the only black woman at either tech company I've worked at. She used to tell me, often, how disappointing that was."

I went to the fridge and returned with a couple beers. Jill was unceremoniously placing the empty beer cans by my bed into the trash. I signaled with a nod that I hoped conveyed both my embarrassment and *thank you.*

"Do you think there should be rules to this?" Jill said.

"Rules to what?"

"Just because we have Margo's password, it doesn't mean we have the right to use it." Jill paused, the obvious question coming to her: "How did you get it anyway?"

"It's a long story. But I only first logged on as Margo so I could deactivate her Facebook account." I stopped, then added "at the request of her mother" to further absolve myself.

"Have you signed into any of Margo's other accounts?"

"Nothing else. Just Fantastic Planet."

"Never her email or anything?"

"Never her email."

"And why did you log into Fantastic Planet?"

"Honest to god, I was just typing in 'Facebook' and 'Fantastic Planet' came up."

"Did her mom tell you that was okay too?"

"No, but I wouldn't have found you if I hadn't. And if I hadn't been lucky enough to have her password, I would never have been able to tell you what happened to Margo."

Jill took a slug of her beer. "But that doesn't mean we shouldn't have rules about this. Margo might be dead, but she's still entitled to her privacy."

I hadn't considered this. I mean, what was privacy to the dead? But maybe Jill was right. I'd have to think about it. In the meantime, I nodded along in agreement.

"So after we find her music from PORK,

that'll be it," she said. "We'll put M4v15B34c0n to rest forever."

"But, like, you're not even a little curious about her email?"

"Lucas, we cannot look at her email. Email is, like, the center of the universe."

Again, I agreed. Mostly. "So once we're done today, I am throwing away this sticky note."

"Yes, we're done," Jill said. "After this."

It seemed a little late to be moralizing about this. The floodgates were already open.

"Okay, here we go." I typed "M4v15B34c0n" in the password field for the last time. Then I tore the piece of paper in half, then quarters, then it was in the garbage bin.

I did a search for audio files but didn't find anything that resembled music.

"Do you think she kept it all on a separate hard drive like you?"

It was possible, but I hadn't seen anything like that in Margo's bedroom. I kept scanning the computer. No music whatsoever. But a search of audio files did reveal a curious folder named "Fantastic Planet." Inside it were a series of WAV files: uncompressed audio. All named and dated. I clicked one and . . .

"The world ends and there are only two survivors: a man and a woman. They escape on a spaceship that exits the Earth's atmosphere just moments before the planet explodes."

"What is this?" Jill asked.

"As the rocket hurtles through space, the man looks back and sees his home crumbling. Fire consumes the globe until there's nothing left to devour, and the planet disintegrates into an infinite number of little pieces, shooting out in all directions toward the unknown reaches of the universe."

"It's . . . Margo."

"The man weeps for the billions lost."

"What?"

"This is Margo speaking."

"The woman is looking forward, her eyes taking in the vastness of space."

The voice was unmistakable. Margo's. The file continued on, telling the story about Earth's only survivors. By some miracle, they crash-land on a habitable planet. The man expects that the two of them will do their duty and populate their new home to assure the continuity of the human race. The woman has no such plans. They've arrived on a new planet, free of expectations of what a woman should do.

"And the woman leaves the man behind.

She sets off toward the jungle to live her own damn life."

The audio file ended. I looked over at Jill, who had been staring at me the whole time.

"That was Margo?"

"It was."

But what was this? What the hell had Margo been up to?

"There's an entire folder of these," I said. I brought the laptop over to the bed and planted myself next to Jill. Together, we scrolled through the Fantastic Planet folder. There must have been hundreds of files. I played another. It was a story about a woman who discovers that she can turn invisible — and that, as a woman in a society dominated by men, it doesn't change her life in any meaningful way. After that, another. This one was about a planet exactly like Earth, but all of the people of color have been eradicated by disease, so the world begins enslaving people with blond hair to maintain a social hierarchy. We listened to a third. Scientists cure death, allowing people to live forever. With no stakes left in the world, everyone starts murdering one another for fun. And the stories kept going.

Some were better than others. Some were more complete than others. Nearly all of them had a dark, cynical plot twist. Neither

Jill nor I could make sense of it, but we knew we would have to listen to them all.

Grief isn't just the act of coping with a loss. It's reckoning with the realization that you'll never discover something new about a person ever again. Here it was, though. Something new.

Hours passed as we indulged in the treasure trove of WAV files, both speechless. We let Margo's voice fill the room with tales of far-flung planets and alien civilizations and interstellar travel. It was less like hearing a ghost and more like witnessing a message from an astral plane, a different dimension, the future. Margo's stories were told with confidence and poise. And yet, she'd occasionally screw up on the recording — she'd misspeak and the tone of her voice would break, maybe she'd laugh a little to herself before starting over — and in those moments, I couldn't help but think that she was alive.

THE_FOLLOWER.WAV

There's this woman on Mars who lives a normal life in the city of Neo Port-au-Prince. She leaves early in the morning to go to work at her menial day job in the city and, in the evening, returns home to the outskirts. The commuter train is fast — it's a hyper-rail, after all — but it takes her two hours each way. She doesn't mind the ride. She spends most of it gazing out the window, admiring the vast expanse of red desert. The mountains are multiples taller than anything on Earth, the valleys exponentially deeper. It is all a wash of crimson sand and dust. The weather systems are violent. Sandstorms and lightning are never far off in the distance. It's a landscape that is somehow at once both bleak and beautiful.

The woman lives alone, which is the way she'd prefer to live. Her apartment is small and on the edge of the sprawling suburban colony just outside Neo Port-au-Prince, but she likes the peace and quiet. At night, there's hardly a sound. She makes dinner for one, and either reads a book or watches a little television before falling asleep. It may sound like a dull existence, but the woman is happy to be alone. But, of course, she is a woman. And women are never just left alone.

One day, on her way home from work, the woman catches a man staring at her. He is seated across from her on the hyper-rail. He is an average-looking person: middle-aged, dressed in business casual, most of his body hidden behind a copy of the *Neo Intelligencer*. They briefly make eye contact before the man looks back down at his newspaper, and the woman thinks nothing of it. The man gets off at the next stop, and she rides another hour and a half to get home.

The next day, she sees the man again — catches a glimpse of him out of the corner of her eye. Again she thinks nothing of it, but he gets off at the stop after the one from the previous day.

On the third day, the woman wonders what the likelihood is that she will see the same man on the same train again. It doesn't seem unlikely, she concludes. Commuters are consistent. She takes the same train home every day; maybe this man does too. And on top of that, what is she even worried about? This man isn't bothering her. He hasn't even said a word to her. She wonders why she's being so paranoid.

Still, she decides to indulge that feeling the

following day. She stays an extra hour late at work — to the surprise of her boss, who remarks that he's never seen her there that late. (She explains that she's trying to show initiative, a little more work ethic, and her boss takes a strange, smug satisfaction in hearing this before telling her to keep up the good work.) When she leaves the office, the woman is surprised just how empty the streets are. Apparently no one stays around the financial district after hours — all the businesses are closed. The silence makes the walk to the hyper-rail feel longer than usual. She thinks about the sound of her footsteps as they echo off the skytowers that block out the sun.

She finally boards the train. It's empty. She takes a seat. But just as the doors are closing, who should appear? The woman's follower. He looks as innocuous as ever, like it was by design. He sits down on the opposite side of the hyper-rail car and opens his newspaper. The train starts moving, and the woman can't take her eyes off him.

The hyper-rail crawls to its first stop. A handful of people board. The man turns the page of his newspaper. Next stop, some people get on, some people get off. The woman still has her eyes on the man, waiting for him to do something. He minds his own business. Several more stops go by until the woman can't take it anymore. She approaches the man. He doesn't seem to notice her. She tears the paper out of his hands and asks why the fuck he is following her. Now she is yelling, and everyone on the train is staring. The man says nothing, does nothing. He stares blankly, as if he doesn't understand. The hyper-rail pulls into another station and the man scurries off.

In the decades following the Great War for the Red Planet, the governing bodies of Mars maintained peace through rigorous and constant surveillance of its citizens. Holo-cameras were installed in every corner of the planet's major cities, allowing the government to record and monitor public spaces at all hours of the day. It is supposed to make everyone feel safe at all times. The woman does not feel safe.

There are many places you can buy a gun legally on Mars. There are just as many places you can buy one illegally, only you can get it faster. The woman asks a friend, who asks a friend, and that evening a dealer appears at her door offering a small arsenal of weapons. She asks for something discreet, something pocket-sized. She explains that it's for self-defense and the dealer says he doesn't care. A small ray gun will do. It's a single shot. Once you fire it, it's done. The woman asks what happens if her target doesn't go down after a single shot. The dealer assures her that there's no chance of that.

She takes it.

On her next commute home, she sees the man again, of course. The woman thinks about the gall this man has to follow her, even after their confrontation the day before. She had warned him. She told him that if he followed her again, she would make him sorry for it. And yet, here he was, as if nothing had ever happened.

The hyper-rail makes its usual stops. The car gets emptier and emptier. The man is still reading his newspaper. What a prick, the woman thinks.

Finally they reach the woman's stop. She gets out of the car. The man follows. She can hear his footsteps behind her. She picks up her pace, and so does he. She can hear him getting closer. And closer. And closer until —

She spins around, withdraws the ray gun from her purse, and fires. It lets out an earsplitting blast, illuminating the dark corridor for a moment in a brilliant swirl of pink and green. The laser pierces a hole right through the center of the man's chest. His final expression is one of surprise, of bewilderment. He doesn't scream, just tumbles to the ground limp.

The woman calls the police, but it doesn't matter. They are already on their way. The holo-cameras have captured everything. The authorities have been alerted.

The woman's trial doesn't last long. Most trials on Mars don't, since they rely almost entirely on surveillance footage. Here's what the holo-cameras show: a woman walking; a man behind her, probably minding his own business. The judge informs the defendant that there is nothing illegal about this behavior. It doesn't matter that he followed her home. There is no proof that he ever intended to do her harm. Feeling unsafe is not a justifiable cause for obtaining a firearm and killing someone.

The woman is found guilty of murder. She will be sent away for a long time, to a prison fortified by impenetrable crystal walls.

But the woman knows that this was her only option, the only possible recourse. Because in the end, Mars is just like any other planet: a giant mass of garbage that orbits through space, barely able to sustain human life.

IV
INVENTORY

After two years of freelance writing, Jill finally landed a full-time staff writer job at a luxury trade magazine. 2002, 2003 — those weren't great years. 2004 was going to be a good one. The pay wasn't life-changing, but the consistency of having a check delivered into her bank account every two weeks was. Direct deposit almost felt like cheating, as though it didn't count if she didn't have to deliver the money to a bank herself. Jill no longer scrambled to make rent anymore, and for the first time since college, she had health insurance.

The irony didn't escape her. Her job involved projecting a high-end life of luxury to people — multimillion-dollar apartments, first-class travel, reports from lavishly bland parties — even though she would never be able to possess that life herself. Her days were spent in a small, quiet office, among only a handful of other staff writers and editors, but evenings often took Jill to press events, gaudy affairs thrown by PR agencies trying to get people excited about a product by handing out free drinks and access to a handful of barely recognizable D-list celebrities.

When she started covering these events, Jill felt the pressure to dress and act the part. But as she eased into the job, she realized nobody cared. She retired cocktail dresses and started wearing jeans (black). She would indulge in hors d'oeuvres (something she never got tired of, no matter how mediocre the spread), and talk to a few people for quotes. The success of a night was measured by Jill's ability to eat an entire meal's worth of canapés before the waiters stopped coming around. A bust of a night would end with Jill stopping for a dollar slice on her way home, so starving by this point that she would impatiently burn the roof of her mouth on hot cheese. On the subway, she'd tongue at the soft, pained parts of her gums.

Like many of their friends in Brooklyn, Jill and Victor had moved in together partly because they loved each other, partly because of convenience. They'd met at a party — Jill drawn to the tall half-Japanese, half-Brazilian with perfectly tousled hair. (It turns out they'd both been raised largely in Connecticut.) They'd been dating for just four months when they realized both their current leases ended at the same time, and it seemed like the sort of New York luck that only an idiot would pass up.

Summers were hot in New York, but they seemed particularly hot in Jill and Victor's one-bedroom apartment in Bed-Stuy. The neighborhood was famous for that one movie that Jill had never seen but always meant to. What was it called? The one about the heat wave? It didn't matter. Jill and Victor had a single air-conditioning unit, but it never seemed powerful enough to keep the apartment cool. Victor's computer — a massive black monolith of a thing — was an unwelcome and powerful heat source. Jill had only ever owned tiny, thin laptops, but Victor had explained, more than once, that to power the 3D rendering engine for his work required a workhorse of a machine.

To be a video game designer, you had to be many things: an architect, a physicist, a novelist, all in one, Victor liked to say. He had mapped out elaborate blueprints to be modeled in three-dimensional space, the evidence of which was scattered about the desk, spilling over onto the dresser and bookshelves and any other flat, elevated surface in the apartment. Jill often saw Victor writing out formulas, doing short-hand math on loose paper — receipts, flyers, drafts of her bad short stories — anything was fair game. He had even scrawled notes on the back of junk mail envelopes; once, after Jill had brought home a couple bagel sandwiches, she found all the napkins from the takeout bag absorbed into Victor's landscape of mad-scientist scrawlings.

Sometimes Jill tried to make sense of the notes to better understand what Victor was working on. He was making a video game, that she knew, but Victor never said what kind. When Jill pressed him on it, just out of loving curiosity, she wouldn't get much more. It wouldn't be like the ones she had played before, he said. Victor wanted to make something more personal. He wanted to create a game that was intimate and quiet. She admired his focus — she was jealous, in fact — so she left him alone to make whatever it was he was making.

With the new stability of Jill's staff job, Victor was able to quit his day job teaching middle-school kids math. As long as he'd make enough from freelance web design to pay for his half of the rent, Jill didn't mind paying for the rest of their expenses. It would be a fine arrangement for a few months while Victor completed his project. They rarely ate out, rarely went out at all, really. And Jill had never seen Victor more thankful than the day she urged him to quit tutoring. Over a long sushi dinner (Jill's treat), a celebration of her first paycheck, he volleyed between saying "thank you" and "but are you sure?" and Jill was filled with a kind of pride she'd never felt before. She could provide for the person she loved, and that delighted her. Even if, when she got home from work every day, the loud hum of the black computer tower always greeted her before Victor did.

Eventually, the secrecy of Victor's project got to Jill.

If Victor had been a painter, she'd have seen his canvases around; if he were a musician, there would at least be sounds of composition coming from the other room. He spent his day obsessing, typing on a computer, his game's contents buried on the hard drive unseen, like it didn't even exist.

Jill finally said these things to Victor. She wanted assurance that what he was making was even real. This conversation, to Victor, felt like a betrayal. How could she not

211

believe him? Could she not see him working? How could he prove it to her without showing something that wasn't ready to be seen? And why was she yelling?

It was true, Victor was working on the game. But he'd found another way to make money, and he was determined never to tell Jill how.

The toughest part of building his game wasn't the programming. It was the graphics. Victor had no formal training in 3D modeling and animation, so he'd started teaching himself. There were textbooks available, but they were all expensive. Instead, Victor cobbled together an education through what was freely available on the internet. There were a lot of tutorials, some helpful, most not. But the best resource was an online community of budding 3D artists.

Victor had also, unwittingly, stumbled onto a community of people with a penchant for computer-animated pornography. On the surface it looked like any other forum, except as he read on he realized users were talking about animating monster orgies. Still, curiosity kept Victor from closing his browser. The videos weren't titillating so much as they were mesmerizing. The animations were crude and unrealistic; the models were undetailed and untextured. The result was a hypnotic kind of sexual fantasy that was weightless, with actors that had skin that was slick and smooth like plastic, bouncing around in 3D space, unbound by the laws of gravity.

There was a section of the forum where people could request specific videos. It was, without a doubt, the busiest part of the message board, and it became clear to Victor that while the community of people making these movies was small, the appetite to consume them was overwhelming.

Victor combed through all the requests — they varied greatly in sophistication — until he found one that sounded easy:

I want a video where a guy is fucking a big titted girl from behind until he cums in her ass. She's blonde and her tits bounce as he pounds her. Also she has wings — not like angel wings but like the kind of wings a bat has. Haha dont ask.

All it took was finding a couple of stock character models and grafting some wings on the back of the woman. The animation was easy too, since it was just a repetitive thrust. The trickiest part was figuring how the wings should move. Should they flap?

213

They should.

It was only five minutes, but he sent the video to the requester, redsox1978, anyway. Within an hour he received a reply:

Goddamn man this is fucking perfect. Thanks so much!!

After that, he began taking commissions.

As Victor took on more and more orders, complicated requests prompted long email chains, lots of back and forth. It was a hassle, for one thing, but Victor also found that getting in discussions with strangers about their specific fetishes was not exactly the way he wanted to be spending the workday.

So he had customers fill out a request form:

SELECT CHARACTERS (MAXIMUM OF 8):

- White woman — blonde, large breasts
- White woman — blonde, small breasts
- White woman — brunette, large breasts
- White woman — brunette, small breasts
- White woman — redhead, large breasts

214

- White woman — redhead, small breasts
- Asian woman — large breasts
- Asian woman — small breasts
- Black woman — large breasts
- Black woman — small breasts
- White man — regular penis
- White man — large penis
- White man — extra-large penis
- Asian man — regular penis
- Asian man — large penis
- Asian man — extra-large penis
- Black man — regular penis
- Black man — large penis
- Black man — extra-large penis
- White woman — blonde, regular penis
- White woman — blonde, large penis
- White woman — blonde, extra-large penis
- Monster — regular penis
- Monster — large penis
- Monster — extra-large penis

Characters can be customized. Please choose a base model and describe which physical attributes you would like altered. Be as specific as possible.

What is the setting?

Detail the scene you want commissioned. Be as specific as possible.

As with Victor's very first commission, people generally had specific ideas of what they wanted, but they tended to be small variations on what was already out there. People would request women with very specific haircuts or tattoos; maybe a demon would have two cocks. It was easy work. Plus the money was good, even better than the freelance web design work he was doing, and it wasn't long until Victor was making almost all of his income from tailor-made animated pornography.

Like any job, the work got easier the more Victor did it — partly because he was getting more skilled, but also because every new request meant a model or animation that could go into his library to be used again. On his desktop, he now had a folder of different porn-actress sounds, sorted and organized by voice type and intensity. Over time, Victor had amassed a collection of different men and women and anything in between, able to fuck in every position imaginable.

Unlike several of the other animators who did commissions, Victor had very strict rules about sharing his work. Any custom porn was made for the client and the client only. If he discovered that it had been uploaded to a public porn site, Victor cut that person off for good. As his reputation grew, he spent more and more time policing popular sites for his own work. Victor knew the value of his art wasn't defined by its quality, but its scarcity.

With these sex animation projects dominating his time, he'd become less interested in physical intimacy. Maybe it was all the breasts and dicks he spent his day around. For Jill, all things occupied one of two states: they were either in a rut or they weren't. Their relationship, once hot, had now cooled. Which she knew was normal. Like all ruts, it would pass.

"You can play the game," Victor said early one Saturday while Jill was drinking her coffee.

"Really?" Jill looked up from her newspaper, which she had folded into quarters to make it easier to chip away at the crossword. Victor motioned toward the office.

Now seated in front of Victor's giant computer, Jill saw on the monitor a sparse menu, just text announcing the game's name: INVENTORY.

"So what do I do?"

"I think it's better if I don't explain it."

"Are there instructions?"

"You can figure it out."

"Can't you just show me what to do?"

"No, I'm going to leave the apartment while you play."

Victor already had his coat on.

"Wait, are you serious? You're leaving?"

"Yeah. I can't be in the room with every person who plays the game, so I should see if it makes sense for strangers."

"But I'm not a stranger."

"I'm just gonna hang out at the café around the block. Just text me when you're done."

And suddenly Victor was out the door, no goodbye, no kiss. The computer was emitting so much heat. *How does Victor sit here all day?* Jill wondered, as her hands began to sweat.

Was she excited? Was she anxious? There was nothing left to do but hit the space bar. She began.

The desktop tower began to hum. On the screen, a door to an apartment.

The game did not, as Victor had promised, explain itself. It took a moment for Jill to figure out how to move. The mouse controlled the first-person view, and eventually she figured out that the arrows on the keyboard would direct her movement. The mouse was like the head, the keyboard like the feet. She moved clumsily toward the

218

door. It didn't budge.

How do I open the door?

Jill tried the space bar again. No luck. Then she tried ENTER. Same result. She clicked with the mouse. The door swung open, the animation sudden and too quick. Jill figured Victor would want feedback, so she found a sticky note by the keyboard and jotted down that observation: *unrealistic door opening.*

Stepping into the apartment, Jill found a corridor. The three-dimensional space was sparse and dimly lit, ominous. Was the game supposed to be scary? If so, Victor had succeeded. Jill walked down the hallway toward a light shining from around the corner. She turned right, into what appeared to be the kitchen and living room. There was no furniture, though. It was an empty apartment.

She kept moving forward. Through the kitchen, she discovered another door. She clicked on it. The door opened with the same unconvincing animation as the front door. Jill underlined her sticky note.

As she'd expected, the next room was a bedroom. The layout of the apartment in the game resembled the floor plan of their actual apartment. It had taken her a moment to recognize it without their stuff packed into the space. This meant that through the bedroom, there should be another door to Victor's office.

Why would Victor put our apartment in his game?

Like the kitchen and living room areas of the game, the bedroom was also without furnishings. It seemed large and cavernous without a bed or bookshelves or clothes strewn across the floor, like in their real bedroom. Jill moved to examine the closet. She clicked it open. It was empty, though there was a set of unused clothes hangers. *Clothes hangers — nice detail!* Jill wrote, thinking it would be encouraging to also catalog things she liked.

She kept moving. There was, as she'd expected, a door to Victor's office. But this door looked different. The other two that she had walked through had been brown, textured to look like wood doors. This one was black. Light peeked out from under it, signaling that maybe someone was inside the room. Jill could feel her heart rate rising.

I am going to kill Victor if something jumps out of this room.

With a tap of the mouse, the door began to creak open slowly, its animation more deliberate than the other doors, revealing a dark room. Jill took a sip of water, exhaled, and stepped through the doorway.

The room she entered was not Victor's office. It was another corridor, just like the one she had walked through minutes earlier. Opening the office door had placed her in the exact spot where she'd started the game. That must be a bug. Jill turned around and tried to go back through the door again, but this time, clicking the mouse did nothing. So she proceeded forward down the hallway, through the kitchen and living room, and into the bedroom again.

This time there was a bed. Its appearance startled Jill. It was their bed, modeled with painstaking accuracy. She walked around it and examined the dark wood frame, with its textured wood grain; the bedding was a replica of their own, a mustard chevron duvet over white sheets. The biggest difference was that the bed in the game had been made, in contrast to the usual state of disarray in real life. Looking away from the computer, Jill peered into the other room at their actual bed.

The bed looks just like ours. Very accurate, Jill added to her note. She was running out of space, so she started a new one.

Through the office door again, Jill found herself looking down the same corridor. As she walked into the kitchen, this time she noticed the appearance of their small dining room table and its two matching chairs. Upon further inspection, Jill recognized the same impressive level of detail that Victor had applied to their bed. She walked through the living room into the bedroom, where she found the bed again, and then through the office door to emerge back at the corridor.

The game was a loop. Each time Jill completed her tour of the apartment, she was sent back to the beginning. And every subsequent iteration of their apartment featured one new item. Victor had started with the big things — their couch, bookshelves, dressers — but as Jill went further and further into the game, the new details were harder and harder to spot — small plants, clothes hanging in the closet, the teapot on the stove. Jill wasn't sure if this constituted a game, since there was no concrete objective, but she did enjoy the small mystery of finding the new object that had been rendered in the apartment with each ensuing version.

Jill had lost track of how many times she'd done the loop. But as she got further and further, the game started to become mundane. The changes were becoming so subtle that Jill lost interest in finding them, and she started going through the loops as quickly as possible. And as the artifacts began to pile up — there seemed to be no end to them — it got harder and harder to see around the space. Oddly, Jill found herself able to move through all of the objects like a sort of specter. The models would clip and glitch out as she passed through them.

At a certain point, once the game had rendered everything faithfully from Jill and Victor's home, new objects began to appear. Extra chairs and tables, imagined plants and lamps and TVs and mirrors. The new items became escalatingly absurd: a beach umbrella, a car tire, a giant menorah, the statue of David. Eventually the apartment became so crowded with things that it was just a mess of botched polygons colliding with each other in a hollow space. Jill had made an assumption that because the game had a beginning, it must also have an end. Clearly it did not.

Victor had explained that adding sound effects and music would be the last step — he wanted to get every other element pitch-perfect first. But he hadn't considered that the absence of sound had a different effect. The game felt hollow, empty. Jill moved around Victor's world like a ghost, floating silently and weightlessly. Or maybe that was the intention. Maybe this is exactly what Victor was trying to tell Jill. The thought infuriated her. This was the art of a coward.

There was one dimension that Victor had not considered. The player could always quit. No matter how much Victor wanted to control the three-dimensional confines of the space, and the fourth dimension of time, there was a dimension he hadn't accounted for.

Jill hit ESCAPE.

MOUTHFULS AND DEEPTHROATS —
    m4w (Upper West Side)
    Come by today and let's have some fun.
Generous, clean, down to earth. Hosting in my safe location. Please be clean and ready to have some fun on this gloomy day.

White Guy Seeks Asian Woman — m4w
    (Astoria)
    I'm looking for a sexy and small asian woman (preferably Japanese, Chinese, or Korean) to have a nice time with.
    I am married, never been with anyone other than my wife but I fantasize about a sexy, tight, asian woman to spend time

with on the side. Maybe you are in a similar situation as me — it doesn't matter to me as long as you are understanding.

I am 30 years old, white, 5'9", 217 lbs (a bit husky), brown hair and eyes with a beard, very clean. I am intelligent and enjoy good conversation. I am willing to take it at your pace and explore this together.

Shoot an email if interested and let's discuss! Please put 'Asian Fever' in the subject line so I know you're real.

Rape fantasy question — m4w (Midtown)
Question for you ladies. Is it true that most of you have some sort of rape fantasy?

Months later, Jill was in her new studio in Cobble Hill browsing the personals section of Craigslist. It had been a slippery slope to get there but what was the harm? Jill was compelled by the way people could be so frank about their desires. Some were crude and gross, but overall it seemed like an act of bravery to vocalize what you wanted most.

After leaving Victor, Jill had been promptly laid off from her fancy magazine job. The stock market had tanked two years earlier, and the world was still catching up to its effects. She moved in with some old friends to stem the financial bleeding and finally, once she'd cobbled together some freelance work, she found her own place, a small studio. She'd taken her clothes with her when she left Victor, but anything with a shared history — the furniture, the kitchenware, decorations, all the things they had picked out together — was left behind. At a department store, she loaded up two shopping carts full of home goods: trash cans, lamps, towels, silverware, pots and pans. She was excited — it had felt like a fresh start. But when she reached the checkout — pushing one cart forward with her left arm, tugging the other cart behind her with the right — she watched the digits on the register climb, each beep of the bar code scanner reverberating in her body, the cost adding up to an amount that she hadn't accounted for during her shopping spree. The cashier was still scanning items when Jill walked away. She abandoned her carts and headed to the exit.

Over a few weeks of obsessive Craigslist searching for free and cheap things, Jill was able to furnish her entire studio. The only thing she struggled to find was a bookshelf, so her hardcovers still sat in small piles at the foot of her bed. She had also discovered the "missed connections" and "casual encounters" categories of the site. It had been too long and she was intrigued. She clicked.

Many of the postings included a photo of the guy, which usually featured him shirtless, never a face, of course. Other times, it was a straight-up dick pic. Jill found these fascinating — less aroused, more curious. Some guys understood that the appeal of a dick pic had less to do with the penis itself but with how it was framed. (It wasn't difficult: good lighting and an angle that wasn't from straight above — really, just a little thoughtfulness.) After leaving Victor, it was refreshing to think about someone else's dick for a while. No sacrifice had to be made for the future. It was about what felt okay and comfortable in the present. And the thing that felt okay and comfortable right now was getting laid.

The first "encounter" wanted to meet at a bar. This seemed reasonable. But when she arrived, she found herself stuck there for the duration of a drink, even though she knew immediately that neither of them was interested in sleeping with the other. (He was too sweaty; she suspected he'd been disappointed by her height.) The small talk they made felt frivolous, and Jill felt her soul slowly leaving her body as she asked a litany of questions like "How many siblings do you have?"

Not to be discouraged, she set firmer rules. They could meet at a bar, but neither was obligated to stay for the entire drink. "Either of us can leave at any point, and the one rule is the other must not take it personally," she wrote to the next encounter. He agreed.

They hit it off. Jill went home with him after a small conversation where they'd established a rapport, a mutual attraction, and so began Jill's campaign of Craigslist hookups. Half the time she bailed, but all of the men she did go home with were for a single night only. (The exception was one man, Garrett, who liked to go down on her while listening to NPR on his headphones. Jill saw him four or five times.) Her strategy was to approach each encounter with no expectations but stick to her rules. If, during their conversation, the man said something she wasn't comfortable with — an off-color comment, joke, or political belief — she'd leave; if he made any mention of her height, she'd leave; if anything was suggested that was outside of what they'd arranged on email, she'd leave.

Craigslist was an ugly website. It was Times New Roman on a stark white background, with functional blue text to denote links — like a website that was never styled. But Jill admired its HTML brutalism. There was something simple and naked that made it feel trustworthy, like it wasn't trying to dress up what it was. Whereas the online dating sites she had briefly attempted to use were styled in bright, nonthreatening colors, Craigslist was stripped down to its bare essentials.

If getting over the loss of Victor meant regaining some semblance of control, in these casual encounters no one had more control than Jill.

Making rent on her own was difficult. The market for full-time writing jobs had completely evaporated, and Jill found herself doing an uneven combination of freelance assignments and administrative temp gigs.

But mostly, Jill had a lot of unstructured free time. So she began to write. She'd fill up those empty hours in the day in front of her computer, working in a text document that had no deadline and nothing at stake. It was calming. She wrote and wrote and it felt therapeutic — or at least she believed that's what something therapeutic would feel like. Eventually, the gigs became more reliable: a couple regular written assignments, three days a week filing at a law firm near her apartment. And Jill would come home, open up her laptop, and keep writing. When her law firm job turned into a full-time thing, it took more discipline to keep writing but she woke up early to write before work. Most nights, she'd come home and continue writing, exhausted, until she would close her computer and climb into bed in whatever she had been wearing at the office.

A year later, Jill had a manuscript. Through a friend of a friend, she had an agent. Through her agent, she suddenly had a book that several prominent publishers wanted. It was stunning that a year of work could culminate in this. And though it was at times difficult, in many ways writing a novel was the easiest thing she'd ever done.

The money was good. Jill hadn't expected that. She quit her law firm job — the first time she had quit anything in her life. (Well, besides Victor, if that even counted.)

The title was *Adult Contemporary*. It felt like she'd finally grown up.

She hadn't talked to Victor in months, but she couldn't help dedicating the book to him. He would never read it — probably never even know about it. But Victor had made a video game to tell her exactly how he felt. Jill had returned the favor.

The art of a coward.

V
MAVIS BEACON

Grief comes in waves. At least according to
a book Jill had read. It was a famous memoir
by a famous California writer, whose famous New York writer husband had died of
a heart attack. Jill said the book fucked her
up. The phenomena — the waves — come
as sudden and unexpected symptoms: short-
ness of breath, tightness of muscles, chok-
ing, weakness.

"I don't feel any of those things," I said.
"The waves. Do you?"

"I don't either. Nothing so acute, at least,"
Jill said.

Jill lent me that book, but I never read it.

CREDIBLE VIOLENCE

ABUSE STANDARDS

"For us to deal with a violent threat, we

have to determine how credible the threat is," I said. I clicked to the next slide.

We aim to allow as much speech as possible but draw the line at content that could credibly cause real world harm.
People commonly express disdain or disagreement by threatening or calling for violence in generally facetious and unserious ways.

I read the slides to the room. I had spent a lot of time working over the language, but realized that I'd never spoken it aloud before. It sounded clinical, cold.

We aim to disrupt potential and real world harm caused from people inciting or coordinating harm to other people or property, by requiring certain details be present in order to consider the threat credible.

An Indian woman raised her hand. She was one of the younger people in the room. Really cute.

"Hi, I have a question."

"I can see. You raised your hand. What's your question?"

"What is a cred—"

"Actually, what's your name?"

"What?"

"Everyone, before you ask a question, just tell me your name so I can remember it."

"Oh, I'm Nina."

"What was your question, Nina?"

"What is a credible threat?"

"I'm glad you asked." I clicked to the next slide. "First, we have to determine if the threat of violence is achievable. That means establishing a time frame."

ACHIEVABLE THREATS OF VIOLENCE
Today
Tomorrow
In 3 hours
Next time I see you,
When it rains
Sooner or later
Etc

NOT ACHIEVABLE
When pigs learn to fly
When hell freezes over
Etc

"Who still says 'when pigs learn to fly?' "

"The point is that any idiomatic or hyperbolic expression makes the threat unachievable."

"Why?"

"Because pigs will never learn to fly."

"And what if they did? What if someone developed technology that could crossbreed pigs with birds, and from that, pigs gained the ability to take flight."

Another person jumped in. An older black guy.

"My name is Thompson. Why would we want pigs to have wings?"

"You know what a chicken wing tastes like," Nina said. "Imagine if that was made of pork."

The class seemed amused by the logic, or maybe they were just hungry. I decided that I liked Nina.

Our first problems with user behavior were related to bullying, which was nearly impossible to police. Context was everything, especially since bullying could so easily be confused with regular, good-natured teasing. There was no way to understand just from messages whether the tone was playful or openly hostile.

But as Phantom grew, bullying became the least of our problems. Suddenly, we were dealing with threats of violence, hostile and graphic in nature.

i'll kill you

i'll put my boot so far up your ass i'm
  gonna knock out your front teeth
come near me i'll skin you like a pig
fuck off nigga
i will kill you i will kill you i will kill you

Like bullying, it was difficult to moderate without full context. But unlike bullying, we actually had to do something about it.

For a week, Brandon and I hunkered down in a conference room attempting to write moderation guidelines, which was boring and tedious and felt like busywork. If we were a much larger company, we would have called in experts, firms specializing in handling sensitive material, hired an expert with moderation experience; we might even have installed a resident academic ethicist. But it was just me and Brandon, two twentysomethings with no idea how to handle abusive language or death threats.

"Were you bullied in high school?" Brandon asked.

"I mean, sure. Who wasn't?" I said. "Well, you probably weren't."

"You'd be surprised."

"You're tall, white, handsome, pretty charming. What would anyone even bully you about?"

Brandon basked in the compliment for a

236

moment before answering. "I wasn't always this confident, or this tall. And harassment is more complex than jocks picking on nerds."

"In my experience, it's just the more powerful making life miserable for the less powerful for the sake of making themselves feel better. I think it's pretty simple."

"If it's that straightforward, then this should be pretty easy for you."

Which is why, a week later, I was squashed into our conference room, presenting a PowerPoint deck to a dozen new hires. They were contract workers, briskly assembled by an outside temp agency. They looked ragtag, unhappy to be there, fully aware that this was just another in a series of low-paying gigs. I immediately loved them.

It'd been since high school that I had to present anything in front of a group of people. I was nervous, even though no one else really cared. There weren't quite enough chairs for everyone, so some were seated while others stood or leaned against the wall. "Hi everyone," I said to the crowded conference room. The response was tepid.

I explained the basics of the job. Every time someone flagged a message, it would be routed to a member of the moderation team for investigation. The moderator would then look at the context of the conversation and decide whether it violated our content guidelines.

At the end of the deck, I had prepared a short quiz. The article I'd read about presentation tips had suggested finishing with something interactive. So I decided to test my new moderators by putting a few statements on the screen and seeing if they could file them correctly as credible threats of violence or not.

Someone shoot the President.

"Is this statement a credible or not credible threat of violence?"

Thompson raised his hand. "Not credible."

"Wrong," I said. "This is a credible threat of violence because it is a call to action and it cites a specific target."

"I disagree," he said. "It would be extremely hard to shoot the president. Like, he's got Secret Service and everything. You couldn't walk up to the president and shoot him. They'd murder you before you could shoot the president."

"But what if you shot him long-range, with a sniper rifle, JFK assassination style," said a white guy from the back of the room. "And that guy got away with it."

"What do you mean he got away with it? They caught Lee Harvey Oswald."

"You think he acted alone, man? You gotta wake up."

"We're getting off topic," I banged my hand on the table, like a gavel in a court-room. "Per our policies, 'Someone shoot the president' is a credible threat of violence. End of story."

Let's beat up fat kids.

"Credible?"

"Not credible," I explained. "Unlike 'Someone shoot the president,' this state-ment doesn't specify a specific target."

"So you have to want to beat up a specific fat kid for it to be a problem?"

"Exactly."

I hope someone kills you.

"Definitely credible," Nina said, brimming with confidence.

"Let's let some other people answer," I said. A few other hands went up. I pointed to one man in the back.

"I'm Lion."

239

"What?"

"You said to tell you our names after we raised our hands."

"Oh, that's right. Your name is Lion?"

"My name is Lion." A white guy, dread-locks. "And that is a credible threat of violence."

"Sorry, Lion, it is not a credible threat."

"But it's talking about a specific person."

"Right, but the qualifier 'I hope' indicates desire but not intent."

Kick a person with red hair.

"Credible threat," Nina said.

"Sorry, it's not credible."

"Again? Is anything a credible threat if it's not against the president?"

"And isn't this offensive to redheads?" asked a man standing in the back, a red-head.

"Right, redheads have it so tough in America," Thompson said.

"All I'm saying is, like, what if the sentence was 'We should kick black people.' "

"Whoa, you need to sit down right now if you think those are the same thing."

"I don't! I just want to understand the rules."

I clarified: "These threats are only credible when they're leveled at what we call a 'vulnerable group.'"

"Hi. My name is Lion."

"I didn't forget that your name is Lion."

"What counts as a vulnerable group?"

Actually, Lion had a good question. I looked through my notes. "Any group defined by race, ethnicity, nationality, sexual orientation, gender, or religion."

"But not hair color?" The redhead again.

"White boy, sit down!"

"I can't — there aren't any more chairs."

"And who defined what a 'vulnerable group' is?" Nina asked.

The answer, of course, was that I did. But I ignored the question. "I should have included that in this presentation. I'll update it and send a new version to you all."

Next slide.

To snap a bitch's neck, make sure to apply all your pressure to the middle of her throat.

Nina put her hand up meekly.

"Credible?"

"Sorry, this is still not credible."

"OH, COME ON!"

Thompson jumped in: "It's just *a* bitch,

241

not *the* bitch."

I nodded approvingly at him. I felt a tinge of pride. "That's right. And it's not signaling a specific threat — it's more of a general statement, even if the language is —"

"Gross? Horrifying?" Nina looked upset.

"The rules don't single out gross and horrifying. Just achievable threats of violence."

We put the moderators to work shortly thereafter. Emil and I had set up an array of computers and desks late the night before. There was already plenty of work to do — the request queue was unending. The members of my team got to their seats and began.

At Brandon's insistence, a large screen had been set up at the front of the room. It displayed two numbers: how many new requests there were and how many had been finished that day. A management tactic. It would motivate everyone, Brandon said. The screen and its counter were visible from everywhere on the floor.

Soon the customer service crew was working quietly. The sound of gentle keyboard taps and mouse clicks filled the room. I walked around, occasionally looking over people's shoulders. When someone had a question, they would raise their hand and I would address it. But mostly people didn't have questions, which I took as a testimony

242

to how well constructed our policies were written. It was all going better than I could have expected.

The second half of Jill's novel *Adult Contemporary* jumps ahead a year. At first, everything seems normal in the household, but in reality everyone is still reeling from the revelation that the mother has been selling herself to support the family.

The kids have reverted back to teenage angst mode. The son appears uninterested in having friends, doing well in school, or engaging in anything but video games. On the surface, the daughter appears to be coping well. She is still a stellar student and a hyper-engaged, college-bound high school star. But in secret, she is becoming more rebellious. And her behavior becomes reckless and dangerous.

The novel feels more intricate, more emotionally complex in the second half. It opens up to include the perspectives of both parents. The mother quits sex work, hoping that it will heal all wounds in the family. It does not. The financial strain is keeping her up at night, and she feels an overwhelming sense of guilt that she is no longer providing. Then there's the dilemma of the father, who feels guilty because he is unable to

243

make ends meet. Even though his wife was a sex worker by choice, he cannot shake the feeling that he has failed her. When he tries to express that feeling to her, she becomes furious. She reminds him that doing this work was her decision and that he has no right to wallow because of it. But he asks her if she would be doing it if they didn't need the money, if the family didn't need so much. She knows, in her heart, that she wouldn't if they didn't. It's a devastating moment.

The headier, smarter stuff comes in the second half of Jill's book. But it feels, on the whole, uneven. The first half is funny, even jaunty, as the mystery propels us forward, but all the vigor and humor of the first half disappear in the second, weighed down by each family member's increasing unhappiness with themselves and one another.

After I finished the book, I looked up its reviews. Most people felt the same way.

Margo's recordings spanned hundreds of hours. Together, we'd listened to many of them by this point. I'd spent an afternoon meticulously compressing all the WAV files into MP3s so I could listen to them on a hand-me-down iPod Jill had lent me. I listened to Margo's stories on my commute and scribbled notes on loose paper, to report them back to Jill later that evening. Sometimes the stories were incomplete, names of characters and planets inconsistent. In many of the recordings it was clear that Margo was drinking, and though those stories were often slurred and on occasion total nonsense, some of them were my favorites, reminders of our meandering nights rambling in bars together. In these recordings, Margo's sentences would trail off, sometimes punctuated by a burp or a giggle.

Our plan was to transcribe all of Margo's stories, though when we decided to do that we hadn't quite realized just how many of these recordings there were. It became clear that Margo must have done this nearly every night for several years. Years of telling stories, seemingly spontaneous and without preparation, from the way she spoke. Jill joked that she herself had enough trouble writing one science fiction story. Sure, not every one of Margo's stories was a winner. But taken altogether, her body of work was stunning.

We usually finished working around midnight. If we weren't too tired, we'd hook up, or at least we would fool around. One night, as we were both half clothed, Jill had an idea.

"You know what we've never done?" She got out of bed and began digging around her closet, retrieving two towels. "We've never used the sauna."

There were luxury amenities available in Jill's condo, she explained. The building was new, built of showy metal and glass to disguise its cheap structural bones. Brooklyn was full of brick brownstones that had lasted the better part of a century, if not more, and still looked good; now they were surrounded by tacky-looking high-rises like Jill's. In her words, she lived among "the cheapest rich people."

"How can you afford this apartment?" I asked.

"Oh," she said, embarrassed, before admitting: "I can't."

I assumed that meant her parents were helping her with rent. Or she was living off a trust fund.

"Do your parents help out or something?"

"What? I would never let my parents pay my rent." She seemed pissed off.

I shrugged. "Hey, if my parents were in a situation to help me pay rent and they offered? I would accept that help in a heartbeat."

246

We walked to the sauna barefoot, in our towels; I had grabbed a couple beers. Despite all its extravagant amenities, the building was a ghost town. I almost never saw other occupants. The condo had been finished for the better part of five years, but still more than half of the units remained unsold, and many that had been sold remained unoccupied — supposedly purchased by people somewhere outside of New York as an investment.

The few apartments that were occupied were a block of units reserved for affordable housing. By law, new buildings like these had to offer a small percentage of their units to poor tenants. To get them, you had to apply through a lottery system controlled by the city.

"Tens of thousands of people apply and very few get anywhere. Getting this apartment is the luckiest thing that's ever happened to me," Jill said. "Maybe the only lucky thing that's ever happened to me."

"But isn't affordable housing for actual poor people?" *And maybe not intended for a well-educated white girl from a middle-class family in the suburbs?* I didn't say it.

"I don't think you realize just how little money I have. My income was way below the threshold to apply."

247

Though I'd rarely seen anyone else in the building, Jill said she'd had numerous encounters with residents who turned their noses up at her because she didn't own her unit.

"None of the affordable housing folks are allowed to use the amenities," Jill said. "But it's really easy to steal one of these." She held up a small, black piece of plastic — a key fob — and swiped it on the keypad by the sauna door. It made a satisfying beep, and the LED light on the lock changed from red to green, granting us permission.

The heat relaxed my muscles, cleared my head; it made a cold beer taste even better.

"When's the last time you were in a relationship?" Jill asked.

I was surprised by the question. "A while ago. When I was living in Oregon. This girl and I would hook up a couple times a week, which was a lot, considering I lived with my parents and couldn't bring her home," I said. "You get pretty good at having sex in confined spaces. Like a car."

"So it never got serious?"

"She actually told me, 'Lucas, you are not a serious person.' Which was rude, but also, not wrong."

"Mmm. Definitely rude, at least."

"And what about you?"

"I lived with a boyfriend for a while. Since then, I've only dated casually. I think it suits me, mostly." Then Jill asked, "What are we doing?"

I didn't want to answer, so I played dumb. "Sitting in a sauna, drinking beer?"

"No, I mean, like, what are *we* doing?"

"Like, with Margo's stories?"

That clearly was not what Jill was asking about, but she sipped her beer and let out a resigned "Sure."

"The stories are good."

"Mm-hmm."

"Maybe it's selfish that we're keeping them to ourselves."

"Do you want to put them on the internet?"

"No, like, we should collect them into a book. Get them published. You're an author, you know how that works, right?"

"Well, sure."

Thinking back . . . Jill never agreed outright.

I leaned over and kissed her when she smiled — either I was too caught up in the moment, or maybe I didn't care if she thought it was a good idea. I ran my hands under Jill's towel, up her back.

"Oh, this is why you wanted to use the sauna," I said, realizing she hadn't worn a bathing suit. Jill removed her towel and lay down on her back.

"So you're good in confined spaces, huh?"

The heat of the sauna had us breathing heavier and louder than usual. I worried that somebody might see us, but of course, nobody ever came.

Lucas, you have to watch this video.

I have a bunch of emails to get through, Margo.

Watch it now.

You know it's hard for me to open a video with my boss breathing over my shoulder. I swear, he spends more time bothering me about what's on my computer monitor than actually doing any work at Nimbus.

Okay, I'll just describe this video to you:

There's a white guy wearing a black hoodie and black beanie. He's on the roof of a single-story house. He approaches a trash can.

A metal one?

No, like one of those big plastic containers. The kind you probably see in the suburbs.

So he's going to jump into a garbage bin?

Seems that way. He's walking toward it. He does a flip in the air, and about

halfway through his rotation, he just yells "fuck," and lands ass-first in the trash can.

I can hear you laughing from the other side of the office.

It's so good. Okay, here's another: There's a white guy, also in a hoodie, swinging around a pair of nunchucks. Oh, he's kind of good at them actually? He's doing a bunch of nunchuck tricks.

Does he hit himself in the crotch?

Oh my god, he just whacked himself in the dick with nunchucks.

You are laughing so loudly over there.

HE HIT HIMSELF IN THE DICK.

Margo, everyone is staring at you.

It's so good. Okay next video.

I don't understand why you like these clips so much. It's just video after video of dudes accidentally hurting themselves.

First of all, they're called "fails." And second, they are so goddamn funny. There's nothing funnier than failure.

I don't get the appeal. Like, you're just watching people get injured and laughing at them.

We work in tech, an industry that fetishizes failure. We celebrate men who start companies and fail spectacularly. People who run startups that don't

work out — they are lauded as men who have come out smarter and more confident for it. It's not even failing upwards. It's failing . . . omnidirectionally.

I suppose there's something subversive about watching videos of dudes getting it in the nuts. It's satisfying to see failure as just failure, and not part of a redemption arc afforded only to white guys.

Yes, exactly — Oh my god, Lucas, look at this one!

I'm not clicking that.

Click it.

No.

Click it.

Fine.

Good boy.

Okay so it's . . . footage from the dashboard of a car.

Yeah, it's called a dashcam.

It's a dashcam. Great. Someone is driving their car and — oh, they just got hit by another vehicle. Oh, this isn't one video. It's a series of car crashes. A dashcam compilation. Margo what the hell, this video is twenty minutes long.

Wild, right? I'm so glad I can't drive.

Why are all of these Russian?

I read that everyone in Russia owns a dashcam. Apparently laws are so lax,

252

plus traffic enforcement is so corrupt, that everyone has these cheap video cameras on their cars to protect themselves in the case of an accident. Like, if you get rear-ended, the person that hit you can claim you're at fault. Or maybe they have more money and can pay off the cops to favor their side of the story. But at least the system respects firsthand footage as evidence. Therefore, everyone has a dashcam.

So the solution is: everyone is surveilling each other.

The best offense is a strong defense, and in Russia, a strong defense is a dashcam.

Who has the time to compile all these car crash videos and then set it to a rap-metal soundtrack?

Lucas, we spent our high school years ripping and uploading music to a forum.

Fair. I can still hear you laughing from the other side of the office. Are you still watching this car crash video?

Oh, I'm going to watch all twenty minutes.

How do you get away with not even pretending to do work?

It's the privilege of being the most

intimidating engineer in the office. Who is going to mess with me if I'm obviously the best programmer here?

Margo, you're so humble.

Listen, there's nothing more humbling than watching video after video of people fucking up.

Nina was the most competent person in my growing pool of customer service reps. And a close second was Thompson, who didn't work quite as briskly, but I'd taken a liking to him just for the way he made the office laugh. No one ever stresses the importance of humor in the workplace. Thompson was a little older — maybe mid-forties — and was less computer literate than the rest. As a form of motivation, there was an extra fifty-dollar incentive for the person who got through the most support requests in a given day — a sizeable amount of money, considering that a day's base pay totaled less than a hundred dollars. In the first week, Nina won the bonus cash four out of the five days. At 5 p.m., when our support was officially offline, I'd hand her a crisp bill in front of everyone, a small ceremony that would hopefully encourage others to compete for the same honor the next day.

But outside of Nina and Thompson, the

cast of characters on the service floor rotated quickly. By the second and third week, nearly everyone from the first training class had moved on. They'd either found better jobs or they'd burned out. Or they weren't cutting it, and had to be let go. Or, as was the case with Lion, they'd been fired after being repeatedly warned about getting high at work. I worried about one day losing Nina and Thompson, so after much pleading with Brandon, I was able to up their hourly salary. They were both happy. I felt like I was doing a good job.

Brandon was satisfied with the work we were doing downstairs, but Emil said we were not producing results.

"Your team is getting through thousands of support requests a day," Emil explained. "For there to be enough information to feed an algorithm, we need to be churning through tens of thousands each day."

I resented the way Emil described his algorithm as needing to be fed, as if it were hungry, as if it were a person — more a person than the people downstairs who were literally hungry and using our meager pay for actual food. But he was understandably frustrated. In the month or so since we'd scaled out the support team, Emil had made very little progress in his attempts to automate the review process.

"If you want more signals to feed your algorithm, then we need to hire more people," I said. "My team is working as fast as humanly possible."

"*Humanly* possible," Emil said. "That's why we need to let the algo—"

"Shut up, Emil," Brandon said. "Don't blame Lucas and his people because your software can't tell the difference between a death threat and Eminem."

"What happened?" I asked.

Emil left the room in a huff.

"I keep pushing Emil to make this system smarter, but he believes the only way it can get smarter is if it can ingest more data." Brandon added, "Machine learning, you know?"

Brandon showed me several tests where Emil's algorithm had scanned several hundred thousand messages, using a combination of language analysis, results from customer service support requests, and a list of flagged words to identify whether a message was acceptable or a threat. The results were wildly inconsistent. Oftentimes "bitch" got marked as inappropriate, regardless of context. "Breast" was an issue, even when used to refer to a chicken breast. The system had flagged nearly every instance of where a racial slur was used — not a violation of our guidelines, since it was impossible to determine if, say, a white person was saying the N-word or if a black person was saying it. But, embarrassingly, it seemed to struggle most with hip-hop verses, even when they came from extremely popular Top 40 songs. (Emil said his future solution would be to integrate a song lyrics database for exemptions.) Overall, when it came to conforming with our policies, the algorithm had been correct only 17 percent of the time. It was clear that Emil's system could only identify things at word level. It still couldn't wrap its head around sentences.

"It will get better over time. Hopefully."

"Well, until then, I think we need another dozen people if we're going to keep up with the support queue."

"Obviously, we can't just keep adding people to our customer support team forever. But in the meantime, keep up the good work down there."

He granted me the employees. Before I headed back downstairs, I asked if I could see Emil's list.

Blacklist (750 terms)

a55, a55hole, aeolus, ahole, anal, anal-probe, anilingus, anus, areola, areole, arian, aryan, ass, assbang, assbanged, assbangs, asses, assfuck, assfucker, assh0le, asshat, assho1e, ass hole, assholes, assmaster, assmunch, asswipe, asswipes, azazel, azz, b1tch, babe, babes, ballsack, bang, banger, barf, bastard, bastards, bawdy, beaner, beardedclam, beastiality, beatch, beater, beaver, beer, beeyotch, beotch, biatch, bigtits, big tits, bimbo, bitch, bitched, bitches, bitchy, blow, blow job, blowjob, blowjobs, bod, bodily, boink, bollock, bollocks, bollok, bone, boned, boner, boners, bong, boob, boobies, boobs, booby, booger, bookie, bootee, bootie, booty, booze, boozer, boozy, bosom, bosomy, bowel, bowels, bra, brassiere, breast, breasts, bugger, bukkake, bull shit, bullshit, bullshits, bullshitted, bullturds, bung, busty, butt, buttfuck, butt fuck, butt-fucker, buttfucker, buttplug, c.0.c.k, c.o.c.k., c.u.n.t, c0ck, c-0-c-k, caca, cahone, cameltoe, carpetmuncher, cawk, cervix, chinc, chincs, chink, chinks, chode, chodes, cl1t, climax, clit, clitoris, clitorus, clits, clitty, cocain, cocaine, cock, c-o-c-k, cock sucker, cockblock, cockholster, cockknocker, cocks, cocksmoker, cocksucker, coital, commie, condom, coon, coons, corksucker, crabs, crack, cracker, crack-whore, crap, crappy, cum, cummin, cumming, cumshot, cumshots, cumslut, cumstain, cunilingus, cunnilingus, cunny, cunt, cunt, c-u-n-t, cuntface, cunthunter, cuntlick, cuntlicker, cunts, d0ng, d0uch3, d0uche, d1ck, d1ld0, d1ldo, dago, dagos, dammit, damn, damned, damnit, dawgie-style, dick, dickbag, dickdipper, dickface, dickflipper, dickhead, dickheads, dickish, dick-ish, dick-ripper, dicksipper, dickweed, dickwhipper, dickzipper, diddle, dike, dildo, dildos, diligaf, dillweed, dimwit, dingle, dip-ship, doggie-style, doggy-style, dong, doofus, doosh, dopey, douch3, douche, douchebag, douchebags, douchey, drunk, dumass, dumbass, dumbasses, dummy, dyke, dykes, ejaculate, enlargement, erect, erection, erotic, essohbee, extacy, extasy, f.u.c.k, fack, fag, fagg, fagged, faggit, faggot, fagot, fags, faig, faigt, fanny-bandit, fart, fartknocker, fat, felch, felcher, felching, fellate, fellatio, feltch, feltcher, fisted, fisting, fisty, floozy, foad, fondle, foobar, foreskin, freex, frigg, frigga, fubar, fuck, f-u-c-k, fuckass, fucked, fucked, fucker, fuckface, fuckin, fucking, fucknugget, fucknut, fuckoff, fucks, fucktard, fucktard, fuckup, fuckwad, fuckwit, fudge-packer, fuk, fvck, fxck, gae, gai, ganja, gay, gays, gey, gfy, ghay, ghey, gigolo, glans, goatse, godamn, godamnit, goddam, goddammit, goddamn, goldenshower, gonad, gonads, gook, gooks, gringo, gspot, g-spot, gtfo, guido, h0m0, h0mo, handjob, hard on, he11, hebe, heeb, hell, hemp, heroin, herp, herpes, herpy, hitler, hiv, hobag, hom0, homey, homo, homoey, honky, hooch, hookah, hooker, hoor, hootch, hooter, hooters, horny, hump, humped, humping, hussy, hymen, inbred, incest, injun, j3rk0ff, jackass, jackhole, jackoff, jap, japs, jerk, jerk0ff, jerked, jerkoff, jism, jiz, jizm, jizz, jizzed, junkie, junky, kike, kikes, kill, kinky, kkk, klan, knobend, kooch, kooches, kootch, kraut, kyke, labia, lech, leper, lesbians, lesbo, lesbos, lez, lezbian, lezbians, lezbo, lezbos, lezzie, lezzies, lezzy, lmao, lmfao, loin, loins, lube, lusty, mams, massa, masterbate, masterbating, masterbation, masturbate, masturbating, masturbation, maxi, menses, menstruate, menstruation, meth, m-fucking, mofo, molest, moolie, moron, motherfucka, motherfucker, motherfucking, mtherfucker, mthrfucker, mthrfucking, muff, muffdiver, murder, muthafuckaz, muthafucker, mutherfucker, mutherfucking, muthrfucking, nad, nads, naked, napalm, nappy, nazi, nazism, negro, nigga, niggah, niggas, niggaz, nigger, niggers, niggle, niglet, nimrod, ninny, nipple, nooky, nympho, opiate, opium, oral, orally, organ, orgasm, orgasmic, orgies, orgy, ovary, ovum, ovums, p.u.s.s.y., paddy, paki, pantie, panties, panty, pastie, pasty, pcp, pecker, pedo, pedophile, pedophilia, pedophiliac, pee, peepee, penetrate, penetration, penial, penile, penis, perversion, peyote, phalli, phallic, phuck, pillowbiter, pimp, pinko, piss, pissed, pissoff, piss-off, pms, polack, pollock, poon, poontang, porn, porno, pornography, pot, potty, prick, prig, prostitute, prude, pube, pubic, pubis, punkass, punky, puss, pussies, pussy, pussypounder, puto, queaf, queef, queef, queer, queero, queers, quicky, quim, racy, rape, raped, raper, rapist, raunch, rectal, rectum, rectus, reefer, reetard, reich, retard, retarded, revue, rimjob, ritard, rtard, r-tard, rum, rump, rumprammer, ruski, s.h.i.t., s.o.b., s0b, sadism, sadist, scag, scantily, schizo, schlong, screw, screwed, scrog, scrot, scrote, scrotum, scrud, scum, seaman, seamen, seduce, semen, sex, sexual, sh1t, s-h-1-t, shamedame, shit, s-h-i-t, shite, shiteater, shitface, shithead, shithole, shithouse, shits, shitt, shitted, shitter, shitty, shiz, sissy, skag, skank, slave, sleaze, sleazy, slut, slut-dumper, slutkiss, sluts, smegma, smut, smutty, snatch, sniper, snuff s-o-b, sodom, souse, soused, sperm, spic, spick, spik, spiks, spooge, spunk, steamy, stfu, stiffy, stoned, strip, stroke, stupid, suck, sucked, sucking, sumofabiatch, t1t, tampon, tard, tawdry, teabagging, teat, terd, teste, testee, testes, testicle, testis, thrust, thug, tinkle, tit, titfuck, titi, tits, tittiefucker, titties, titty, tittyfuck, tittyfucker, toke, toots, tramp, transsexual, trashy, tubgirl, turd, tush, twat, twats, ugly, undies, unwed, urinal, urine, uterus, uzi, vag, vagina, valium, viagra, virgin, vixen, vodka, vomit, voyeur, vulgar, vulva, wad, wang, wank, wanker, wazoo, wedgie, weed, weenie, weewee, weiner, weirdo, wench, wetback, wh0re, wh0reface, whitey, whiz, whoralicious, whore, whorealicious, whored, whoreface, whorehopper, whorehouse, whores, whoring, wigger, womb, woody, wop, wtf, x-rated, xxx, yeasty, yobbo, zoophile

I had to laugh a little, imagining Emil, who rarely cursed or raised his voice, writing up a list of the most offensive words he knew. I had a strange impulse to look up "chink" to make sure it was on the list. In high school, I'd been called a chink. It didn't happen often anymore — maybe once every few months — that someone might say it to me on the subway.

One time, in the elevator of a department store, an older white man standing behind me muttered that he couldn't believe that the gooks had made it to America. He said it quietly, but just loud enough for me to hear it. I turned around to face him.

"What did you just say?"

He repeated himself, this time at full volume: "I said I can't believe the gooks have made it to America."

The man stared me straight in the eyes. He was easily in his seventies, shorter than me too, but I shrunk back. The hatred in his eyes was so clear and pure.

"Oh my god, Grandpa." He was with a younger white woman, about my age, now identified as his granddaughter. She must not have heard him at first, but she was embarrassed now that she had the second time.

"I killed people like you in the war."

"Grandpa, stop!"

"You fucking animals."

"Jesus, Grandpa, leave him alone!"

With a polite *ding,* the doors opened and the woman tugged her grandpa out of the elevator. She turned to me and apologized profusely.

"I'm so sorry. He's not of right mind —"

"Fucking gooks!"

"Grandpa, we're leaving."

I would have told her that it wasn't her fault, that it was fine, really, but the elevator doors closed before I could. The woman had begun scolding her grandfather, and I felt bad for them both. She was mortified. The whole confrontation was tense, but it had happened so fast. Walking away, I even thought it was kind of impressive he had used the word "gook," because it meant he had rightly identified that I was in some part Vietnamese.

When I told Margo, she hadn't understood.

"I would have lost my shit," she said.

"If someone called you a 'gook'?"

"Do you know the roots of that word? You know, we're both technically gooks."

"Unless you're secretly Asian, I don't think you count as a gook," I said.

She was dead serious. Its origins as a slur, she explained, went back long before the Vietnam and Korean Wars. "Gook" began to be used in the 1910s, during the U.S.'s occupation of Haiti. Marines called black Haitians gooks. Any idiot could look it up on the internet.

"I've got Haitian roots, along with some Jamaican. I know that 'gook' mostly refers

264

to Asian people now, but historically we are both gooks," she assured me. "Look it up."

"I'm not going to look it up."

I wasn't going to fight Margo, and I certainly wasn't going to fight history.

"Why do you even know the etymology of 'gook'?"

Margo didn't answer. She was already waving down the bartender for two more beers.

To celebrate the raises I'd gotten out of Brandon for Nina and Thompson, I took them out for drinks after work.

"Beers are on me," I announced proudly. (I'd borrowed Brandon's corporate card.) "What do you guys want to drink?"

"Whatever the happy hour deal is," Thompson said. "I only drink at a discount."

"The funny thing about 'happy hour' is that it assumes the rest of the night isn't happy," Nina said. "Like the night begins well, and only gets worse."

"Why is everything you say so bleak?"

Things got bleaker. Nina had complaints about every single person we worked with. Everyone was either too lazy or too overeager. Thompson complained about the bathroom situation. Our floor, with two dozen people, had one dingy bathroom. There was an unspoken rule that you could only use it for quick business. He told us about the afternoon he'd spent wandering the neighborhood looking for "a fancy place to take a dump."

"You know I'm your boss, right?"

"Please, I've seen the other people we work with."

"Wait, I want to know where Thompson ended up . . ." Nina trailed off.

"Taking a shit?"

"I mean, who doesn't like a nice bathroom?"

Two blocks from the office was a hotel. If you walked in with enough confidence, Thompson said, no one would doubt that you were staying there. I looked over at Nina. She was entering notes into her phone.

As we finished our first drinks, Thompson excused himself. "I gotta get home. Kids and such."

"I didn't know you had kids," I said.

"Four of them."

"How old?"

"I can't be expected to remember all four of their ages."

"Yes you can," Nina said.

"I can barely remember their names!"

Thompson thanked me for the drinks, and on the way out shouted, "The kids are six, eight, thirteen, and sixteen!"

I went to the bar and returned to the table with two more beers.

"I'm actually fine. I don't need another drink."

"Oh, you're leaving?"

"No, I can hang out. I just don't want another."

"I should have asked."

"It's okay," she said. And then: "Actually, do you want to go for a walk?"

"What about these beers?"

Nina was already putting on her coat and slinging her purse over her shoulder. "Who cares? They were free."

It was dusk and Nina was determined to squeeze every drop of sunlight out of the day. Bryant Park was nearby. We could hang out there. Nina walked quickly, weaving through people with the kind of graceful aggression that only lifelong New Yorkers possessed. ("Born and raised," she said.) She dashed across the street when we didn't have a WALK signal, totally unafraid of oncoming cabs. I thought I might die at least a couple times on our way to the park. But Nina had turned a twenty-minute walk into ten.

Bryant Park was, as always, a swarm of tourists. Nina surveyed the park like a falcon, and when she spotted an open bench darted immediately to it, tugging my arm along with her.

"Do you like working at Phantom?" she asked, once we'd sat.

"I mean, it's a job."

"But do you find it fulfilling?"

"I've never had a job I would describe as 'fulfilling.' "

"My parents are both history professors. They went straight from college to grad school, where they met. They've never known anything outside of academia, and yet they've always seemed satisfied — emotionally, spiritually." Nina exhaled. "I don't know how they do it."

"Were you a good student?"

"An excellent student," Nina clarified. She slouched in her seat. "But being good at a thing doesn't mean you like it."

It was a warm summer day, but as the light disappeared, a chilly breeze swept through the park. Nina shuddered suddenly, almost violently, and instinctually I put my hand on her arm and asked her if she was okay. Of course she was fine. Her skin was soft, smooth. I could feel the goose bumps prickling up on her arm.

"You're . . . still holding my arm?"

"Oh, uh, sorry?"

"I thought you were going to kiss me?"

"Oh" — I took a step back, hesitated — "I mean, should I?"

"Probably not, right? Like, you're my boss and all?"

"Yeah, that's true?"

Everything we said had the rising intonation of a question.

"We'll keep this relationship professional?" she said.

"I guess so?"

I thought I might still kiss her. But the moment, however brief, lingered too long, and I thought about Jill. So we had a New York goodbye, which was always logistical: Which train are you taking? We both needed to get on the N train. She was headed downtown, and I was going whichever was the other way.

"We're getting nearly a third of these correct now," Emil announced proudly one week at our staff meeting. "I know it's still a long way off, but at this rate I think we can get to over fifty percent in the next two months."

He was talking about progress on his

269

algorithm. When Brandon and I had first started having weekly check-ins on the customer service team, Emil was often sheepish since there was little movement. But after a few more weeks, Emil was making small breakthroughs. Suddenly the algorithm had a success rate of 32 percent.

"Two months is too long. Every day we support the twenty-plus people below us. We're bleeding money," Brandon said. "You have one month to figure this out."

Rationally, I knew that my team was competing against Emil's moderation system, which would only get better over time. But the early results had convinced me that I had months — maybe even up to a year — before it would improve enough to catch up.

Emil shuffled out of the room, laptop in hand, beaming.

"Lucas, wait." Brandon gave me a pat on the shoulder. "I'm sorry Emil isn't making progress more quickly."

I wanted to tell him that it was fine. In fact, if Emil wanted to keep not making progress, I'd be more than happy with that.

"I know it's been tough," he continued. "It can't be that fun down there, managing so many people. But you've been doing a great job."

I thanked Brandon for the compliment and returned to the customer service floor below. The room was quiet except for the diligent sound of keyboards tapping; nearly everyone had their headphones on. I knew the customer service operation was not a priority, but I had never realized just how temporary the space was. No decorations, not even a plant. I barely knew most of the people I'd hired, but I thought about how they all had bills and rent to pay. They were my responsibility.

That night, I was late meeting Jill at the bar because of a subway delay, and I found her by herself in a booth playing something on her phone. She motioned that she would show me. I scooted myself into her side of the booth.

"It's the worst," Jill said. "But I can't stop playing."

It was a puzzle game. There was a grid of brightly colored blocks — on closer inspection, different kinds of candy — that needed to be rearranged and matched in threes. Simple in concept, but challenging in execution. Jill let me play. She was on level 67. I asked how many levels there were and she shrugged, like the game could go infinitely and it wouldn't matter to her. The game was both maddening and satisfying — a kind of perfect alchemy of pleasing colors and sound effects, masking an underlying system built to exploit the most addictive tendencies of the human brain. It was genius.

"I'm already too embarrassed how much time I've sunk into it. And I'm even more embarrassed that I pay to keep playing."

As I continued to play I remembered something. "Did I ever tell you Margo was obsessed with Pac-Man? Like, we'd always go to this crappy bar solely because they had this old-school Pac-Man machine. And Margo would order a beer and ask for five dollars' worth of quarters and just stand in front of the arcade cabinet until she was too drunk to play anymore."

Seeing how poorly I was performing, Jill took her phone back. I watched her eyes widen as she tapped and swiped.

"Why Pac-Man?" she asked.

"She had a total engineer brain about it. She could see the patterns of the ghosts chasing you around the maze. The game was designed to be easy enough to feel beatable, but tough enough that it wasn't. That way people would play again and again."

Jill finally put her phone down.

"That's depressing, isn't it? That you can

272

trick people into doing a thing indefinitely."

"Humans will never commit to something forever. But they will do a dumb thing as long as you keep stringing them along," Jill said. "Like my exes."

When I didn't laugh, Jill added, "That was a joke."

I hadn't really heard the joke because I was thinking. If a game could do it, so could I. By stringing Emil along, I could extend the lifespan of my team.

"Brandon's always saying this thing at work: Don't ask for permission, ask for forgiveness."

"That sounds kind of rape-y."

"What?" I hadn't quite caught what she said. "Sorry, but I have to go back to work."

Every resolved customer service ticket was saved in a database that fed directly into Emil's algorithm. The more completed tickets, the more the system would improve. At a certain point, it would have enough tickets, enough data, to automate the process.

But what if that data were altered slightly? If Emil's system was ingesting false data, it would be learning from false signals. And instead of making progress, would it instead take steps backward?

By the time I arrived back at the Phantom office, everyone had left for the day. There were still blinking lights and the glow of screensavers coming off monitors, connected to computers that had been left running even though no one was using them. I spent nearly all my time on the customer service floor, but on the main floor I still had a desk and a computer. I hadn't used it in weeks.

My plan was simple: change the status of a few hundred random tickets so that it would throw off Emil's algorithm. The system was attempting to find consistency across the tens of thousands of customer support requests we'd handled. If I could introduce a little more randomness into it, it would make it impossible for the system to find any patterns. Emil's progress would stall and people on the customer service floor would keep their jobs. But my process had to be as unpredictable and haphazard as possible — introduce a deeply human kind of chaos.

It crossed my mind that Emil might notice something was amiss once his algorithm's accuracy plummeted. But it was more likely he would blame himself rather than the data. Unlike people, data was neutral; data was infallible; the raw numbers were never self-interested.

And on some level, engineers were right about data. They were just wrong about people.

When I got back to Jill's apartment, I found her cooking . . . something.

"I didn't realize you'd be back so quickly," Jill said. "And I also didn't think I'd be running behind so much. I was hoping to have this done before you returned." She seemed a little frazzled, moving between a large pot and a pan on the stove with unease.

"What are you making?"

"Pasta." She clarified: "Spaghetti."

"Well, it smells great," I said, which is what you're supposed to say.

I offered to help, but Jill insisted that she had it under control. I noticed she'd diced her onions in an uneven, haphazard manner. Also, her pasta had definitely been left in the boiling water for too long. And I doubt she'd salted the water first. Still, I appreciated the gesture. I usually did all the cooking, and was more than happy to. But everyone deserves a night off.

"What did you have to do at work?" Jill asked.

"It was nothing interesting."

Jill seemed annoyed by my reluctance to

say anything. "Who do you talk to?"

"What do you mean?"

"Like, when you have something on your mind, something weighing on you" — she looked up from her spaghetti — "who do you tell?"

"Do you want that person to be you?"

"No, it doesn't have to be. But there should be someone in your life that you actually talk to."

"I mean, it used to be Margo," I said. "Obviously."

Jill went back to her cooking, but the questions kept coming. "And you and Margo never dated?"

"You asked me that the night that we met. No, we did not date."

"And you guys never hooked up?"

"Not even once."

"And that's not something you thought about?"

"It. Was. Not." Jill's insistence was making me defensive. And angry.

"Even though she was someone you admired, talked to about everything, and wanted to be around all the time."

"Why are you grilling me on this?"

"You're obviously obsessed with Margo, and I find it hard to believe that the thought of sleeping with your beautiful friend never

276

ever crossed your mind."

"Just because she's attractive —"

"She was beautiful."

"Okay, fine, Margo was beautiful. Where are you going with this?"

"I just don't believe that you weren't in love with her."

"Of course I was in love with her! But what if I could love someone and not want to fuck them? People always talk about romantic relationships as being more than friends. What if friendship is actually the greater form of connection? What if being close to someone doesn't require being physical? What if, actually, it's better if it isn't? What if there are people more important than the ones you sleep with?"

"This is a really strange thing to tell someone you're fucking," Jill said.

Even now, I couldn't explain this to her. She wouldn't understand what Margo and I had. She couldn't even imagine it.

"It's just, you talk about Margo all the time," Jill said, "but you make her sound less like a person and more like a monument."

"Your onions are burning."

"What?"

I pointed to the smoking pan.

"Fuck!"

I put on my coat and told Jill I would go to the bodega and get another onion. When I got back, I showed her how to slice an onion more evenly: half moons first, then longer slices vertically; keep moving the onion to maintain a grip. She insisted that she didn't need the help. So it was past 10 p.m. by the time dinner was served. The spaghetti was good, the sauce a little under-seasoned.

"Would you tell me if you didn't like my cooking?" she asked.

"Of course," I said, probably lying.

Every Thursday at 6 p.m., a group of four engineers always met in one of the Phantom conference rooms to play a board game. I was impressed by their consistency.

One week, an engineer was missing. Brandon had taken him along to San Francisco, where he was meeting investors for the next round of funding. So I was asked to fill in for the absent player. I agreed reluctantly.

There is only one thing more painful than listening to someone explain the rules of a board game, and it's when that person is a server engineer.

"What am I trying to do in this game?" I finally asked, as one of the engineers droned on and on. The group of players laughed, as if for the first time acknowledging that the collective end goal derived from the combination of cardboard hexagons, playing cards, and a set of wood pieces might not be self-evident. Thematically, the game was set on an unsettled island. You, an explorer of sorts, were tasked with colonizing it — and not just colonizing it, but colonizing it better than the other players. In the abstract, the goal was to accumulate points, which could be earned by building small wooden houses. The houses were built by getting resources. Resources were allocated based on where each player had houses. The logic was circular. The engineers liked the game because it was a closed system, and within it they could compete.

I stumbled my way through the game. Rules were clarified and reiterated to me by kind but slightly frustrated opponents. But as I began to comprehend how the game worked, it started to feel more fun. I was gaining a sense of control. After a couple hours, the game was over and I had lost pretty badly, but I felt accomplished in my newfound rudimentary grasp of the game's mechanics. It was 8 p.m. and everyone else had vacated the office for the day. We started over.

We were all about six or seven beers deep

by the time we were nearing the end of the second game. I lost that one too, though I had made some moves that even surprised the veteran players. And I'd had some fun, too, surprisingly. I don't know why I thought Margo and I were the only people who bitched about Brandon and Emil. Well, they had even more complaints about Brandon than we'd had — less about his privileged behavior, and more on the directions he'd chosen to take the company. Scott, who had been at Phantom the longest (before it even had a name), said we shouldn't be pandering to investors just to secure more funding. Did we really want to build a service for teenagers, just to appease venture capitalists? Tom disagreed. He felt like the idealistic mission of Phantom had not panned out, and now users were finding a new, better use for the service. We were lucky, really, that teens had come along to provide us with a new, more viable business. Josh had concerns that we would never make money from teenagers. As soon as we made attempts to create a business around them — to encourage, even force them to pay — they would flee en masse to another free messaging service. Someone would rip us off, fund their own version with venture capital, and we would be left high and dry.

"I don't know," Scott said. "What do you think, Lucas?"

I was surprised they wanted to hear my opinion. I tried to dodge. "Honestly, I don't understand enough of the tech world to really know what makes sense for Phantom."

"None of us do," Tom said. "I mean, Brandon is a twenty-four-year-old CEO."

Josh said, "You're in customer service. You actually spend time dealing with our users all day long. You probably have better insight into Phantom than anyone else at the company."

"I read their complaints, but it's not like I've met people who use Phantom," I said. "I've never really used it."

I pulled out my phone — my flip phone.

Josh laughed. Tom told me I was ridiculous. Scott assured me that the company would buy me a smartphone.

"Would anyone trade an ore for two sheep?" I asked.

There were no takers.

What's the most surprising thing you ever saw Margo do?

Once we were riding the subway, and there was a woman seated across from us, reading a book, minding her own business. She was tall, beautiful, white. Kind of had

281

the look of a model, but maybe not. Anyway, the man sitting beside her — he's middle-aged, totally unassuming until the moment he pulls out his dick. He just starts quietly jerking off. I never thought I would be able to describe a stranger whacking it as "subtle," but the act was subtle enough that the woman next to him didn't notice. She just kept reading her book.

Margo starts flipping out on the dude. "Put your raggedy-ass dick away, you lowlife piece of shit." Something like that. The entire train is suddenly at attention. "You put that away! Away with that, you sick freak!" By this point, the woman has leapt up from her seat and everyone is staring at the pervert, who is now attempting to stuff his cock back in his pants. "This is no place for that! No place at all!" And now people are laughing. Everyone in the train is cracking up, even though they're witnessing this horrible thing. Margo has somehow defused the whole situation. The train pulls into a stop, and the man flees literally with his tail between his legs.

The pretty woman thanks Margo, who says it was no problem at all. Another man on the train moves to pursue him, but she grabs him and tells him to let it go, that it's not worth it. By letting the pervert flee,

Margo had saved all involved.

What is the meanest thing Margo ever did?

Why do you want to know that?

A person's not really a person without flaws. I want to have a complete portrait of Margo, not just an idealized version of her.

Don't get me wrong. She could be mean. She just never meant to be mean, you know? Like, there wasn't one specific instance I could point to where Margo was trying to be terrible. But there were times when she could be cruel. Mostly when she was drinking. Times when she'd had just a little too much whiskey and she'd see you vulnerable and just twist the knife because she could. She could dismantle any person limb from limb with her words whenever she wanted. That was, like, her X-Men mutant power: the ability to destroy a person. But she kept it hidden, to herself. Did you ever read *X-Men*?

No. I thought it was a movie.

It was a comic book series first. But anyway. There is this character in it named Jean Grey and she's the world's most powerful psychic. Even more powerful than Professor X.

Who is Professor X?

He's formerly the most powerful psychic. Not important. What's important now is that Jean Grey is.

Okay, so —

— But a transformation happens and Jean Grey becomes possessed by her powers. Now she's the Dark Phoenix.

Wait, I don't —

And suddenly, the world's most powerful psychic is a different person, and able to destroy entire galaxies. She's a cosmic-level threat, one even greater than Galactus. I know you don't know who that is, but his nickname is "Destroyer of Worlds." So Phoenix is now more dangerous than THE DESTROYER OF WORLDS.

So Margo when she's drunk turns from Jean Grey to the Dark Phoenix. And that's when she's meanest?

What?

I'm just trying to follow.

No, it's just, like, Margo was very smart — smarter than anyone. She was very powerful with her words. And she could crush you at any moment with them. But she usually chose not to. There were just these rare moments when she drank a little too much and that power slipped out.

When she becomes the Phoenix?

Yes, that's what I mean. That's the metaphor. Or whatever.

You realize the point of a metaphor is to make an idea clearer.

Right.

And you've chosen a frame of reference that I have no familiarity with.

It's an imperfect metaphor anyway. The Dark Phoenix Saga ends with Jean Grey suddenly reclaiming control of her body and sacrificing herself in order to save her friends and the universe.

Is that what you think Margo did?

What do you mean?

Sacrifice herself?

What? No. Why would you say that?

Well, the circumstances of her death are vague.

She was drunk and she got hit by a car.

I mean, it sounds like she was drunk a lot.

Yeah, but it wasn't a problem.

Then it's not possible that Margo . . . chose to walk into the street.

I said it's not a good metaphor. You have to understand: Margo was happiest when she was drinking. Occasionally mean, sure, but mostly she was fun, unburdened. It was a release for her.

And have you had too much to drink?

Maybe. Yes. Just maybe, actually. Unlike

Margo, I am not high-functioning after several beers. More than several. Hmm. Are we done with this exercise?

Yes, that was my last question.

Okay, okay. Sorry I got hostile.

You're drunk and you care a lot. It happens. I actually have one more question.

What is it, Jill?

Do you think you knew Margo better than anyone else?

I thought I did. But I think I just wanted that to be true. You can spend all your time with someone and still not know the entirety of them. All you know is what they've shown you. And even the things they show you, you won't even understand them at the time. You won't get it until it's too late to do anything about it.

A_POPULAR_DECISION.WAV

The tribunal had come to a conclusion: mankind was not worth saving.

The debates were civil, sure, but they'd been prolonged — years long by this point. Decades even. A council of Earth's brightest delegates sent from every country to observe the planet, from the Citadel, a gigantic space station that represented the sum of all modern technology and human effort. It orbited the Earth coolly, from a distance, to act as the moral arbiter of man.

It was strange to be so removed. To witness everything from the cold blackness of space should have made humanity's appeals clear. But nothing on Earth seemed warmer or kinder than nothingness. In fact, it was worse than space. It was one thing when it was disease. The plague had been a common enemy, one that brought the world together to combat through science and collaboration. Seeing that unfold, even with the massive loss of life, was encouraging. Humankind could band together in times of crisis. The hegemonic shape of society had broken down in the face of survival. It turns out the threat of extinction brought out the best in people.

But while disease was not a man-made problem, everything else was. In fact, it seemed like the eras of prosperity bred the most inequality. Wealth created poverty; inequity instigated war. People loved killing one another to further themselves. It was the only thing that human beings could do efficiently.

In the beginning, the tribunal was more than just a gesture. It weighed in on political matters as third-party observers, all of whom were unaffected by any terrestrial consequences. The idea was that absolute morality could be achieved through total objectivity. In the century since the members of the tribunal had been aboard the Citadel, they rarely agreed on anything. As a result, the council's advice became largely ignored, its existence merely a symbol. But if there was one thing they could all consent to, it was that things were not getting better.

Earth is burning up. Each year, the global temperature rises three degrees. The sun bears down across the planet, its rays blasting through an atmosphere that has been decimated by just a couple short centuries of pollution. Ah, "pollution" — such a great euphemism when really what we mean is the consequence of humanity.

In just a decade, Earth will be uninhabitable. Hot. No crops will grow. The oceans will dry up. Human life, as we know it, will cease to exist.

But it will be a slow death. Years of drought, hunger, suffering. Terrible stuff. So the tribunal comes to a conclusion. They set coordinates for the Citadel to collide with the Arctic. The impact will create a tidal wave that swallows the Earth, drowning every human being.

[Margo burps]

And that was humankind's last great act: taking matters into its own hands. Who knows? Maybe the threat of extinction would bring out the best in people again. Go out on a high note.

[Margo rips an even bigger burp]

Hehehehehehehehe

VI

HUMAN RESOURCES

I'd underestimated the resilience of cruelty. We all had. The customer service floor had now ballooned to nearly forty people. We were running out of space. Emil's system was coming along too, even despite my attempt to delay it. It had begun auto-flagging suspicious messages, creating a new queue of things to look at, deemed questionable by the algorithm. But no matter how quickly we scaled up our operation — with manpower or technological power — there was too much hateful and toxic language for us to investigate. The more effort we put into it, the more the problem seemed to grow.

If someone was harassing another user on Phantom, we would disable their account after three strikes. But that person could just open a new account and start again, now with a fresh slate. I'd proposed making it more difficult for users to create a new account — maybe force accounts to be tied to a single phone number or email address — but that idea was instantly vetoed by Brandon, since it violated Phantom's utility to people who needed to be anonymous to change the world. You know, the corporate whistleblowers, the investigative journalists. It didn't matter to Brandon that, in two years, these righteous folks had never materialized.

The reality is that Phantom was still largely being used by mean teenagers. The other reality was that investors didn't care about our issues. The only measure of success — and continued funding — was user acquisition. They needed to see that Phantom was growing. Any impediment to growth was a signal that things had stopped working, and that it was time to turn off the faucet to the money.

Meanwhile, as we were getting better at identifying abusive language, users had found new ways to skirt our moderating abilities. Since Phantom didn't support the sending of photos, they began sending image links. Whereas before we could blacklist certain words, URLs obfuscated the things they pointed to: Graphic images of war. Sexually explicit pornography. A lot of swastikas.

Nina was the first one to catch what was

happening with the links.

"So our users are Nazis?" I asked.

"No, they just like Nazi imagery," she explained.

"What's the difference?"

"Most of these kids don't know what Nazis actually are. They just know that Nazis represent a kind of extreme version of evil. Nazis are scary and bad even without the context of, y'know, stuff like the Holocaust."

"Stuff like the Holocaust, huh," I repeated. "Hmm."

"Don't be a smart-ass," Nina said, nudging me on the shoulder.

I had to admire such cleverness, even if it was disturbing. The brutes understood how we were policing their language, so they had found an entirely new medium.

Nina's proposal began to set out moderation guidelines, like the ones we'd had for written threats of violence. I quickly flipped through the copy she had printed.

"This is . . . excellent work," I said.

"Thank you," she said. "I want to do my best for you."

"That's good, because I —"

I lost my words for a second. Nina was smiling, awaiting my approval. I wanted to tell her more about how impressed I was by her work, how she'd really thought things through in a way that I could barely begin to fathom. But the best thing I could do for her was to bring this report upstairs to Brandon.

"Where are you going?" Nina asked.

Waving the report at her, I replied, "None of this matters if Brandon doesn't sign off on it."

Before my parents owned the bed-and-breakfast, my father worked as a chef at a Japanese restaurant situated in a strip mall. It was just one of many franchises in a chain of teppanyaki places, which seated guests around a hibachi grill. The main draw of these restaurants was that the chef would cook in front of the guests, performing knife tricks and telling little jokes. Both dinner and a show.

The chain had been started by a Japanese wrestler in the '60s who'd been disqualified from the Olympics for getting into fights with his teammates. He had more success in the restaurant management business than in wrestling. Like most non-Western food, it was difficult to charge a premium price on Japanese food, no matter the quality. Ethnic food, especially at the time, was considered gross by Americans. It was inferior cuisine made by inferior people, so it could at least be cheap. But having been born in Tokyo, the wrestler realized he could wield that foreignness if it was exoticized. Impress diners with the outlandish, other-worldly appeal of the East, and customers would pay up.

My father was obviously not Japanese, but none of the patrons ever knew. Some kind of Asian was authentic enough. All of the chefs took on pseudonyms that were stereo-typically Japanese names: Haru, Yuki, Ha-ruki. As a joke that only he would find funny, my dad picked Sony, which was not in any shape or form a real Japanese name. Patrons often told my dad about how they loved their Sony television, as if my father were responsible for their high-quality technology just by bearing the namesake. He'd bow and say, in his best fake Japanese accent, "Oh thank you, thank you."

To nail the accent, he'd studied his favorite Bruce Lee movies, where Japanese people were vilified, depicted as conniving busi-nessmen named Mr. Suzuki. As a child, I remember him watching those films while practicing knife tricks. He'd quickly dissect grilled shrimp, then flip them into his shirt pocket, his chef's hat. He would stack slices of grilled onions to form a volcano. Oil was poured in the top. "Fire!" he'd yell as it ignited, flames spouting out. I would clap at the spectacle.

He performed this routine day in and day out. He was always amazed that people came to the restaurant more than once, since all the chef's tricks were the same each time. But the pay was respectable, the hours reasonable for a cook's gig. It never bothered him that he was posing as a Japanese man. I doubt he ever thought about that, even as he feigned a different kind of accent. This was a rare situation, in which my father — an immigrant from Vietnam — could use his appearance to get away with something. What did it matter that people thought his name was Sony?

The wrestler's obituary appeared in the paper the year before I moved to New York. He had died of pneumonia. In addition to launching an empire of lucrative Japanese restaurants, he'd been inducted into the wrestling hall of fame, started a pornography magazine, had a short career as an offshore powerboat racer, and fathered nine children. One of them became a famous model, another a famously mediocre DJ. He represented every American ideal of a man: an athlete, a businessman, a daredevil, a father, a womanizer.

In the paper's write-up, the wrestler was credited for introducing America to Japanese food. It was a dubious claim — it was just steak grilled on a hibachi and doused in soy sauce — but there was a modicum of truth to it. Unlike any other kind of Asian food, be it Chinese or Korean or Vietnamese, Japanese food was seen as a high-end cuisine. It was respected, revered. You could charge real money for it too. And what was more American than that?

After three straight weeks of repeating the same routine every night — bar, small dinner, work on Margo's stories — Jill began to go a little stir-crazy.

"I spend all day writing in my apartment, and then you come over and I write some more. Can we go out? See friends?"

I didn't have any other friends. Jill barely did either. Which is how we made plans with her old roommate and her new boyfriend. They hadn't hung out in forever. Dinner and drinks, it would be easy — fun even. I wasn't particularly interested in going out, but I was curious about Jill's friends. She rarely mentioned other people in her orbit.

The restaurant they picked was the New York location of the teppanyaki chain.

This place reminded me of the one where

my dad used to work, only larger and more crowded. We arrived early, and were the first ones seated. I told Jill that my dad used to be a chef at one of these places. She asked if that made it weird eating here. I told her it didn't, but I appreciated her asking.

Jill's friends, Jackie and Jeremy, arrived late.

"Sorry, the train," Jeremy said. He shook my hand, gripped it hard.

"It's so nice to meet you, Lucas," Jackie said, giving me an unexpected hug. She said Jill had said nothing about me. A joke?

Jackie and Jeremy were an attractive white couple. Both had come straight from work and were dressed up — professional, somewhat conservative outfits that could best be described as Connecticut chic. His shirt was starched crisp, well-fitted, and the blandest shade of blue. His suit, too, was prim, its only flourish a checkered pocket square barely peeking out of the breast pocket. Hers was slightly trendier, a blazer with sleeves made to be rolled up, the sort of outfit that could be worn during and after work hours. Jill and I, as people who worked from home and at a startup with no sense of dress code, had put no mind into what we wore: T-shirts, jeans, old sneakers.

Maybe it was because we were quiet

people, but throughout dinner, Jackie and Jeremy did most of the talking. Their stories were about work and how hard work was and how hard they worked. But there were few specifics. Jackie worked in PR and spoke vaguely about difficult clients; Jeremy, from what I could gather, was in finance, but anything more specific than that never surfaced, other than that lots of money was involved.

"Jeremy travels so much that he sometimes prefers to sleep sitting up."

"It's true. Some nights I sleep in the living room on the couch with my travel neck pillow. I'm such a freak sometimes."

"You just work so much, honey."

"Gotta bring home the bacon for my baby."

The two kissed and Jill looked at me, eyes wide with some combination of horror and distress.

"You know, Lucas's dad used to be a chef at one of these places," Jill said.

"Oh really?" Jeremy said.

I nodded.

"That's cool," Jackie said.

I nodded.

Jackie and Jeremy, surprisingly, had nothing to say. Jill, maybe embarrassed that she'd brought it up, asked if I'd looked at

298

the menu yet.

I didn't need to. I already knew everything on it.

The chef's routine was — without missing a beat — exactly the same as the one my father had performed nearly two decades earlier. There were shrimp tosses; an onion volcano. Jeremy kept trying to make conversation with the chef. Jackie wanted to do "sake bombs," which were less a kind of drink and more of a hazing ritual. She explained: you balance a shot of sake on two chopsticks above a glass of beer. Then, in unison, everyone bangs the table until the shot drops into the beer, then you chug the whole thing as quickly as possible. Jill protested, but Jackie assured us it would be fun. When a waiter came by, Jackie held up four fingers to make it crystal clear. The waiter apologized, and pointed to a sign behind the bar: NO SAKE BOMBS.

When the bill arrived for our steaks, Jeremy insisted he pay. Then he and Jackie insisted we go out for another drink. There was a great bar around the corner, apparently.

At the bar, Jeremy wanted to know where I worked — the first question he'd asked me all evening.

"No shit! I use Phantom all the time. Great service. You folks do good work."

"Oh thank you," I said. It was the first time I'd met anyone not affiliated with the company who used Phantom. "Everyone works really hard on it, so it's nice to hear that someone likes it."

"Like it? I love it. Disappearing messages — so much fun. Genius idea. You come up with it?"

I told him I didn't, but Jeremy's compliments kept coming. They were aggressive, disingenuous. A sales tactic, it seemed, but I wasn't sure what he was selling.

Jackie interjected. "If you two are gonna talk about work, I'm getting another drink."

"It'll be quick. I just want to ask Lucas a few questions. Phantom — it's such a big deal."

Jackie sighed. "I'll grab the next round but I'm putting it on your card."

Jeremy opened his wallet and found his credit card. It was a pale green card with the word CORPORATE stamped across it.

"You're gonna expense this?"

"Yeah, talking to Lucas about Phantom is . . . research for a future investment opportunity." Jeremy laughed to himself.

"Come on, Jill. I'll need a hand with the drinks." And the two of them headed through the crowd, toward the bar.

Jeremy continued.

"Can you keep a secret?" he asked. I never said yes, but he kept going. "I gotta admit: I use Phantom to talk to this one girl. It's perfect. The messages just disappear. No way Jackie would ever find out."

It was strange how Jeremy trusted me with this information so quickly. Even stranger was how he so readily volunteered it, thinking that I would be impressed. I kept waiting uneasily for him to try to high-five me, and if one part of this conversation was not a disaster, it was the fact that the high-five never came.

"The things I can say on Phantom — it's so freeing. You can say the dirtiest, nastiest shit. Real, deep, primal human things because it'll never come back to you. And if it did, what proof would they have? Their word versus yours."

He went on.

"Are you guys going to add the ability to send photos? Because right now it's just text. You guys have to be adding photos soon, right? Phantom would be perfect for sexting then."

I was tempted to tell him the workaround the bullies used — send links to pictures, the trick to sending unsolicited swastikas.

But Jeremy barely let me get a word in. He went on and on and seemed to know a lot about "sexting." A mayoral candidate for New York City had just been busted — his entire career and future upended — because he was caught sexting. If he had used Phantom, Jeremy argued, he'd still be in the running.

"That's not exactly what we built Phantom for."

"If not that, then what?"

"The idea is that the self-destructing messages would enable people to make brave acts without worrying about the paper trail, like corporate or government whistleblowers, or undercover journalists." I was at once defensive of Phantom and disgusted with myself for sounding like Brandon practicing his pitch deck.

Jeremy scoffed. "But how many whistleblowers and journalists use Phantom as opposed to dudes like me talking dirty to their side pieces?"

"To be honest, it's almost entirely teenagers."

That shut him up. Jackie and Jill returned with four beers. I drained mine quickly and helped Jill finish hers.

"Sorry Jeremy was . . . the absolute worst."

I assured Jill that he was fine. I'd had a nice time.

"You don't have to pretend," Jill said. "Especially because you are terrible at holding it in when you don't like someone."

"You don't know me. Maybe I love to be lectured about . . . markets."

"Business transactions."

"Investing."

"And let me tell you all about my Starwood points."

"It's funnier if you imagine that Starwood just means 'space boners.' "

I never thought someone would kiss me immediately after I uttered "space boners," but here we were, making out in the street. Jill apologized again for subjecting me to an evening of Jeremy. Maybe the strongest bond two people could have was hating the same person.

That night, I slept at my place so I could be at work before anyone else. I looked up Jeremy's Phantom account. It took a minute to verify it was the right Jeremy, but once I dug into his message history — the feature that Emil's team had newly created — it was easy to confirm. Now that all messages were archived in Phantom's database, I had the ability to look up any user's past messages. It was for customer service purposes, but this seemed like a reasonable use case. Jeremy wasn't joking. He had been full-on sexting with someone named Lily:

J: baby i'm so hard for you
J: i'm going to do all sorts of things to you
L: your getting me so wet
L: tell me what you want me to do
J: suck my balls baby
L: ok yes
L: i want you inside me
L: i want your hard cock in me
J: i want to be inside you too
J: but i also want you to suck my balls first
L: ok ok i am sucking your balls now

I printed out the entire transcript. Then I texted Jill for Jackie's mailing address. She asked why, and I told her that I'd promised to send Jeremy some Phantom swag — a T-shirt, some stickers, that kind of thing. Jill seemed skeptical, but surrendered the address of their condo on the Upper East Side.

Funnily enough, the most time-consuming part of this whole task was finding an envelope and a stamp. I thought about including a note, explaining that these were Jeremy's secret messages, but I decided against it. Jackie would know what these were, or at the very least, she'd confront Jeremy about them.

As I dropped the envelope in the mail I had a thought: *When was the last time I mailed a letter?*

After a series of fluffy magazine interviews aimed at drumming up investor interest, Brandon was finally getting meetings with people who'd previously turned down the opportunity to hear him pitch. But the newfound attention on Phantom also raised the company's profile for criticism. Two weeks after Emil began work on the new algorithm, I received a flurry of emails from Brandon early in the morning, telling me I needed to get to the office immediately.

"I emailed you like a dozen times," he said when I walked in.

"I don't have a smartphone." I raised my flip phone in the air. "You can text or call me."

Brandon hardly glanced up as he motioned me over to a conference room, and on his laptop he had open a story that a tech publication had run about a photo we'd censored. The piece, which didn't include any comment from us, ran under the headline "Is Phantom Censoring Your

Private Messages?"

Apparently, a journalist using Phantom had had one of their messages flagged and deleted.

"People can't know that we're doing this," Brandon said. "It would be disastrous to the company's reputation."

I'd known that our moderation operation was not exactly aboveboard. Sure, we'd updated our terms and services to cover our ass legally, but the language was deliberately vague, elastic.

Still, the specifics of our moderation guidelines could never be a secret forever, especially given how many temporary employees we were churning through. They'd all signed nondisclosure agreements, but hunting out leakers and litigating would draw more undue attention.

Brandon was beside himself, frustrated and anxious in a way I'd never seen him before. He paced around the room. He flapped his arms wildly as he talked, which reminded me of the way stand-ups might punctuate a punch line, save for the fact Brandon was screaming. I tried not to laugh. I understood the severity of the situation. But seeing Brandon out of sorts was, as always, a delightful experience.

"We get called out for a cyberbullying

problem, so we find a way to solve it. What do these people want?"

It was unclear who Brandon meant when he referred to "these people." I tried to calm him down by assuring him that I'd look into the records and figure out what happened.

"Emil's stupid fucking algorithm," Brandon said. "He wanted to test it against your team, prove that it could hold its own against human judgment. I never should've signed off on it."

"Wait, Emil's algorithm is active? I thought he was still just testing internally."

That same algorithm had been eating two weeks' worth of poisoned data. No wonder it was shitting all over itself.

"We rolled it out a few days ago. We were only going to do it for a week and see the results. I'm sorry we didn't tell you, but Emil said that if you knew, you might adjust how the team downstairs was moderating and it would make the test less scientific."

"I'm glad that making a test 'scientific' was more important than my trust," I snapped. I hadn't cared much about the power dynamics in the office. But suddenly I had leverage. And I felt a desire to play a new role: I was going to be as entitled and self-righteous as possible.

Brandon apologized. He admitted his

mistake — something he'd never done before. And I let him talk through what he was thinking: The piece that had been posted was incomplete, published by a half-assed twentysomething writer with no real proof that Phantom was censoring messages, even if he was right. But that would spur the real journalists with an investigative background, with clout, who worked at real, legitimate newspapers and magazines, to find the truth. And that was the worst part, according to Brandon. They had the truth on their side. Phantom was a compromised service. It advocated a set of values publicly, while privately and selfishly adhering to a different set of rules. People wouldn't get up in arms about the company's treatment of user privacy. They'd be furious about the hypocrisy.

Even though he was raving (again, loud and hilarious), I couldn't help but be impressed by how quickly Brandon had worked through the press cycle. Hopefully he wasn't right, but rationally, I knew he was.

Through the glass door of the conference room, we both spotted Emil.

"Get in here now," Brandon yelled. Emil rushed over, not even taking a moment to remove his jacket or put down his backpack.

Brandon told me to figure out what exactly had happened. I headed downstairs.

Most of the support team was already at their desks, but it was weirdly quiet — no keyboards tapping. I walked around to Thompson's computer and saw that he had the article up.

"Everyone's reading it," he said.

"Do we know what happened?" I asked him. Then I turned to the room and asked again. Sternly. I figured this would be a good time to wield some authority. It was likely Emil's automated moderation system that fucked this up, but I wanted everyone to know this was a serious situation. No one should take it lightly.

I got zero response.

"Listen, uh," Thompson said quietly, "I pulled the customer service log."

"And?"

"Well . . ." He gestured toward the stairwell.

"What?"

"It's Nina. She's . . ."

Everyone was looking at us. Apparently the rest of the team understood the gravity of the situation, had already deduced exactly what happened, even if they didn't understand the implications it would have for

Phantom.

"Everyone back to work," I instructed. People returned their attention to their monitors half-heartedly, and I walked toward the stairwell.

I could hear Nina's gentle sobs echoing from a couple flights above. I asked her if everything was okay, but she couldn't stop her jagged breathing. Her face was pressed into her palms; she was weeping with an intensity that I would've found cartoonish if I didn't feel so bad for her.

"I can't lose this job," she finally said.

"No one said you're losing your job."

"People have been fired for so much less."

"Like who?"

"Like Lion."

"Lion showed up to work high four times. Do you know how bad you look when you warn someone that it's three strikes and somehow you still let it get to four?"

Nina let out a choked laugh. It felt like progress.

"It was my fault, though."

She walked me through it. When the article broke this morning, Nina used the name of the writer to do a reverse-search through the Phantom user database. She'd assumed the photo had been deleted by one of the newer temps, and had mostly tried to find out who screwed up so she could scold them. To her surprise, it was herself.

Nina barely remembered handling the flagged message. It was one in a queue of hundreds of messages she had looked at the day before. But she did recall some hesitation around the image. It was a black-and-white photograph from the Vietnam War, wherein the camera captured the execution of a handcuffed Viet Cong soldier at the hands of South Vietnam's chief of national police. The image was iconic — a Colt .45 just fired, the bullet penetrating the skull of a prisoner.

She'd hesitated flagging it, but the image had violated our policies for graphic content: regardless of the fact that it was well known, the photo was still violent and barbaric. For a user to send another user a depiction of a murder could be easily understood as a threat of violence. Nina had judged it as such, and moved on to the next image in her customer service queue.

"It's a famous photograph," I said, unhelpfully.

"Don't you think I know?" Nina finally looked up at me. Through her tears I could sense anger, though it was unclear toward whom.

"Then why did you flag the image?"

"Because there's nothing in our guidelines that exempts photos of historical significance. It's still a violent image."

Nina was right, of course. We hadn't specified what to do with art.

"This is why we have humans handling these requests. A person should be able to identify this picture and understand that this is an edge case. Or at least know that this particular instance is more complicated than what the policies cover."

"The point of rules is that they should cover everything!"

"I still think you should have caught this. You know that when support cases are questionable, we can spend the extra time to talk through them."

"But we're supposed to get through as many cases as quickly as possible," Nina said. "We have quotas. There are bonuses. We have a fucking leaderboard."

I didn't have a response for this. Again, Nina, even in her state of despair, was thinking clearly, rationally. We'd created an environment that rewarded people for being as efficient as possible, rather than thoughtful.

"I really can't lose this job," Nina said. "I'd have to go home and move back in with my parents. This job is already embarrassing enough as it is."

I tried not to take offense.

"I did everything I was supposed to do. I studied hard. I got good grades. I graduated with fucking honors. And still, not a single job I applied for even bothered to call me back."

She explained that she had earned a bachelor's degree in American history and student debt from an Ivy League school. Her focus was the second half of the twentieth century. She knew everything there was to know about the Vietnam War. Definitely more than I did.

"Have you heard of the Hamlet Evaluation System?" she asked. "That's a rhetorical question; no one knows what it is. Which is maybe the point of writing a thesis: to dedicate months and months researching a topic that nobody would ever care about —"

The talking seemed to be calming her down.

"— Not many people realize this but Vietnam was the first war that was believed could be won using machines —"

What would I report back to Brandon?

"— General Westmoreland believed in something he dubbed 'the electronic battlefield,' that by using a systems-oriented

313

approach, he could more efficiently manage everything in the war —"

I was confident I could save Nina's job, but the responsibility ultimately fell on me.

"— So his strategists devised the Hamlet Evaluation System, which quantified the Americans' efforts into a series of metrics that could be used to understand how much progress was being made toward winning the war —"

My team screwed up, so I should take the blame.

"— The attempts to statistically measure the war effort meant advisors were filling out worksheets based on eighteen different indicators —"

It crossed my mind that I could lie — protect Nina by saying that it was the fault of Emil's moderation algorithm, as Brandon had originally suspected.

"— Most of these were subjective, though, on top of being near-impossible to gauge in the first place, so advisors' reports always showed progress —"

But Emil would have access to the logs and could easily dismantle that story.

"— I mean, it makes sense, right? If you're under pressure to turn in good news, and no one can really prove otherwise, wouldn't you just say that everything was going swimmingly? —"

Still, I could maybe spin it in my favor.

"— On top of everything, all of this data collected was used not just so the Americans could convince themselves they were winning the war —"

The needs of Emil's system pushed my team to resolve tickets at a rate that was untenable.

"— But so they could also convince the media that they were always making headway —"

Really, this was all Emil's fault. I could make that case.

"It was true because no one could prove it untrue." Nina paused, as if having a minor revelation. "God, even that is ironic too."

I didn't understand what she meant, but I also knew that it didn't matter much.

"Are you even listening to me?"

I reached over to touch her arm, to comfort her. It was sudden.

"Really?" Nina pushed me backward. Hard.

Upstairs, Brandon was screaming at Emil and making no effort to hide it. The room had a glass door, and did not keep sound in very well. Everyone at Phantom could hear. Emil was seated, just taking it all in while

Brandon berated him. He looked attentive, but still unfazed, which I imagine was making Brandon even angrier.

I waited for a pause in the conversation. A few minutes passed before there was a lull in Brandon's yelling. I knocked on the glass. Brandon exhaled and gave me a hand motion that indicated I could come in.

"We were just discussing the possibility of taking Emil's moderation system offline, at least until it improves enough that we can feasibly start testing it in the wild."

"That's what I wanted to talk to you about," I said.

I sat down at the table. Brandon finally seated himself too.

"The censored message from the article — that wasn't flagged by Emil's algorithm. It was someone on my team."

"What?"

Emil looked surprised too, but didn't say anything.

"It was an image — an old war photograph, kind of famous. The moderator identified it as such, but removed it because it still violated our policies about graphic imagery."

Emil let out a chuckle — tried to keep it in — a small, satisfied betrayal of his cool indifference.

316

Brandon didn't apologize, only let out a long sigh. Back in levelheaded CEO mode.

"Emil, go back to your desk. Lucas, lay out all the details."

Emil left, and I walked Brandon through what had happened step-by-step. I explained that it wasn't Nina's fault. (Brandon had forgotten who she was. "One of our most senior moderators," I said; when he still didn't know, I further clarified: "short Indian girl.") We had set policies that were rigid, and we encouraged consistency rather than flexibility.

"If you have an entire floor of people making those judgments, why can't we take things on a case-by-case basis?" Brandon asked.

What a gift, and Brandon didn't even know it. If I played it right, I could land a finishing blow to Emil's algorithm and protect my team.

"We've been treating the customer support team as temporary, and preparing for a future where Emil's automated moderation system handles all requests. For his system to work, our guidelines need to be consistent — even if it means making the occasional mistake like this."

"We can't make a mistake like this again," Brandon said. "The press is gonna kill us."

"Then maybe an automated future is not what we should be planning for."

Brandon sunk back in his chair. It looked like he was considering it.

"And what kind of changes would we have to make to accommodate this new course we're charting?"

I tried to not let the weak nautical reference distract me.

"Right now, we incentivize everyone to get through as many of these tickets as possible. They're encouraged to work quickly, not thoughtfully. We hire with high turnaround in mind, so even if we did have people with expertise, we'd expect them to leave with it after only a few months, maybe even weeks. They don't care about Phantom because we make it clear we don't care about them."

And here's where I planted my flag: "Make them full-time employees, with salaries and benefits and a stake in the company. Give them a real reason to want this."

Brandon started nodding. He said this was a strong case and promised to "run the numbers," a phrase he always used that I didn't really believe meant anything. But Brandon seemed to have been listening, maybe even convinced. We talked through several more minute details about how we would change our moderation policies, specifically to avoid cases like this one. Brandon said that the clearest way to illustrate a change publicly was to make an example of someone. I told him that wouldn't be necessary — I'd hold myself personally responsible.

"Fine, I trust you," Brandon said.

This was the most encouraging thing he had ever said to me.

I headed downstairs, feeling victorious. If it wasn't 11 a.m. and I wasn't at work, I would've celebrated with a drink.

But by the time I had returned to the customer service floor to tell Nina she didn't have to worry about her job, she was nowhere to be seen. I checked the stairwell again. She wasn't there. I asked Thompson if he'd seen her.

"She left."

"Where did she go?"

"No, you don't get it, man," Thompson said. "She *left.*"

"I didn't know you had a car."

"I barely ever use it," Jill said. "I mostly keep it around because I love to spend what little money I have on auto insurance. Plus, I love re-parking the car across the street every few days to keep it from getting towed."

"At least it gets you out of the house."

"God, I was joking but I think you're right: I might never leave the apartment if I didn't have this stupid car."

With our bags in hand, we walked down the tree-lined street in search of Jill's car. She'd lost track of where she'd parked it. Somewhere on this block. We looped back a couple times and when we found it, a beat-up 1994 Honda Accord, Jill lifted her hands in mock celebration at the absence of a parking ticket on the dirty windshield.

After the Friday I'd had, with the negative press around the moderation team, Jill decided that we should get away for the weekend — maybe the most thoughtful thing anyone had ever done for me. I printed out directions, two pages' worth. On our way out of Brooklyn, we got caught in stop-and-go traffic headed toward the George Washington Bridge. But once we'd cleared it, it was smooth sailing headed upstate.

"Do you want to put on some music?" Jill asked, passing me the aux cord.

"What if we put on some of Margo's stories?" I suggested. "There are still a bunch I haven't listened to yet."

"Oh, cool. Sure. That's a good idea."

"Do you want to listen to something else?"

"No, let's do Margo. For sure."

I plugged in the iPod, and it took us the rest of the way there — out of Brooklyn, up I-87, away from the city. We arrived at the house Jill had rented after two and a half easy hours of driving. As we pulled in, Jill joked that her favorite part of going upstate was being able to park wherever the fuck she wanted.

The exterior of the house was quaint, the interior immaculately adorned by mid-century modern furniture and tasteful art. No gaudy flat-screen television; instead there was a vintage record player with an impressively curated milk crate full of LPs. Similarly, in the bedroom, a meticulous selection of paperback books, nearly all of which, Jill noted, she had read.

Jill had made dinner reservations near our place. I wished I'd known ahead of time so I could have packed a nicer shirt, but I made do with the collared one I'd brought. It was wrinkled from being stuffed in my backpack. I spent a few minutes trying to smooth out the wrinkles with my palm. It only sort of worked.

The outside of the restaurant was innocuous, like an old house. Inside, though, it

321

was something else: dark wood floors — new but made to look old, possibly "reclaimed"; dimly lit by Edison bulbs, their filaments offering more of their wiry figure than functional radiance; small tables paired with big chesterfield couches; a bar with a bartender; a bartender with a vest; at the center, a carefully manicured fireplace below a massive taxidermied head of a buck, his glassy-eyed expression appearing less sad to be mounted on a wall and more bored by what he was forced to look at for eternity.

It was rustic country lodge meets dark Victorian opulence. I had never been to a restaurant like this, one that was as concerned about its mood as it was with its food. My family rarely ate out, not that there was much in the way of fine dining in eastern Oregon. Sure, I'd been to nice restaurants before in New York. But nothing quite like this. Who could afford it?

We were seated near the fireplace. A waiter asked what kind of water we'd like: our choices being still, sparkling, and tap. I was about to ask which one was the free option when Jill said we'd both prefer sparkling. "Very nice," said the waiter, as if it was a thing worth complimenting.

The menu was intimidating. Swordfish

would be plated on a potato emulsion, topped with an herb-and-chili vinaigrette, also dandelions. The potatoes were "young potatoes," and they came with three-year aged gouda, caraway, whey-cured fennel. Even the ravioli would be a combination of cheese and pumpkin, served with preserved citrus. It all sounded very appealing, even if I couldn't imagine how anything would taste.

Jill must have caught my expression when I looked at the prices on the menu, because she assured me that dinner was on her.

I was embarrassed. "Oh no, I was just . . . You don't have to pay for dinner."

"Relax, it's my treat. I've been meaning to come here for a while anyway. It's nice to eat an expensive meal with good company."

The waiter came back with our sparkling water.

"I've honestly never eaten at a place like this before," I admitted.

"A farm-to-table restaurant?"

"No, like, a fancy restaurant."

The waiter laughed. Jill smiled.

"Don't worry, we'll take care of you here. I'm happy to guide you through any items on the menu. Is there anything you like in particular?"

"I like spicy food. Is anything on here spicy?"

The waiter thought for a moment. He then picked up my menu to scan it himself.

"I don't think we have anything spicy, unfortunately. We're more about the fresh, locally sourced ingredients."

I went for the ravioli. Jill picked the swordfish and a bottle of wine for us to share. The waiter nodded approvingly.

"Do you eat at places like this often?" I asked.

Jill told me that when she worked at her last job — well, the only job she'd ever had, years ago — she would get expensive dinners paid for by publicists. It was the best perk of the job, the chance to eat at some of New York's finest restaurants, many of them the best in the world, on someone else's dime. I was surprised by the specificity and accuracy with which Jill could recall these meals, like old friends she hadn't thought about in a while.

"This place is fancy, but it's not, like, a three-Michelin-star kind of place," Jill said.

Right, not a three-Michelin-star kind of place. Sure.

"I can see you're uncomfortable. We can go somewhere else if you want."

"It's not that. It's just not something I'm

used to."

"I didn't think it would be such a big deal to go out for a nice dinner."

"This is the type of place that Margo would've hated," I said. I immediately regretted it.

"How do you know that?" Jill poured herself more wine. "Sometimes I wonder if we really knew the same Margo. It seems like your Margo hated everything. I only know the things my Margo liked."

"Would you have taken Margo to this restaurant?"

"I don't know. Maybe. But I didn't take Margo here. I took you."

I had more to say, but our waiter arrived at the table, this time with another server. In unison, they placed our dishes in front of us. I bit into my cheese-pumpkin ravioli, its preserved citrus. The thing was too salty.

After dinner, we didn't talk much. We went to bed without saying much either.

The next day things were better. We woke up, pretending the night before never happened, with the exception of Jill's hangover. She apologized vaguely for being too drunk, which explained away our argument at dinner. It worked. I said I was sorry too, though neither of us said why.

We decided to sneak into the indoor pool of a local hotel, a trick she'd learned from her luxury magazine days. The key, Jill said, was to act confident, like we owned the damn place, like we were entitled to it, and no one would doubt that we'd paid to be there.

To my surprise, the plan went off without a hitch. In the pool, I told Jill she looked good in her swimming suit, a black two-piece. She said thanks and that I just looked okay in mine. My stomach hung just over my board shorts.

"I look like a teenager, huh?"

"With the belly of a dad."

We both laughed.

"My mom always said everyone is either a lake person or an ocean person."

"What are you?" I asked.

"Definitely an ocean girl. We spent a lot of summers driving up to the beaches in Newport, Rhode Island. Waves and Slushee lemonade. The best."

"We only have lakes in eastern Oregon, obviously. So no waves. Just lots of calm, clear blue lakes."

I splashed water in her direction. She splashed back.

"Can I get either of you anything?"

From nowhere, a waiter had materialized.

The man was wearing a flannel and jeans — an unassuming uniform for a server.

"Two beers please," Jill said.

"I'll get those for you right now. What room are you staying in?"

"Two forty-two," I said.

Jill shot me a look.

"Very good. I'll be back with two beers."

"You're gonna charge our drinks to someone's room?"

"If we didn't say anything, they'd know we don't belong here. Plus, anyone who can afford to stay here is not going to notice two beers."

"You're a bad influence."

"Me? I'm not the one who ordered beers at ten a.m."

"Oh Jesus, is it only ten?" She splashed me again. "You're a lake boy. I'm just an ocean girl. It'll never work."

We started making out in the pool. I lifted Jill up by her hips, and she wrapped her legs around my waist. The beers arrived. We downed them immediately, and put two more on the tab for room 242. We were drunk by noon.

The rest of the weekend was delightful. We had grand plans to go for a hike, but realized we would rather lounge around at the house. I cooked dinner while Jill read on the couch. It was the first time in a long time that I wasn't preoccupied by work. Occasionally I checked my phone, expecting a missed call or a text from Brandon. But he hadn't reached out. It was a relief.

Everything went smoothly until our ride back Sunday afternoon. We got caught in traffic just outside the city.

"Can you put some music on, or something?"

We'd been listening to MP3s of Margo for most of our trip back.

"Oh, okay," I said, pausing the iPod. "What do you want to listen to?"

"I don't know. Just not Margo right now."

I flipped the stereo to the radio. I hit the scan button, which cycled through FM stations five seconds at a time. There was very little music. We mostly heard ads for car dealerships in New Jersey. The point of scan is to let it go until you hear something you like, but we rarely did, so the radio mostly skipped through its frequencies for the rest of our drive.

When I arrived in the office on Monday morning, I found the customer service floor completely vacant. All of the equipment was still there, an array of computers and monitors propped on the folding tables we'd gotten in lieu of desks. Had we done that to save money? Or because this entire operation was never going to last?

Upstairs I found Brandon at his desk, clicking around on his computer like nothing had happened.

"Where is everyone? Where's my team?"

"Lucas, let's step into the conference room."

"No, I want to know where everyone is right now."

"We let everyone go. We're no longer doing customer support. I can explain. Let's just go to the conference room."

"What do you mean we're 'no longer doing customer support'? Why wasn't I consulted?"

"Don't be hysterical. I knew you were on vacation, so I thought I would do you a favor by taking care of the layoffs myself. I called everyone over the weekend and told them we were terminating their temp contracts early."

"That was my team."

"They were just bodies, in seats, on a floor below this one. I really think we should talk in the conference room." Now Brandon wasn't suggesting.

Brandon had taken my proposal to make

the customer support team full-time employees very seriously. He said I was right. The way it existed currently was untenable and shortsighted. If we were going to moderate Phantom's messages, we needed to either commit or not do it at all. And the solution, apparently, was to not do it at all.

More articles had broken over the weekend. I hadn't been checking. Soon, all the details of our moderation process would find their way to the public. All of our guidelines and policies would inevitably leak. Everyone would not only know that Phantom was censoring its users' messages, but exactly how we went about doing it. A PR nightmare.

"We stand behind our policies, though," I said.

"It doesn't matter. The fact that we're doing it at all is enough to make people upset."

"Is the plan to deploy Emil's system? Because it is so far from ready."

"We're not using Emil's algorithm either. We're trashing that."

"What? So without people responding to flagged messages or Emil's algorithm, how are we supposed to protect our users?"

"We don't."

"At all?"

"We take no responsibility for users on

330

Phantom anymore. We produce the platform, the technology that people use. We're not accountable for how people use it."

"How can you say that?"

"Look, even with a team of a hundred, or a thousand, moderators, or if Emil's algorithm actually worked with 99.9 percent accuracy, we still wouldn't be able to catch everything. And every time something slips through the cracks, we're going to get called out on it, no matter how hard we try. People are always going to find new ways to be terrible and cruel."

"You're just giving up?"

"Ever since the first story about Phantom having a bullying problem broke, we have spent countless hours — and a huge swath of our budget — trying to solve it. And even though we've made progress, publicly no one has noticed. We're still the messaging service with the bullying problem."

"It's worse than that. It's harassment, it's violence. People get death threats."

"That's our problem unless we declare, outright, that we are no longer responsible for it. Use Phantom at your own risk."

"You'd rather willingly make Phantom a worse, a dangerous environment?"

"We can't keep taking these hits. We need to raise capital, and I can't do that if the press is going after us every week."

And there it was: Brandon's real motivation.

"I started Phantom with lofty principles, and I haven't given up on them," he said. "But we'll never achieve those ideals — never make a real difference in the world — if we run out of money first."

The situation was more dire than I had realized. Without major cost-cutting, Phantom would be cooked in six months, if not sooner. Brandon assured me that he had really given thought to my proposal. But the cost of salaries, benefits, and vested shares of the company would cut the lifespan of Phantom from six months to three.

"Plus, I can't go out and raise money from investors and tell them that half of the people I just hired are on the customer support team."

"Why not?"

"Because a tech company is supposed to be making technology, not apologizing for it."

Brandon said I could take the day off, but really, it was an offer predicated on the fact that I no longer had anything to do in the office.

I couldn't bear the thought of going home

and sitting in my apartment, so I wandered around the city, trying to find a way to distract myself. I had three frozen margaritas at the Mexican place down the block, the only place serving alcohol before noon. I stopped by a movie theater, but nothing playing sounded appealing. I thought about texting Jill, but couldn't imagine how to explain that I had the day off because I was a complete failure as a manager. Instead, I wandered around until I found a quiet park. I sat on a bench, put my headphones in, and there was Margo.

"Earth is burning up. Each year, the global temperature rises three degrees. The sun bears down across the planet, its rays blasting through an atmosphere that has been decimated by just a couple short centuries of pollution. Ah, 'pollution' — such a great euphemism when really what we mean is the consequence of humanity.

"In just a decade, Earth will be uninhabitable. Hot. No crops will grow. The oceans will dry up. Human life, as we know it, will cease to exist."

I still had plenty of un-listened-to Margo stories, but there were a handful I kept returning to every time I was stressed out from work. I would never describe Margo's voice as soothing, but the familiarity was calming. There was one about a tribunal of the world's smartest people who oversee the planet's affairs from an orbiting space station. Their job is to observe Earth objectively, from a distance — quite literally — and act as a council that can advise world leaders from a non-terrestrial vantage point to prevent future geopolitical conflicts.

Decades pass and the situation on Earth doesn't improve. In fact, things only get worse, and after witnessing years of violent, cruel, and selfish human behavior from space, the tribunal comes to the conclusion that man's only achievement is the ability to inflict pain and suffering upon itself. People are irredeemable. The planet is doomed. The smartest thing the tribunal can do, it decides, is to put the human race out of its misery. They realign the space station's orbit so it collides with the Earth. The impact will shatter the Arctic ice cap, causing the tides to rise across the Earth, the seas to swallow civilization whole and end human suffering. *"And that was humankind's last great act: taking matters into its own hands."*

The audio file ended with Margo laughing. In the park, sitting alone, I laughed too.

That night I went to Jill's, but was reluctant to tell her about what had happened. The next morning, we both took the N train, a subway that connected both Brooklyn and Manhattan's Chinatowns and extended upward toward Queens. I was headed back to the office, and Jill had to meet with her agent in Midtown. We decided to grab some food somewhere around Canal Street, maybe dumplings.

After we boarded the subway, Jill fished a pair of white earphones from her jacket pocket. They were tangled, scrunched together tightly like a dry brick of instant ramen. Jill went about trying to pull the strands of cord apart.

"Are you listening to music?"

"Oh sorry, force of habit. I usually just wear headphones on the train to make sure nobody talks to me."

I realized we'd rarely ridden the subway together before. Usually, I met Jill at her place, and we wouldn't go anywhere.

The train car was mostly full of Asians — likely Chinese, given the trajectory of the subway. Standing by the door was a large white man, dressed in the outfit of a construction worker: boots, paint-splattered carpenter jeans, a neon yellow T-shirt.

"This train is full of chinks," he said to himself. "Chinks everywhere, as far as the eye can see."

He continued on, shifting into an impression of Chinese.

"Ching chong chang, chinky chink chink."

It was the kind of lazy racism you witnessed on the train every once in a while. I'd certainly seen it before. It shocked me the first time I heard the word "chink" on the subway. But in the months I'd been in New York, I'd learned to tune it out.

"Excuse me, sir" — it was Jill — "what you're saying is extremely offensive."

Out of nowhere, she had leapt up and was walking across the car toward the man.

"What does it matter? These people can't understand. They only know Chinese."

"First of all, that is an assumption you're making."

"Lady, why don't you just mind your own business instead of yelling at strangers?"

"You're being racist."

"Come on, it's not racist. They don't speak English. If you come to America, you better talk the way the rest of us talk."

"I speak English," I said.

"Who is this? You're just saying this to me to protect your yellow-dicked boyfriend."

"How fucking dare you —"

"Jill, come on, it's not worth it." I pulled her back.

"Yeah Jill, come on, it's not worth it," the

336

man said, kicking his voice up an octave. "Listen to your chink before you make him upset."

"I'm technically more of a gook," I said, figuring that I could end this before it turned into a confrontation.

"Now who's the racist?" The man began to laugh.

The train came to Canal Street, and the doors opened.

"This is our stop."

Jill and I exited the train. She was livid — partly at the man, partly at me.

"I can't believe that guy. WHAT AN ASS-HOLE."

"It happens. This is how people are."

"Yeah, and they keep acting that way if nobody says anything."

"You're not gonna change someone's mind by harassing them on the subway."

"I'm the harasser?"

"I just don't think you need to stand up for us when it happens. Like, I don't need to be protected from a guy saying 'chink.' I hear it all the time."

A moment passed, and it seemed like the whole incident would blow over.

"I don't know why you're not angrier," Jill said.

Now I *was* getting angry. But not at the

guy on the subway. At Jill. How did she think it was her place to tell me how to feel about being called a chink? I didn't like it. But I also wasn't going to let it ruin my day by making a big deal out of it.

"Would you have stood up and confronted that guy if I wasn't there?" I asked.

I'll never forget the look Jill gave me then.

"How could you ask me that?"

When we arrived at the dumpling place we were both still fuming. We ate in silence, then went our separate ways.

As I walked in the door, Brandon told me I looked unwell, like I might need another day off. I debated telling him that I hadn't slept the night before, but instead laughed dismissively in his general direction and walked straight to my desk. I clicked around on my desktop, not exactly doing anything for a minute, before I realized Brandon was standing behind me.

"Just wanted to follow up on the project."

"Mmm?"

"The email project."

Brandon had assigned me the "email project" a few weeks before the layoffs. I'd been too busy managing the customer support team to make any meaningful progress. Now I had no excuse.

"Oh yeah, I am working on a planning document." (I wasn't.) "Should be done by the end of today."

"Excellent, excellent." I could never tell if Brandon repeated words to add emphasis, or because he often struggled to think of another word.

I turned back to my computer, assuming Brandon had left. He had not. He pulled up a chair next to me.

"You know you can take it easy. I know you're still feeling a little raw about the customer service stuff. If you want time off, I can pass the email project off to someone else."

I wanted to appreciate Brandon's offer, but I didn't want to give him any path to feeling less guilty about what he had done: suddenly and swiftly robbing people of their jobs. I thanked him, assured him I was doing just fine, and wondered if he would leave me alone this time. He did.

The growth of our user base had flatlined, and a larger and larger piece of the pool that remained was dropping from active to dormant. Active users were people who opened Phantom regularly, sent messages often enough for us to consider them valuable. Dormant users were those who had at one time used Phantom and had since fallen off. I'd always found that phrasing to be peculiar, as if dormant users were just asleep, waiting to be awakened once again.

"We just have to reengage these people," Brandon explained. "Remind them how great Phantom is."

This meant email. Lots of email. Brandon said these kinds of projects were called "win-back campaigns," and they were the most effective ways to reactivate dormant users.

I'd first heard the term "win-back" from Margo back at Nimbus, which had been an operation that was large and organized enough to have already automated something like this. She'd hated saying "win-back." It supported her theory that all of technology was invented by horny ex-boyfriends who assumed the affections of another person could be won, like a prize, with enough perseverance. What if these startup bros could just understand when some things were gone, they were gone forever? What if they considered that with some things, you only get one shot, and if you blow it, you've blown it for good?

The first step was to come up with email copy. We would test different messaging to determine the most effective "win-back" language. I created a new document and started writing down ideas.

Subject line: Long time no see
Subject line: It's been a while
Subject line: See what you've been miss-
ing

No matter how I wrote it, it sounded pathetic.

Subject line: Did you forget about us?
Subject line: We miss you
Subject line: Come back

Brandon told me to run copy ideas by Emil, since, like me, he had nothing to do once we'd decided Phantom was a lawless platform. Emil suggested that I come up with ten to twenty variations, and explained that we could "A/B test" them. I asked him what that meant. Emil rolled his eyes, expressing just how ridiculous it was that someone wouldn't already know. He explained: We could send different groups of users unique subject lines and test to see which one was most likely to be opened.

"It's like creating parallel dimensions," he said, "except the only difference between the two is that in the A universe we've sent the subject line 'Long time no see,' and in the B universe we wrote 'It's been a while.'"

I told him that if we had the technology to create parallel dimensions, this was the most boring thing we could possibly do with it. He did not appreciate the joke and moved on to something else.

I went back to my desk and attempted more subject lines. I stared at the screen for a long time, hoping the words would just materialize. Somehow hours passed, and when Emil came by again to express his polite impatience, I told him he'd just have to make do with what I had.

Subject line: ajdklfja
Subject line: askdjklfajsdl
Subject line: aklsdjjskldjfalksjfjio

After our argument on the subway, Jill and I didn't speak for a few days. I wasn't mad, but I didn't feel like talking.

Without evenings at Jill's or any steady thing to do at work, I found myself sliding back into the same habits I'd had earlier. I showed up late to the office, barely did anything at my desk, went home and drank by myself. At night, I could just focus on transcribing the rest of Margo's stories, which I'd do until I passed out.

At work, Emil was frustrated with me, since I was the only thing holding up the win-back project. All he needed was copy for the email, and I kept reassuring him that I was working on it even though I clearly was not. I promised that it would be done by the end of the week. By Friday, I still hadn't written a word.

I woke up on Sunday to a string of frantic texts and voicemails from Brandon. I was feeling groggy, but I showered quickly and headed into the office. As I approached the building, I saw Emil by the elevator.

"Do you have any idea what's going on?" Emil asked, looking both concerned and pissed off that he had to be at work on a weekend.

We found him in the conference room.

"I sent the win-back emails," Brandon said, as if it was some kind of confession.

"Those aren't ready," Emil said. "Lucas hasn't finished copy for them."

"I know. I wrote them myself."

"Oh, okay. What's the problem then?"

Brandon turned his laptop around to show us his screen. It was his inbox, and the most recent messages were:

Subject line: Long time no see
Subject line: It's been a while

343

Subject line: See what you've been miss-
ing
Subject line: Did you forget about us?
Subject line: We miss you
Subject line: Come back
Subject line: ajdklfja
Subject line: askdjklfajsdl
Subject line: aklsdjjskldjfalksjfjio

I didn't understand what I was looking at.
Brandon leaned back in his chair and put
his hands over his eyes. "I fucked up."

"What am I looking at?"

Emil was typing and clicking furiously.
"Why didn't you wait for us to do this?"

"I thought if I could send these win-back
emails over the weekend, I could cause a
spike in active users."

Brandon was flying out to San Francisco
tomorrow to meet more investors, and it
had been a last-ditch attempt to make it appear like Phantom's growth hadn't flatlined.

"What is up with these subject lines
anyway?" he asked.

"I just had some placeholders in there
until I could finish writing," I said.

"And what was taking so long with the
writing anyway?"

"You're not going to turn this around on
me. I'm not the one who sent out the emails

before they were ready."

Emil wasn't finished, though. He was slowly understanding the gravity of what Brandon had just done. "Instead of receiving one of the test treatments, every person got nine separate emails with nine different subject lines all at once," he explained.

So what Brandon had showed us in his inbox — the consecutive messages in a row — was what everyone had gotten. Best-case scenario, it had flagged spam filters and maybe no one would see them. But more likely than not, users were probably confused as to why the messaging service they no longer used would send them nine emails in a row, asking for them to come back, like a wildly needy ex.

"That's not great, but it's not the end of the world," I said. "It's embarrassing but we were only targeting a few thousand people for the first test anyway."

"It . . . went out to more people than that," Brandon admitted.

"How many more?"

Emil tapped around a little more on the laptop.

"Holy shit. You sent this to two hundred million people? Where did you even get a list like this?"

But I knew exactly where Brandon had

345

gotten those email addresses. I hadn't a single doubt where they came from. Emil kept yelling, but I was staring straight at Brandon. He looked upset, but not nearly upset enough. Brandon knew exactly what he had done.

I understood that even quiet people need to let off steam. And Emil really let it off, for about half an hour, at Brandon, basically until he had run out of things to yell about. With that, Emil packed his stuff and headed out, fuming. On his way out, he asked if I wanted to grab a drink — the first time he'd ever offered to spend time with me — but I told him I'd catch up with him later.

Brandon and I were silent until Emil cleared the vicinity, until we heard the front door of the office close and the locks click into place.

"I know what you did."

Brandon eyed me for a moment, then let out an unconvincing "I don't know what you're talking about."

"The list. From Nimbus." I stepped closer, didn't break eye contact. "I know."

He didn't seem intimidated. Or surprised. He betrayed nothing.

"Before Margo and I quit Nimbus, we copied the database of all their users,

346

including all of their email addresses. There were two hundred million of them. Kind of an odd coincidence, isn't it?"

Now Brandon looked annoyed. "Is that what you think happened?"

"It's exactly what happened," I said. "But what I want to know is: How did you get the database from Margo?"

"She came to me, after you two stole Nimbus's data — which I might add was hugely unethical and immoral."

"And what does that make you, the person who bought it?"

"I didn't buy it."

"Then how did you end up with it?"

"She gave it to me."

"Bullshit," I said. "You know what I think? You used that as leverage. You used her offer as blackmail, to get her to come here and work for you."

"Don't be ridiculous. Margo came to me because she knew what she'd done was wrong. And she wanted me to tell her how to fix it. She was terrified."

"Why would she go to you?"

From the breast pocket of his collared shirt, Brandon pulled out a cigarette. From his pants, a lighter.

"You smoke?"

He lit the cigarette.

347

"You smoke in the office?"

"I only allow myself one cigarette I bring from home, and I only smoke it on the weekends, when no one else is here."

Brandon spoke with a long, exaggerated drag and exhale. He looked like an idiot.

"Lucas, you act like you're the only person that knew Margo. Like you were the only person in her world."

"You two were friends before she started working here?"

"I would say it was . . . more involved than that."

I didn't believe it. I couldn't.

"There's no way you two were together. I would have known." I was yelling now.

"Well, you didn't. So I don't know what to tell you." Brandon took another drag. "You're not the only one who lost something."

I felt the anger welling up in my stomach, my body getting warmer. I was furious at Brandon, even though, rationally, I knew he'd done nothing wrong. Really, I was mad at Margo for keeping this from me — why wouldn't she tell me? — but you can't yell at a dead person.

"What kind of boss dates one of their employees?"

"Okay, let's not pretend that you didn't

have a thing for Nora —"

"Nina," I corrected, which I realized immediately was a confession.

"Margo and I were involved before she started working here. You were Nina's manager and you acted inappropriately with her. So don't lecture me about inappropriate behavior in the workplace."

"Wait, how did you know about that?"

"She filed an HR complaint. And since there's no HR here, it just went to me."

I'd had no idea. I mean, Nina had not reacted positively when I was trying to comfort her. But to write a formal complaint about it?

"Why would she tell you about it? She could've just . . . told me that I'd done something wrong." I felt the need to explain myself, but could only muster, "We were close."

"How do you tell your manager — who creepily touched your arm at the office — that he's a complete asshole?"

"I was just trying to do the right thing."

"Well, she doesn't feel the same way." Brandon rolled his eyes. "Don't worry, though, Lucas. I took care of it. Because that's what a good boss does."

"What do you mean you took care of it?"

"In exchange for a couple weeks of severance, Nina signed some paperwork. You're off the hook."

I'd fucked up, and Brandon was priding himself on protecting me from the consequences. I was mad at myself for not understanding the situation. It was humiliating, and that feeling now translated into anger at Brandon for hiding it. I wasn't exactly the kind of person to get in a fistfight, but the thought of pounding his smug face was deeply satisfying. I'd just watched Emil yell at Brandon for half an hour and it seemed not to have any kind of effect on him. What I wanted was for Brandon to feel bad. As bad as possible. Not physical but existential pain. For him to question the decisions he'd made that had brought him here, the very nature of who he had become.

But I didn't know how to make a person feel that way, so I reached across the conference table, pulled the cigarette out of his mouth, and tossed it on the floor.

"Come on, man."

"You shouldn't smoke." I stood up and walked away. Just as I reached the front doors, I turned, searching for something to say, but he was lighting another cigarette, the fucking liar.

The first bar I found was bad. Very bad.

But it didn't matter. I'd never understood people who were picky about where they went to get very drunk.

I rolled into a place by my apartment around midnight and ordered a beer and a shot of whiskey.

"What kind of beer?" the bartender asked.

"Your cheapest."

"And whiskey?"

"Your cheapest."

I must've looked like hell. By that point, I'd been drinking all day. The bartender — a clean-shaven, mostly trim guy in his early thirties — looked me up and down with the casual concern of an off-duty cop. He asked if he was going to have to keep an eye on me, which was less of a question and more of a warning. I waved him away.

I'd sent Nina an apology text, and immediately started drinking. I don't know why I thought I would hear back. Five drinks later, when they were closing, the bartender asked me to settle up. I fished a handful of loose bills out of my pocket and started counting. He poured two more whiskeys, drank one in an impressive gulp, and said the other was for me.

"This one's on the house, but these drinks aren't helping, kid."

I usually hated being called "kid," but this

time it didn't bother me. He was right. My behavior was downright childish.

I started talking and couldn't stop. It was late and there were just the two of us. I talked about Jill, about Brandon and Phantom, about Nina and how I was a complete creep, about the headache that seemed to weigh me down as I rested my head face-down on the bar. But mostly, I talked about Margo.

He was putting away glasses and wiping down the long wooden countertops from end to end. Barstools were turned upside down and set in their place.

"I have this friend," he began. "Her mother passed recently. It was sudden. A car accident — just driving along one day, it's rainy, car spins out and hits a tree. She dies immediately. Awful, awful story. My friend, she gets a phone call with the terrible news in the middle of the night.

"That friend is bad at checking her voicemail. All people are, I guess. What kind of person is good at checking their voicemail? Psychopaths, probably. Anyway, after the wake and the funeral, she enters a deep state of mourning. When she's not crying, she's barely living. After a few weeks, she is looking through her recent voicemail messages. And that's when she finds it: a voicemail

352

message that she hasn't heard yet. It's from her mother. From the day she died.

"This is how my friend and I are different. I would've listened to it right away. But she doesn't. It's too hard. Can you imagine that — your mother's last words for you are saved on your phone? How could she bring herself to listen? My friend feels like as soon as she listens to the message, her mother is really gone forever.

"That's sort of the thing with grief, right? You realize the saddest part isn't that you'll never see this person again. It's that you'll never hear them say anything new.

"Anyway, days go by, then weeks. I'm begging my friend to listen to this voicemail because I can tell it's killing her not to. So finally she does. She lights some candles, has a few drinks, and gets ready to say goodbye to her mother forever. My friend opens her phone and checks her voicemail.

"The message is strange: she can hear her mother vaguely in it. But it's mostly rustling, nothing coherent. The message, it turns out, is two minutes of this. There's nothing for her in it. And that's when she realized that the last voicemail from her mother — the one that she's been avoiding listening to for weeks, that she feels guilty for not picking up — is just a butt dial."

When the punch line comes, we both start laughing. I don't know why. It's not funny, but I let out a sickly cackle that I can't keep down. I laugh so hard that my throat gets dry and I start coughing.

"How many times have you told that story?"

The music was off now, so I just heard the clinking of pint glasses as the bartender carried a plastic tray of them to the back. Out of sight, he answered, "Definitely more than once."

He came back with an empty glass and poured himself some water.

"A lot of people who come in. Late, when the bar is quiet, folks who are in the shape you're in like to get plastered and lay a bunch of heavy shit on me like we're old friends. Which I'm more than happy to oblige."

He drank almost the entire glass of water in a single gulp. He wiped his mouth.

"Most people have problems with work, so I've got a story about that. A lot of people have issues with their spouses or significant others, so I have three or four stories like that." He paused. "I don't get quite as many people in here with dead friends or loved ones. So I don't tell that story as often."

He motioned over at the clock, which I

had a hard time reading, but I got the hint that I should finish up.

"Is that story true? The one about the friend and the dead mom's voicemail?"

The bartender put on his jacket. He flipped off the remaining lights.

"You strike me as the kind of person who asks a lot of questions he doesn't really want the answer to."

Jill told me I smelled like a bar.

"Like, the whole bar. Like someone took all the liquor and boiled it into a cauldron, cast a spell, and a young man came out of it."

She was in surprisingly good spirits considering I had shown up at her apartment in the middle of the night and we hadn't spoken in a week. She said she was awake anyway, and even though I was in fairly rough shape, she appeared happy to see me. Maybe she'd missed me.

Jill poured me a glass of water and set me on her couch.

"How drunk are you right now? On a scale of one to ten?"

"I've just been . . . thinking, you know?"

"Oh good, you're a fifty."

"I feel like we're not making enough . . . progress . . . on Margo's book."

"Lucas, it's three a.m."

"I just feel like we could be working harder at it."

"What if we have this conversation when you're not wasted?"

"I want to talk about it now."

"Clearly."

Jill disappeared into the bedroom, then reemerged with a blanket and an extra pillow. She set them beside me on the couch.

"Just get some rest and we'll talk tomorrow."

She turned off the lights and went back to her room.

I closed my eyes. It was hot, humid. I was restless. I was out of my mind. Unhappy and angry and sweaty. I drank some water from the tap, hoping it would cool me down. But it just made me more agitated, a pool of cool liquid sitting in my belly. I went into the bathroom and splashed water on my face. Was my face always this red and puffy? My eyes this bloodshot? I splashed again but the face remained.

I opened the door to Jill's bedroom. She was reading in bed, her desk lamp pulled over so that it perched over the edge of her bed, giving just enough light to illuminate the page.

"Everything okay?" she asked.

"You don't want Margo's stories to be published."

"What are you accusing me of?"

"I can tell. I can sense it. You don't want to do this."

"Lucas, of course I want to do this. Why do you think I have spent hours of my life with them? Hours that I should be dedicating to the thing I am supposed to be writing?"

She closed her book and set it on the desk. She looked at me for a moment, seeing if that answer was enough for me to drop the subject. It wasn't.

"Lucas, this shit is really hard. You have to get an agent on board, then sell it to a publisher, a place that's made up of editors and marketing people. If you want to make something that lasts, it takes a lot of work. I spend all day trying to do this. No one cares about Margo's stories except us."

"What do you mean?"

"Here's the truth: Margo's stories are never going to be published."

"Then why are we doing this?"

"I don't know. We're both grieving and it felt good to be writing again, even if the stories weren't mine. And it feels like the right way to memorialize Margo —"

"No," I clarified. "Why are we doing *this*."

Jill scooted back in her bed so she was upright.

"Oh, we're having *that* conversation. Right now. At three in the morning. Like this."

"Let's have it! We've never said anything about it."

I don't know why I did it. I had nothing but gratitude for her. She was the only other person who knew the pain of missing Margo like I did. She was kind and warm and thoughtful. And all I wanted to do in this moment was make her feel bad. If she could share the grief of Margo, maybe she could share the sting of disappointment. She could take part in every shitty thing that I felt.

"Fine, I'll start," Jill said. "I was sad and you were sad and we could do that together, and you turned out to be a surprisingly good lay."

"Why surprising? Because you assume . . . ?"

She cut me off. "Because you are strangely considerate for a twentysomething who drinks too much and doesn't know anything about the world," Jill said. "And I really, really hate that I know you well enough that you were going to imply I was being racist."

"You assumed correct."

"Lucas, you need to stop blaming every-

358

thing on how shitty other people are."

"That's easy for a white person to say."

"Exactly! God, I knew you were going to say that. I'm sorry I am white, Lucas. There's nothing I can do about that. Usually relationships work better when one person isn't constantly throwing that in the other person's face."

Jill was right. But I was furious, and drunk, and that doesn't excuse it but I wasn't going to let her have the last word.

"I'm glad Margo never had to meet you," I said.

It wasn't true. But I knew it would hurt her. And it did, and as she began to cry, I left. I walked out of Jill's apartment, knowing it would be the last time I'd probably ever see her.

There weren't any cabs out at that hour in the morning, so I started walking north. I figured a taxi would eventually pass me and I could hail it. Somehow, none ever appeared. Maybe this is what I deserved. I did the entire trip on foot. It took me three hours, and I listened to the iPod the whole way. When I finally arrived home, I collapsed into my bed, clothes and shoes still on.

But I still couldn't sleep. I opened my

phone. I had texted Brandon that I quit as I was walking home, and he had responded that I couldn't quit because I was fired. I was going to blow everything up. What was left?

That's when I eyed Margo's laptop. I'd vowed never to log in to it again. But I had kept it around, so some part of me must have known that was a lie. But Margo was dead. And Jill and I weren't together anymore, so she couldn't tell me what I was allowed to do. What did it matter?

I had torn up the sticky note with Margo's password, but I had the password memorized. It only took a few tries, and I was in Margo's email.

I don't know what I expected to discover, but all I found was myself:

Subject line: Long time no see
Subject line: It's been a while
Subject line: See what you've been missing
Subject line: Did you forget about us?
Subject line: We miss you
Subject line: Come back
Subject line: ajdklfja
Subject line: askdjklfajsdl
Subject line: aklsdjjskldjfalksjfjio

VII
Six Weeks at
the Crystal Palm

Week 1

According to men, men need to be heard. This is why they approach women at bars. They think they're making conversation, but really, they want to do most of the talking. It's not so much about getting in your pants — well, they want to sleep with you too, but their needs don't stop there. They need to be listened to, validated. This is why they will tell you stories at a bar. Men want not just your affection, but your approval. They will buy you drinks in hopes of getting one of those things, or both. It's transactional. And on some nights, it's even a fair trade. I'll take that free drink and I'll listen to your sad story because I am broke as hell. People say they "need" a drink. Nobody needs a drink. Lucas always said he needed a drink, but he just wanted an excuse to feel sad.

But I was sad now, and I had convinced myself I "needed" a drink. And I needed one at the same time every day in the same place. Getting back on track meant scheduling my sadness so I could organize my life around it. If I was gonna get through this, I needed to write and I needed to feel sad. I spent all week writing — and being extremely disciplined about it — and then I brought my sadness to the Crystal Palm every night.

This was not some upscale cocktail bar with dark wood and perfectly calculated ambient lighting, or a throwback tiki joint with teak furniture, the faint glow of neon. Brooklyn is filthy with these places. Nor was this an ironically named dive bar with cheap beer, an arcade machine that lets you slaughter deer, and an unusably dirty bathroom — a kind of performative grittiness that New Yorkers love. No, the Crystal Palm was a bar with exactly zero distinctive characteristics and an aesthetic that could be described as "no comment." They served drinks, but there were no beers on tap, and you couldn't ask for a cocktail that involved more than two ingredients.

In some ways, the Crystal Palm more resembled an airport or a bus station in its utility. A liminal space, where you might find yourself on your way to someplace better. Well, I loved it.

■ ■ ■ ■

If you write books, you get an agent so you never have to be the bad guy. A good agent negotiates on your behalf. She's incentivized to get you the best deal, because she takes a 15 percent cut. I'm told that that's the reason the best agents aren't your friend. The good ones are focused on that 15 percent. They don't get paid if they spend all day trying to be your pal.

A draft of *Mining Colony* had gone out to publishers, and unlike with my first book, no one had shown the slightest interest. My agent had urged me to start a new project, but I was convinced *Mining Colony* could be reworked. At her suggestion, I started new drafts of things — only to abandon them. My agent hated this, telling me to just commit to something. I sometimes wondered if she cared about the books themselves. But if I didn't sell another book, she'd never collect another 15 percent.

The Rut, I called it, and I always wrote it out with a capital *R*. It felt serious and specific enough to be a proper noun. Treating it like a person made me feel less insane every time I'd email my agent things like "fuck the Rut," like I was referencing some asshole person instead of an ambiguous inability to write anything worthwhile. Without Margo, I was taking my sweet time and it was slowly killing me.

I still spent most of my days with the intention of writing. I stared at my computer, waiting around for something to happen. It was easy to get distracted by the internet and its unending fountain of articles. You'd read one thing, then click through to another, and suddenly your afternoon had been consumed by a black hole of hyperlinks. Sometimes I'd hit the back button on my browser as many times as I could to retrace my steps. It was like traveling back in time, if time travel made you feel bad about how you'd wasted a perfectly good day.

Every few weeks, my agent would email me to ask how things were going. I would answer these messages immediately with reassurances that the book was going great. Writing never came easier to me than when I was lying to my agent.

When Lucas and I were working on Margo's stories, we'd had a firm schedule. I would meet him at the bar near my apartment at 6 p.m. each day for one drink. It marked an exact end to my workday, which was something I'd never put limits on before. Before Lucas, I had let my writing bleed out into the evening, until the point where I got hungry and tired. I realized after a few days of licking my wounds, letting the day stretch on and on, that structure was much better.

The first day I went to the Crystal Palm, I was the only one there. Well, there was the bartender too — a goth chick rocking a sleeve of tattoos and a septum piercing — who made polite conversation. But mostly I sipped my rum and coke and read my book in silence. It was a perfect experience. And after I finished my drink, I went home and made dinner. Okay, "made dinner" might be giving myself too much credit. I was teaching myself to cook. It was all part of the plan.

The second day, there was a man at the bar. He was handsome, looked early thirties, and he asked if he could buy me a drink. I said I was just staying for the one I had already ordered. Then he introduced himself as Alex, and I told him I just wanted to read my book. And then Alex asked me why I was being such a bitch when he was just trying to be friendly, and the bartender — the one from the day before — told the guy to get the fuck out of there. "We have a policy at the Crystal Palms: No assholes."

He stormed out.

"Is that why no one is here?" I asked.

She introduced herself: Megan, but her friends called her Charlotte.

"Why Charlotte?"

"Because Megan is a stupid fucking name."

You could always call yourself something different, she explained. No reason to let the name your parents chose — which they picked before they met you, before you were a real person — define you your whole life. I liked that idea.

"So what's your name?"

"Jill," I said, and I hardly thought about it as I continued, "but why don't you call me Margo."

"It's a pleasure to meet you, Margo."

"The pleasure is all mine."

AFRONAUT3000: Hi, we've never messaged before, but we have interacted a bit on some Fantastic Planet threads. Anyway, I just wanted to say that I loved your first book, and that I'm even more excited about the science fiction novel you're working on. It's very cool that you came to our message board looking to solicit help from a well-read community (even if it is a little dorky that your username shares the name of your book). But if there's anything I can do to help, please, just ask.

MINING_COLONY: Hello! This is a very flattering message to receive, especially from someone who is so prolific on this forum. I feel a little intimidated, a little out of sorts here. But the community has been very welcoming, in no small part because of people like you, but also very specifically you.

Week 2

It was fucked up, I know. But if I'm being totally honest, it felt good to be Margo, satisfying in a way nothing had satisfied me in months, maybe years. Margo was who I was at the Crystal Palm.

For the first time in a long time, the novel was going well. I was writing just enough each day, enough that I might turn in a manuscript to my agent before she dumped me. I'd begun incorporating some elements of Margo's stories into my work — nothing that she'd said in her recordings, but ideas. The real difference in my writing was that I began to think of how she would write. The Margo I'd communicated with was open and optimistic. But in these stories, I discovered a perspective that was skeptical of everything, that thought of the world as an adversary, that believed interesting characters should be at odds with their surroundings. At the very least, it gave compelling (if not cynical) stakes to all her stories, and it might help mine too.

The bartender, Charlotte, at least she was in on it. Not that she knew who the real Margo was, or what she meant to me. We never got that deep, but we were friendly enough that I received the occasional free drink, even if it was always some awful shot of a dark purple liquor that we drank together. ("It's an amaro," Charlotte explained. "All bartenders like it.") By the second week, we had a rapport. I came to have a drink and read by myself at the bar; Charlotte would chase away men and I'd leave her a nice tip.

At 6 p.m., I was almost always the first person at the bar, but one night there was a man sitting with his laptop before I arrived. He looked like, well, any guy, not dissimilar from that awful dude whatshisname that gave me a hard time when I didn't accept his drink the week before. He was asking Charlotte if they had wifi, and when she said no, he said that most of the places he went in San Francisco, where he was from, had internet access for patrons. Charlotte said sorry, but she wasn't really apologizing.

I sat down and she served me a rum and coke.

Usually I read a book at the bar. But this evening I had gone to a copy shop and printed out every single one of Margo's stories that Lucas and I had transcribed. Some of them I had begun to rewrite — clean up the language, make them into real stories. But Lucas had outpaced me with his transcriptions, so most of the stack had not been edited — or even looked at yet — by me. I had hit a sticky point in my work that day. I'd written myself into a corner and needed a break. Maybe I'd find some inspiration in Margo's stories. Skimming through the printouts, I marked passages that I liked with a highlighter, doodled notes in the margins.

"Are you a student?" asked the man.

I looked up, made eye contact for a second, and said, "No."

"Lawyer?"

"Certainly not."

He nodded to himself, seemingly to acknowledge that he understood I was to be left alone. He ordered another drink and closed his laptop, having conceded that, without internet access, he wasn't going to get any work done. I went about my business.

From his messenger bag, the man pulled out a book. I recognized it immediately. It was the paperback of my book.

"Where did you get that?"

"Huh?"

"That book. Where did you get it?"

"I took it out from my bag?"

"No, why are you reading that book?"

"Is this book bad or something? I don't know. A friend lent it to me for my trip, and now I am reading it because there is no wifi at this bar."

"You don't understand —"

"I clearly don't."

"I wrote that book."

"What?"

"You're" — he looked at the cover — "Jill August?"

"In the flesh."

The back cover of the book had a small black-and-white portrait of me. He held it up next to my face, squinted. "Okay, I guess I see it."

"What do you think?"

"Well, now that I know you wrote it, I'm obviously going to say I like it."

"You can be honest."

"I like it."

"Oh really."

"No, I really do. I honestly don't read much, and I am flying right through it. I read, like, the first one hundred pages in a row on the flight here."

"You're from San Francisco?"

"Yeah. The Bay Area, at least."

"That's a five-hour flight. It took you five hours to read only a hundred pages."

"I'm a very slow reader. Watch me sit at the bar all night and knock out another twenty."

I don't know why I laughed, but I did. I shouldn't have but it happened, and it was too late to do anything about it.

"Can I buy you a drink?"

Charlotte moved toward us like she was just seconds away from telling the guy off. I put up a hand to wave her off. She nodded and went to make the drink she'd assumed I wouldn't want.

He introduced himself. "Michael."

We shook hands for some reason.

"I'm Margo."

"Not Jill August?"

"That's a pseudonym," I lied.

"A nom de plume," he said, like he was correcting me. "Okay, 'Margo.' It's a pleasure to meet you."

Charlotte plonked down our drinks.

■ ■ ■ ■

He had a startup and was in town for work, trying to raise money. He'd already hit up every investor in San Francisco. Maybe there were folks who would be willing to take a risk on him in New York.

"The last thing a woman wants to hear at a bar is a guy telling her about his startup," I said.

"Fair point."

"Like, nobody."

"Okay, okay."

"But here's a deal," I continued. "If I listen to you, you have to listen to me after. I'm gonna tell you a sad story and you're gonna listen, attentively, to every second of it."

Michael looked suspicious, but maybe his curiosity got the better of him. Or maybe he just really, really wanted to tell me about his startup.

"Also," I added, "you're gonna expense all our drinks."

Two more arrived, neither of us having asked Charlotte for them.

Michael's startup had a backstory. He used to be in love, you see. The woman's name was Kristen (of course), and he remembers the day they moved in together. At the time, they were both too poor to afford movers, so they rented a truck and did it all themselves. It was an exhausting day, one that involved a lot of tired bickering from all the stress of manual labor. By the end of the move, the fighting had gotten so bad that Michael and Kristen weren't even talking, and suddenly the entire cohabiting thing didn't seem like such a good idea anymore.

They showered off and planned to order takeout. But to Kristen, the thought of them eating shitty Chinese food in silence was just too much. Instead, she suggested they go out. Like, really go out. Dress up, find the nicest restaurant they could get into without a reservation. Michael thought this idea was crazy. They were worn out. The last thing he wanted to do was to celebrate a day of arguing. But he went along. They dug through their boxes to find their best outfits — Kristen found a dress she'd worn only once; Michael, his one and only ill-fitting suit — and they left the unpacked, barely furnished apartment.

At dinner, they spent too much money and began fighting again, of course. An expensive meal wasn't going to alleviate any of the pressure that had been building throughout the day. It would also not bode well for their relationship, which would slowly deteriorate over six months until Kristen moved out and the two would never speak to each other again. But on the way to that dinner, everything felt different. The promise of treating themselves to a nice meal after a long day of moving signaled that they had made the right decision, that living together was the next step in a long and fulfilling friendship, the road to marriage, a home, maybe even kids. All that potential felt so present on the thirty-minute subway ride headed to the restaurant.

The subway car was mostly teenagers and tourists. The teens were loud and joyous and keeping to themselves, as if no one else in the world existed. There was a group of three women in their mid-forties, likely tourists, considering their fanny packs, speaking a vaguely Scandinavian language (Swedish? Danish maybe?). One of them, armed with a large camera with an intimidating lens, approached Michael and Kristen and asked if she could take their picture. She said they looked so perfect together. Flattered, they obliged.

When she was done, she turned the camera around to show Michael the photo. He could only see a thumbnail-size rendering.

Kristen looked beautiful, of course, in her black-and-white dress; her features looked vibrant, gorgeous. Michael's suit, which rested so baggily on his thin frame, looked trim and tailored from the angle of the photo.

Michael asked the woman to send him the photo. He found an old receipt in his pocket, fished around for a pen (one of the other women had one), and jotted his email address down. She nodded, promising to send the picture when she got to a computer.

The photo never arrived, though. Maybe Michael had written his email down illegibly, or maybe he'd written it incorrectly. Or perhaps the woman just forgot and never sent it. But Michael thought back to that picture often. And he got a little weird about it, he admitted. In the months that followed, he scoured the internet in search of the photo. His relationship with Kristen didn't last, but if only he could hold on to how it felt when he thought it might.

There was no promise — really, not even a strong likelihood — that the picture existed anywhere Michael could access it. The photographer would've had to upload it to a photo sharing site, and a public one. In all likelihood, it was probably sitting on the SD card in her camera. Or maybe she'd deleted it, wiped its existence from the face of the Earth.

And yet, Michael kept looking for it. He spent tens of hours looking through photo sites. There were rough ways to search and filter by metadata, since digital photographs stored certain kinds of information when they were taken. He knew the day it was taken, and, if it was a newer model of camera, it would even identify the city. Michael tried to recall the make of the device, though it was hard to summon that detail. But even filtering as thoroughly as he could, Michael found himself with a pool of millions of images — impossible for a single person to get through.

This is what inspired his company. They did facial recognition, he explained. With machine learning, his technology would be able to identify people, and scan thousands of images per second in search of them.

"It would be like having a million of me looking for this picture at once," he said.

"Does it work?" I asked. "Could you take a picture of my face and then use it to find every photo of me on the internet?"

"Yes and no," he admitted. "The foundation is there. It just requires more time to develop. But if I can actually secure some funding, yes, one day you'll be able to locate every photo of yourself on the internet."

"At first I was skeptical, but that actually sounds like a smart idea."

"Thank you," he said, acknowledging that he'd won my approval.

"What's it called?"

"Panopticon."

I scoffed. "Isn't that, like, a kind of prison where the inmates are observed from every angle?"

"Nobody knows that. Panopticon is a word that sounds cool."

It did sound cool, if you didn't think too hard about it, which probably meant no one was thinking very hard at all.

"So you're here, in New York, looking for money because investors in San Francisco don't like that story?"

"I don't tell it to many people anymore."

"Is it even true?"

"It is true. But it's not exactly the kind of context people who finance companies are interested in."

"Investors aren't so sentimental, huh?"

"They are, actually. Surprisingly so." Michael took a moment to figure out how to explain it to me. "Investors don't want to think of the girlfriend they lost. They want to think about the better girlfriend they can have next."

I tried (and failed) to hold in a groan.

This is when Michael got sad. Sometimes, he found himself restless at night, unable to sleep. So he would just go to his computer and scroll through public photo sharing sites, looking for that perfect image.

"Why don't you just use Panopticon? Didn't you create it for this express purpose?"

"I have. Of course I have. I mean, I've tested Panopticon more than anyone else, so if the technology can identify anyone's face accurately, it's mine. It's scanned through millions — maybe billions — of photos by this point," he said. "But now it's just a ritual. It's familiar and calming. I can't explain it."

Panopticon was a prison after all.

"Your turn."

"What do you mean?"

"That was part of the deal. You would listen to my story, and I had to listen to yours."

I'd forgotten our bargain already. I signaled to Charlotte for two more drinks.

"Oh, I actually think I'm okay for now," Michael said.

I glared at him and he capitulated.

"Okay, another."

So I told him my sad story, the whole damn thing. How I'd had a friend online — my closest friend for a year — and how she'd died, and how I met her other friend in real life and we had staved off our collective grief by sleeping together. I told Michael about the massive archive of Margo's recordings we'd uncovered and been committed to transcribing, with Lucas's lofty and naive hope of a book.

I kept waiting for him to bow out, but he didn't. He was actually a really good listener.

"It's such a shame," he said, when I'd finished. "You and Lucas sound like you two had a good thing going."

"We were fucking to get over the loss of our friend." It seemed like he didn't know how to respond, though he must've realized by this point that if he wanted to take me home, he could.

"Can I say something?"

"Please," I said. "It's just been me talking for the past hour."

"If you knew that it was unlikely Margo's stories weren't publishable, why didn't you make that clear to Luke?"

"Lucas," I corrected, as if it mattered. "He was so hopeful and so confident that this was what we were supposed to do. It gave our relationship a purpose," I said. "And I had been stuck on my own novel for so long — in a real rut. It felt good to be writing again, even if the words weren't mine. I guess that sounds selfish?"

I continued, not ready for a response. "I was never dishonest with him. I said I'd show my agent Margo's stories, and I did. She said, 'Absolutely not, no one would publish these,' which is exactly what I expected her to say."

I finished the last few sips of my drink. Finally, a moment of silence while Michael finished his drink and asked for the check.

"So, are you gonna invite me over or what? Clearly I could use a rebound fuck."

"Ah, I wish I could, but I probably shouldn't," Michael said. Then sheepishly: "The girlfriend, you know how it is." As if he had mentioned her once in our hours-long conversation.

"You know, I'll be completely honest with you: I don't know how it is. Why don't you tell me, Michael. How is it?"

I'm not sure why I was suddenly so forceful, but it worked. Two minutes later we were in a cab to his hotel.

MINING_COLONY: Okay, I've attached an outline of my new book. You're the only person who has seen this. So please be kind. But also honest. But also kind.

AFRONAUT3000: Don't worry, if it's terrible, I'll have you run off Fantastic Planet.

MINING_COLONY: I wouldn't have it any other way. I appreciate you taking a look. I know it's a lot to ask of a stranger.

AFRONAUT3000: Not at all. We're not strangers anymore!

Week 3
I still thought about Lucas often. We did spend nearly every night together for four months. I must have liked him even if I never took him that seriously. He was endearing, honest. I admired that. He liked to go down on me. I liked that too.

Jackie told me she wasn't sure what I saw in him, which was rich coming from Jackie, who had just gotten engaged to Jeremy, that horse's ass. But he'd made a big production out of it — a ring in a glass of champagne at a Michelin three-star restaurant — and even if it lacked any sort of imagination, the photos on Facebook were good (Jeremy had hired a professional photographer), and I hit LIKE and wrote "Congratulations!!!"

Apparently the engagement had come out of a tough time. Jackie had learned that Jeremy was cheating on her, though she wouldn't reveal how she discovered that. Instead of breaking up like normal people, Jackie explained that the "ordeal" had strengthened their relationship. That was even the word she used. Ordeal.

Jackie met me at the Crystal Palm, and she was immediately unimpressed. She only drank white wine, but she liked fancy cocktail bars. (She'd always ask for the wine list, then ask for the house chardonnay regardless.) We hadn't hung out in a while — not since she'd gotten engaged, nor since Lucas and I split — and it was just like old times: Jackie's life moving forward, mine seemingly stalled in place. After college, while I'd struggled, Jackie found herself immediately in a PR job. It demanded long hours for a grabby asshole boss, but the money was decent and her career progressed to the next benchmark. I wondered if, on some level, that was why she'd agreed to marry Jeremy: to check the right box. But I could be wrong. Maybe he had a great dick.

We ordered drinks (a rum and coke, a

glass of the house chardonnay) and Jackie was scrolling through the engagement photos on her phone. I'd already seen them, but I indulged her. Your friend only gets engaged three or four times, tops. There were rough wedding plans (next summer) but the location was to be determined (probably New York, but maybe Paris?). For a moment I was terrified that Jackie would ask me to be a bridesmaid, or worse. Then she told me she'd already lined them up, and I felt disappointed that I hadn't been asked.

"Anyway, enough about me," Jackie said, while simultaneously signaling the bartender for another glass. "How are you?"

"Good. I'm good." The redundancy was not exactly convincing.

"You got that yellow fever."

"Yellow fever?" I was shocked that she'd said it.

"You know those guys who only date tiny Asian women? Because they're so tiny and quiet and thin? That's yellow fever."

I must've made a face.

"Relax, Jill, I'm just kidding. You don't have yellow fever, obviously," she said. "Yellow fever is not a thing for women."

"What does that mean?"

"Like, some women are into Asian guys.

But no women are *only* into Asian guys," she said. "Except you. You're the closest woman I know, especially if the next guy you date is Asian. Two is a coincidence. Three is a trend."

I felt the overwhelming urge to correct her, explain that Victor was only half Asian and that Lucas and I hadn't really been "dating," but it seemed beside the point.

"So what is it called when a guy only dates black women?"

"That doesn't exist. But there is a thing where girls only date black guys."

"And what is that called? Black fever?"

"Jungle fever."

I waited for Jackie to show some self-awareness about using that phrase, but part of me knew she wouldn't. I didn't want to have to explain it to her. Maybe I should have. And I wondered if that was what friendship was: caring about someone enough to keep them from embarrassing themselves. But I didn't want to take responsibility for Jackie, because I realized that I didn't care. We'd been friends since college, and I just didn't give a shit about her anymore.

As I was leaving the Crystal Palm, I felt a strong urge to call Lucas. I'd wanted to talk to him every day since we ended things, but now I felt it more acutely than ever. I wanted to tell him about Jackie and Jeremy's terrible engagement. And how she'd actually said "jungle fever" out loud, with zero remorse. I wanted him to hear about how I'd vowed to myself never to see Jackie again, knowing that he would have been proud.

AFRONAUT3000: I have to be honest — I love it. It's incredible.

MINING_COLONY: What a relief! I am glad you like it. And you're not just saying that to make me feel good, right?

AFRONAUT3000: There are a lot of things wrong with me, but I have certainly never said a nice thing to someone just to make them feel better. What you have so far is very good. I have some notes, which I have also attached. But so far, it's very exciting and I am thrilled that you're even letting me give feedback on this.

MINING_COLONY: You know you're really doing me the favor here.

AFRONAUT3000: If I am, it doesn't feel like it.

Week 4

It was a strange impulse, but immediately after Margo died, I had gone to a copy store and spent upward of fifty dollars to print out our entire message history. I knew I could access it online whenever I wanted, but there was something more permanent-feeling about having it on paper.

As I struggled to rework the draft of *Mining Colony,* I referenced my archived messages with Margo regularly, hoping that I could summon some of the energy I'd had to write the book when we'd been talking every day. Instead I'd get lost in the pages upon pages of our messages — reading and rereading just to hear her voice in my head.

As usual, there were no customers at the Crystal Palm, just Charlotte reading a book behind the bar, delighted to see me, she said, because the book was dreadfully boring. She showed me the beat-up paperback. The title page read *The Redemption of Zora.*

"Fantasy? Sci-fi?" I asked.

"Romance. Basically, a bunch of cyborgs fuck." Charlotte laughed. "A friend gave it to me, and I tore off the cover because I was embarrassed about reading it on the subway."

From her purse, Charlotte revealed the torn cover: the lithe hand of a woman stroking a well-defined male chest, one pec made to look metallic by lazily coloring it silver, set atop an even more impressive set of abs.

"Cyborg romance is a real thing?"

"It's a huge thing. Cyborgs are usually warriors —"

"Of course."

"— and they all have inner conflicts between the cold logic of their robot programming and the desires of their human emotions. Plus, imagine a man technologically advanced enough to actually be good at sex."

"The dream, I suppose."

"Don't judge me. I know it's smut, but I love it."

"I thought you said it was boring."

"This one is boring." Charlotte tossed the book to the other end of the bar, which she could do, because no one else was there.

"I thought you had a girlfriend."

"Who do you think gave me these books? Anyway, I am a very complicated woman, who likes other women and men with robot dicks."

I stepped off my stool, crossed the room,

and picked up the copy of *The Redemption of Zora* that Charlotte had so ceremoniously hurled across the room. And I started reading. It was . . . good. No, great even. I'd never read a romance novel before. The writing was effortless, and even though the plotting was fairly by the numbers, I was impressed by how it established characters, moved through scenes, never tripped over itself trying to express an idea.

And the sex scenes! Sure, they were full of clichés and strange euphemisms, but they were effective, especially the one in zero G, which I was so taken by that I began reading it aloud to Charlotte. I finished the whole damn book at the bar that night, while she plied me with free drinks. She joked that maybe I should write a cyborg romance rather than whatever it was I was writing, and I told her that I would, if I ever thought I could do it this well.

MINING_COLONY: Okay, this is a dumb question.

AFRONAUT3000: No such thing as a smart question.

MINING_COLONY: Why are all computer and internet terms so dumb? I'm obviously not that technically literate, but I don't understand why everything is a metaphor. Like, as if all our data goes into a magical "cloud," somewhere in that beautiful blue sky, waiting to be summoned again at a person's convenience.

AFRONAUT3000: The way we talk about technology is always in metaphor. It's the easiest way to describe, somewhat functionally, how something works. But more often than not, I feel like it's a crutch — a short-term way to explain something that robs a person of a full and real understanding of how a computer or the internet works.

Like, we always think about files living in folders, a rigid hierarchy. That's easy to understand because it has a real-life parallel in how we organize documents. But files aren't actually organized that way. They don't live inside things. And the image of a piece of paper with information living inside a manila folder inside a file cabinet — that establishes a kind of limitation of how someone understands what that file really is. It doesn't have to live in one place. It lives everywhere and nowhere at once. It exists.

MINING_COLONY: It's funny you say that. In fiction, we use metaphors to simplify things — to make an abstract concept more . . . palatable? Less annoying? But sometimes I feel like relying on metaphors does a disservice to the reader. They're useful, when properly deployed.

AFRONAUT3000: "Properly deployed" is the key. Most people who write the language of user interfaces are not extraordinarily talented, humanistic authors, capable of showing empathy.

MINING_COLONY: Now you're just flattering me.

AFRONAUT3000: Maybe I am.

Week 5
I never thought I would see Michael again, but there he was, sitting at the bar of the Crystal Palm, alone.
"What are you doing here?"
"Hey, Jill, how are you?" Michael said. "This is like . . . what's that word? When

something feels like it's happening again?"

I knew the term, but I pretended not to and shrugged.

"Hmm."

I sat next to him. I didn't really want to talk, but I also didn't want to seem impolite. After all, we did fuck that one time.

"I'm back in town for work," he said, explaining himself.

"Looking for more money?"

"I sold my company, actually."

"You sold Panopticon?"

"I did."

"Well, congratulations."

"Thank you."

It didn't explain why he was here, at the Crystal Palm, clearly waiting for me. How long had he been here?

"Do you want a drink?"

"I'm at a bar, aren't I?" I said. "I guess I should buy you a celebratory drink."

"Let me get the drinks. I mean, I just sold my company."

"So I take it you made out pretty well in the sale?"

Michael's grin fell somewhere in an uncanny territory between self-satisfied and still shocked, like he hadn't yet processed it.

Charlotte wasn't working that day. It was some other guy, a beardy dude with classic rock vibes. It explained why the speakers were blasting squealing electric guitars rather than the usual tropical elevator music I'd come to love. We ordered a couple drinks. Michael said he couldn't get into the specifics of the deal, just that he had felt very lucky and grateful.

"I can't tell you who the buyer is," he said. "I'm sworn to secrecy."

Two cocktails later, Michael told me it was a large U.S. defense contractor. He didn't give me the specific name — not that it would have meant anything to me — but he assured me it was one of the big ones. The biggest, maybe.

"What does a weapons manufacturer want with facial recognition technology?"

"Facial recognition — you remembered!" Michael swirled the straw around in his drink. "I don't know what they'll use it for exactly, but you can imagine how useful identifying faces in photos and video footage would be to the government."

"I think there's a word for that."

"Security?"

"It begins with an *s*, but that's not the word I was thinking of."

"Safety?"

"Never mind."

Michael was starting to slouch. I wondered how many he'd had before I arrived.

"Are you going to stay on with the company?" I asked.

"Yeah, the deal is contingent on it. There are certain features we have to add and a few quality benchmarks we have to pass first."

One drink later and Michael spilled the beans.

"It only works on white people."

"What?"

"Like, we can identify a white person with incredible accuracy. But if they're black or Latino or Asian, the technology has a hard time distinguishing them."

"So your software is . . . racist?"

"It's not software," Michael said. "And it's not racist."

"Okay, but it sounds racist."

"No, it's just — it will be fine. The reason Panopticon can't identify nonwhite faces is because of the original data set that we started with. When we were training the algorithm, we collected hundreds, sometimes thousands, of photographs of people we knew personally. Then we fed that to Panopticon and said, 'All of these photos are Kristen. Now try and identify when people in pictures are or aren't Kristen.' "

"Wasn't Kristen the name of your ex?"

"Then Panopticon would train itself to know when photos contained Kristen's face and when they didn't. And we ran that with a few hundred different people, just to get started. The early days of the company were just me and a couple engineers asking friends and family if we could use images from their Facebook accounts, and also old family photos and any other pictures they had of themselves. Anything we could get our hands on."

"So I take it most of the people you trained Panopticon on —"

"— Were white. Yes. Just at the start, but yeah, it was largely white people, and I honestly never thought about it in the early days."

Michael took a moment to collect himself.

"Also, I can't believe you called me a racist."

"I didn't say you were racist, just . . ."

I was about to make a distinction, but Michael returned to his drink, his fifth since I had sat down. He wasn't taking the accusation too seriously. But at the Crystal Palm, I was supposed to be Margo. Or more like Margo. Or something.

Michael laughed more to himself than to anyone. "Thankfully, this defense contractor has the means to supply us with rich data sets to use. And it actually won't take much longer, since Panopticon doesn't have to work on everyone."

"What do you mean?"

"It just has to identify" — and Michael was very deliberate with his language here — "people of Middle Eastern descent."

It all made sense now. And what followed was not pleasant.

"You made software that makes it easier for the government to racially profile people?"

"Come on, that's not fair. It's not racial profiling technology."

"That's what it does!"

We kept arguing. Michael made technology; he wasn't responsible for what people did with it. I told him he did if he profited. He said that was unfair, and, without a real comeback, that was the point when he decided to just be a dick.

"I finished your book, Jill, and the ending sucked." He drained his drink. "Why was everyone so unhappy?"

I signaled for the check. We were screaming at each other, and the idiot behind the bar still took his merry time calculating our bill.

"So why are you here again?"

"What do you mean? I just spent the last

two hours telling you about selling the company."

"No, I mean, why are you *here*. At the Crystal Palm?"

"To see you, obviously. Is there any other reason to come to this bar?" Michael gestured toward the rest of the room, empty, save for our bearded bartender. "I thought you would be happy for me."

"I don't even know you."

"We slept together."

"That doesn't mean anything."

"Well, I thought you might want to do that again."

"You seriously think I'm gonna fuck you after this?"

And at that, Michael slammed his laptop shut, tossed it in his messenger bag, and marched out. Poor Michael. Boo-hoo Michael. I imagined him storming off to his hotel room and scanning the internet for that old, magical photo of him and his ex-girlfriend, futilely thumbing through thousands of images, probably jerking off the whole time.

He had come to the Crystal Palm looking for my approval, and I wouldn't give it. There was a small victory in that.

Then I realized that asshole had left me with the bill.

"Motherfucker," I said under my breath. The bartender thought I wanted another drink and asked me to repeat what I'd said. "MOTHERFUCKER!"

AFRONAUT3000: I was thinking about what you said about technology.

MINING_COLONY: Oh yeah?

AFRONAUT3000: About how all the ways we dumb things down to make them seem safer and easier.

MINING_COLONY: I remember. It was a very specific conversation. Which we had yesterday.

AFRONAUT3000: Don't be a jerk.

MINING_COLONY: I can't help it.

AFRONAUT3000: Anyway, I wonder if we lose something else in that language. Like, in simplifying the ways in which technology works, we also lessen the seriousness of it, which allows an erosion of our morality. A transgression suddenly doesn't feel real or of consequence because it's talked about in phrases that make it sound like it's just magic.

MINING_COLONY: . . .

AFRONAUT3000: I committed a crime.

MINING_COLONY: Wow, okay. Now I'm an accessory.

AFRONAUT3000: It's not serious. Well, it is and it isn't. I should take it more seriously.

MINING_COLONY: Listen, I murder all the time.

AFRONAUT3000: Okay, relax. I stole company data. I thought it might impress this boy.

MINING_COLONY: You stole something to impress a boy?

AFRONAUT3000: Shut up.

MINING_COLONY: He must be a hell of a boy.

AFRONAUT3000: But in the moment, even though I knew it was wrong, it didn't seem *that* wrong, because what I was stealing wasn't real. I couldn't hold it. I couldn't even really take it. I just had a copy.

I sort of imagined myself as Indiana Jones in . . . whatever the first Indiana Jones movie was called. Remember the part where he steals the idol, and swaps in a bag of sand? The temple notices that he's swapped the idol out, either because the sandbag is not the exact same weight, or something mystical about the temple knows that the real idol has been taken. Who knows?

MINING_COLONY: Right, and the temple sends a boulder to crush him.

AFRONAUT3000: So imagine instead, if Indiana Jones were able to create a duplicate of the golden idol. Like, a perfect replica. And the temple never even knew the original was gone.

MINING_COLONY: Okay . . .

AFRONAUT3000: And since the temple didn't know, it never tried to drop a boulder on him.

MINING_COLONY: Okay . . .

AFRONAUT3000: Has Indiana Jones really done something wrong, then? He didn't take what wasn't his, so much as he copied what isn't his.

MINING_COLONY: This logic is sort of convenient.

AFRONAUT3000: What do you mean?

MINING_COLONY: Basically, you're justifying Indiana Jones's crimes two ways. First, the temple didn't try to murder Dr. Jones, meaning he got away clean. Getting away with something doesn't change the morality of it. Second, the idea that making a copy of something isn't without consequence. There are now two of that golden idol in the world, meaning that the rarity of the original is lessened.

AFRONAUT3000: Hmm . . . I see what you mean.

MINING_COLONY: Sorry, that's probably not what you wanted to hear.

AFRONAUT3000: It actually was. It's why I asked.

Week 6

I was there the day the Crystal Palm closed, helping Charlotte more or less dismantle the bar. There were no customers to serve, which was exactly the reason the joint was going out of business, which meant Charlotte was mostly clearing out cabinets and drawers behind the bar. Her plan was to pocket anything that wouldn't be missed: bottle openers, ice cube molds, scissors — things that she didn't need but could at least serve as a conciliatory gift to herself, now that she no longer had a job. She stashed a few expensive bottles of booze too, though she knew those would be inventoried and maybe missed.

Charlotte placed a bottle in front of me.

"Japanese whiskey," she said. "It's all the rage."

"I wouldn't know."

Charlotte groaned, and reluctantly opened the bottle's seal. She poured a small taste for each of us. We clinked glasses. I gulped mine down.

"Jesus, Margo, you're supposed to sip it." As if to illustrate, Charlotte took a delicate sip from her glass. "Like an adult."

"Whatever, I can't tell the difference."

"Good booze is wasted on the likes of you."

"Booze is wasted on everyone."

Charlotte also downed her fancy Japanese whiskey. Then went back to boxing bottles of liquor, while I watched. I told her about Michael.

"I get my shift covered for one day, and of course, that's the one time anything interesting happens at this bar."

She was most amused by the fact that, after our long argument, Michael still wanted to sleep with me. Charlotte assured me that this is "some straight-people shit."

She also asked me how my book was going, making her the first person to ask me since my agent. There was something pure about Charlotte's curiosity, like she actually cared. It made me feel good in a way I hadn't felt good in a long time.

"I actually started a new book," I said.

"Oh yeah?"

This was true. Just a few days ago, in a rare moment of clarity, I realized that I would never get *Mining Colony* into workable shape. The only time I made real progress on it was with Margo giving me constant feedback. And now that Margo was gone, it wasn't right attempting it without her.

"What's the new one about? Also sci-fi?"

"It's so early that I barely even know. It hardly matters. The point is that I've moved on."

I hopped off my stool and began helping Charlotte with the bottles. I got another box from the back room and just started loading it up. I asked Charlotte if there was any order or reason to how the alcohol got sorted, and she said there wasn't. And I realized then that a bar isn't a place; it isn't the people; it's not the mood or the feeling evoked. Really, a bar is just a large, haphazard collection of bottles.

AFRONAUT3000: Have you thought more about Japan?

MINING_COLONY: I want to go so badly, but I just don't think it's in the cards for me this year. And by "in the cards," I mean I am so broke.

AFRONAUT3000: What if money wasn't a problem? Would you go?

MINING_COLONY: I mean, of course.

AFRONAUT3000: So let's say money isn't a problem then!

MINING_COLONY: What do you mean?

AFRONAUT3000: I'll front your plane ticket.

MINING_COLONY: No! You can't do that.

AFRONAUT3000: Really, it's no big deal.

MINING_COLONY: As much as I'd like to go to Japan with you, I wouldn't feel comfortable letting you pay for me. It's a very generous offer, but it could never sit right with me.

MINING_COLONY: You understand, right? How weird that would be?

MINING_COLONY: Hey, are you still there?

VIII
TOKYO 2011

Mom's favorite show was still a suburban drama set in the '70s about a curly-haired young white boy in a white town and his pursuit of a white girlfriend. Unlike my father and his *Paris by Night* collection, she didn't have tapes but she watched reruns in the early evening, just before the local news.

I didn't like the show at all, but I was back at home in Oregon, back to watching weird TV with my mom, feeling like the loser I was. This show's main character was Kevin, who I was almost named after, my mom informed me. She would have gone through with it if I didn't already have a cousin named Kevin. I'd never met a cousin Kevin, I told her, and she said he was the son of an estranged sister, whom I'd also never met.

The white girl that Kevin spent the show attempting to woo was named Winnie.

"What kind of name is Winnie?" my mom would say at least once per episode.

On this particular evening, from the other room, Dad had an unhelpful response. "There were some guys who used to call me Winnie."

I'd never heard this before. "Why did they call you Winnie?"

"It was a nickname," he said, noting that our Vietnamese last name was sometimes pronounced "win" after it was bastardized into English.

"I don't think this white girl is named Nguyen."

"I liked the nickname Winnie, actually," Dad said.

"That's not what Mom was asking."

"Winnie Nguyen, they'd call me."

"They were making fun of you."

"Both of you be quiet. I am trying to watch the white people."

The show was about nothing — a family and a romance — but it was set during the Vietnam War. I didn't know much about the war, which felt like a distant atrocity that didn't have much to do with our family. My father didn't want to talk about it, despite having lived through most of it as a child in Saigon. In the show, though, Winnie's older brother Brian had gone off to fight in the war. You knew what happened when a TV character shipped off to Vietnam. You know, Chekhov's Indochina conflict.

In the episode we were watching, Kevin runs off to the woods to find Winnie after she receives the news of her brother's death, hoping to comfort her. Conveniently, he discovers her by the town's famous climbing tree. She's in shock, grieving. This is the perfect moment for Kevin to make a juvenile advance on her, to show her just how much he cares. This seems to be the plotting of every American show: someone named Kevin trying to win the heart of a girl by being the nicest guy possible, pursuing her with unrelenting kindness and incessant affection. Exert yourself enough and you can have everything you've ever wanted. Perhaps that was the greatest fiction of TV, that hearts could be won over with enough hard work, that romance followed the same ideals as capitalism.

I am not sure why we are supposed to think Kevin is doing the right thing by discovering her there. A girl who wants to be left alone gets followed into the forest by a guy who wants something from her, and we are rooting for that? But it gets worse. Kevin finds her, sitting by herself, staring off into the middle distance, so overwhelmed by her sadness that it has pos-

407

sessed her entire being. And what does he do? He tells her it's going to be okay, and sticks his tongue in her mouth, Percy Sledge's "When a Man Loves a Woman" plays. The camera pans out.

"What the hell?"

"What is wrong?"

"Kevin kissed Winnie while she's mourning her dead brother."

"Yes, she is very sad because of the brother."

"No, I understand the plot. It's just messed up."

"Why is it messed up? She is sad because the brother is dead."

"He's taking advantage of her."

"You are too critical. It is just a TV show."

"A TV show with a fucked-up message."

Mom let out a huff, disappointed that I had cursed in front of her. But she let it go.

"It is just a TV show. You watch it. You don't have to think about it. Just let it go, Lucas."

But I knew I couldn't let it go. Which was worse: The Vietnam War, an atrocity that killed three million people, boiled down to a stupid plot device on a mediocre TV show? Or that we were watching a mediocre TV show that encouraged boys to take advantage of vulnerable girls? I got up from the couch and exited the room, fully aware that I was no longer the sort of person capable of letting anything go.

I went to my room and sat on my bed. I thought about how I'd spent most of my life sleeping on it, and maybe I would for the rest of my days. I'd tried to move out and I'd failed. I was frustrated with myself because it's not like I'd gone across the country with big aspirations. I had no dreams other than to just live somewhere else for a while, and looking around my room was a reminder that I couldn't even do that right.

It had been a month since I'd moved back. I hadn't bothered with my stuff. I abandoned everything in my shit room in Queens: my clothes, my computer, everything else I'd accumulated throughout my two years in New York, which was mostly junk. I'd even given up Ozymandias, the last reminder of my PORK days. I'd hoped leaving behind all my material possessions would mean leaving behind all the things I'd become: a cruel friend, a workplace creep, an alcoholic. Or maybe I was all those things to begin with.

My roommate had received a note that simply said *I'm leaving* and a check for last month's rent. I headed to the airport and got a one-way ticket home. The only thing I took with me was the iPod. I guess I still had one more reminder.

The phone rang, my parents' landline. I could hear my dad answer it from downstairs. It was for me.

"Who is it?"

"He says he is your boss."

I had no interest in talking to Brandon, and even less interest in hearing what he had to say. We hadn't spoken since I had been fired, though he'd called me a handful of times and I just let it ring out. Brandon had sent a half dozen emails that just said "call me," the demanding tenor of which made me want to talk to him even less. I'm not sure how he figured out where I was.

Reluctantly, I took the receiver and waited for my dad to exit the room.

"What do you want?"

"Most people say 'hello' or 'how are you,' " Brandon said.

"I worked for you long enough to know that you only call when you want something."

He got straight to it: "We sold the company. We're being acquired."

At first I thought he'd called to gloat, which seemed needlessly petty. "Congratulations, Brandon. That's really good news for you."

"Listen, you may not work here anymore, but you do still have your shares. Which means you get a cut of the sale."

I asked him how much the acquisition was for. Brandon told me. It was an impressive number.

He didn't sound proud or excited or even happy.

"You know, most people would celebrate becoming a millionaire," I said.

"No, it's good news. It's as good of an outcome as possible, considering our situation. Things were getting bleak around the time you'd left. They only got bleaker."

"I didn't leave."

"You know what I mean," Brandon said. "And you know that my plan for Phantom was never to sell it . . ."

"And now all you have is money."

It was an unfair jab but I didn't have patience for Brandon's shit anymore. He cleared his throat, shifted his tone.

"From the acquisition, you'll receive" — I could hear him rustling some papers — "one hundred and thirty-four thousand, seven hundred and eighty-eight dollars."

"Say that again?"

"One hundred and thirty-four thousand,

seven hundred and eighty-eight dollars. I know it's not a lot, but only a fraction of your shares had vested by the time you exited the company."

"No, that's a lot of money. I've never had that much money."

I was aware that everyone else at Phantom had probably made much, much more than that. But it didn't matter to me what they had. This was three years of salary for me. An incredible sum.

"I thought you would be disappointed but I'm glad you're happy with it," Brandon said. "I know you're just learning about it now, but do you know what you'll do with it? That right there is enough for a down payment on a condo."

"A condo?"

"Yeah. You might as well reinvest it in property. The market is great right now. Everything is dirt cheap."

"Isn't the housing market the reason the country's in a downturn?"

"By the time the economy recovers, housing will be back in fine form and you'll have made a killing."

"Hmm."

Brandon sighed. "I'm sorry, I shouldn't be telling you how to spend your money. I am thrilled you're happy with it."

"I can leave." It just came out. "I'm leaving."

"For where?"

"I'll figure it out." But the reality was that I already knew.

That felt like the natural end of the conversation. But before we hung up, Brandon wanted to say one more thing.

"This is probably inappropriate for me to say, especially since the two of you were much closer. But I think if Margo was still here, we would've made it. I capitulated to investor pressure. I made a bunch of bad calls. Margo would never have stood for my bullshit."

"There's no way to know."

A pause.

"You know how I tell that story about the origins of Phantom? About how I was inspired by a breakup and the texts that remained? I remember telling that spiel to Margo, and she told me, 'That story is bullshit.' Even before we started seeing each other, she was calling me out. But you know what? She was right. I made that story up. The whole damn thing. And she could tell."

"That sounds like Margo."

"But that story worked in all the pitch meetings I had. It's what made the product relatable to investors," he said. "I thought I was building something meaningful, but I'd sold out my ideals from the beginning."

I laughed. "Margo always said that technology was made for sad white boys."

I wasn't angry at Brandon anymore. I was over his relationship with Margo — it no longer bothered me. I wasn't the only person allowed access to Margo's life, I'd come to realize. And to be honest, while I cared little for the lamenting of a twenty-five-year-old millionaire, it was nice to talk about Margo again. It'd been a while since I had someone to do that with.

Brandon couldn't tell me who had acquired Phantom, not quite yet. Later, I'd learn that it was one of the major technology companies from California. They were the internet's largest search engine, and had the lofty goal of cataloging all the world's information, though for what purpose it was unclear. They digitized books and built maps of the Earth. In many ways, Phantom was a good fit for their portfolio: imagine if you could know what everyone was saying to each other. The company could use that information for any purpose — nefarious or not. But mostly it seemed like it would be used for targeted advertising. A company with incredible ambitions to catalog the world's information in all its forms — hiring and exploiting some of the world's greatest minds with innovative ways to do so — couldn't come up with a more creative way to use that information than sell ads. In the end, it was the system that Emil had built that became the most attractive part of Phantom. Everything about Brandon's political and humanistic aspirations for Phantom was forgotten.

Another reason Brandon had called me, instead of simply having the company lawyer inform me of my earnings, was so I could help him settle Margo's affairs. She also had equity in Phantom, and when he told me just how much she took home, it confirmed my suspicion that this money I was so thrilled to have, that felt like a life-changing amount, was just chump change to everyone else.

I promised to forward on the contact information for Margo's mother, Louise. I'd let someone else deal with it.

The money arrived more quickly than I'd expected, just a day after the acquisition was announced.

My first purchase: a smartphone. I drove to the nearest electronics store, which in eastern Oregon was an hour drive away. But I was finally able to afford a modern phone and a data plan. The device felt nice in my hand, the glass front, the smooth, cool aluminum back. Holding it outside the store, I marveled at the device in a way that should have embarrassed me. Such a symbol of opulence, and yet I was drawn to it. I knew my old flip phone had no value left to me. I tossed it at the nearest garbage can. I miscalculated my throw and watched it bounce off the lip of the trash receptacle and land on the ground nearby. I didn't bother to pick it up.

The first thing I downloaded was Phantom. When I opened it, I got hit with a pop-up that explained that the service had been acquired. There was cheery language about the company's "incredible journey" and excitement about "the next adventure" — a string of startup clichés — as if the lifespan of Phantom had just been a series of quests in a video game. For the first time, I recognized that I was genuinely glad to be out.

Buried in the copy for Phantom's acquisition message was the acknowledgment that the service would be gradually sunsetted over the course of three months. I always found that image funny, that a piece of software could be given some kind of sailor's funeral, its remains placed in a boat, pushed into the sea to drift toward a setting sun.

My next purchase: a plane ticket, the second one I'd bought in a month and, again, headed one way.

I'd expected Tokyo to be something out of the future. Instead, I discovered the city was quiet and subdued. It had the scale of New York. There were towering buildings and people everywhere. And yet, somehow, Tokyo was nearly silent. People seemed to move through the city with ease. The subway arrived on time every time. The streets were immaculately kept, cleaned by a sanitation crew that swept through and restored Tokyo to its pristine state each morning.

My imagination of Tokyo had involved more noise, more lights. The one neighborhood that lived up to this expectation was Akihabara, full of large electronics stores signaled by the blare of arcades and blinking neon. The retail of Akihabara resembled something of a technological junkyard. One store was famous for accumulating old devices and selling them at steep discounts. It had bins of loose cords, mysterious peripherals, and obsolete devices sealed in plastic. Digging through those containers of old gadgets felt like excavating years of consumer technology, each layer of goods representing an era of human progress in the way sedimentary rock formations show their age by strata.

I wandered into a multistory arcade with five floors of games. I didn't recognize most of them. I put a token in one cabinet that featured a large drum made to look like a gigantic plastic melon, and a set of drumsticks that looked like carrots. The instructions were in Japanese, meaning I couldn't understand them. I attempted to hit the drum to the beat of the music, but I couldn't tell if I was doing it right. The game was noisy — a string of disappointed blips and bleeps that indicated I was doing a piss-poor job. The sounds kept coming until I was finally struck with a *"game over,"* the first time the game had presented me with an English phrase.

I wandered upstairs, looking for something I might be able to play without instruction. On the third floor, I found a Pac-Man machine. But it wasn't traditional Pac-Man. It was a new variation that involved four players. I watched as a group of Japanese teens played, their eyes trained on the game. The concept seemed similar — eat white pellets, avoid ghosts. But it wasn't clear whether it was meant to be played collaboratively or competitively. The teens teased each other whenever one of them was caught by a ghost, let out a celebratory holler every time a Pac-Man ate a ghost. It looked like fun. When the round was over, one of the kids offered his spot to me. I said I was happy to spectate, but he insisted, gesturing emphatically toward the arcade machine.

There were two boys — a taller one and a shorter one — and a girl, her hair cut with severe bangs. They nodded excitedly as I approached the game.

"What am I supposed to do?" I asked.

The two boys said nothing. The girl giggled and said "Pac-Man." It appeared that they did not speak English.

"You know, I had a friend who really loved Pac-Man," I said. "She told me all the tricks."

The game announced itself beginning with a chirpy jingle, and suddenly our Pac-Men were chomping little orbs, letting out a repetitive squishy trill with each consumed pellet.

"The blue ghost is the one to look out for," I advised. "It tries to get ahead of you, and then trap you."

"Ano jiisan wa zutto hanashi wo suru no ka?" said the short boy.

"Zenbu torikku wo shitteru you na hito ni

419

meccha yabai nee," said the tall boy.

"But the blue ghost, his movements are relative to the red one too, so you have to keep track of him too."

"Ano yarou wa geemu dake shite, tada damare."

The girl giggled.

When the game ended, the three teenagers bowed and said thank you in English. They couldn't stop laughing, and suddenly I was laughing too. I wasn't sure what was so funny, but for a moment, I felt welcome.

Jill, hi!

You probably don't want to hear from me right now (I barely want to hear from me right now). But I'm in Tokyo (it's a long story) and it felt wrong not to email you (I realize this is the first time we've emailed since we met in person).

We once talked about how Margo was obsessed with Japan, that she always wanted to come here. I get it now. It's a metropolis for introverts. The thing, though, is that almost everyone here is Japanese. I can go a whole day without seeing a white person, days without seeing a black person. Margo would've stuck out. I don't know if that would've made life difficult or inconvenient for her in Tokyo, but she's always wanted to be in a place where she felt she belonged. Tokyo is that place but isn't that place. It is like a city constructed for her, but filled with people who do not look like her.

I went to the cemetery you told me about (the future cemetery, with the thousands of LED Buddha statues, you showed me on your phone that one time). It's more magnificent in person — smaller and more intimate than the video let on, somehow more brilliant. The way the colors shift feels more like a subtle change in the direction of the breeze rather than a pre-programmed experience. I found the whole thing very moving. Maybe one day you will come here and experience it for yourself.

Anyway, my thinking was that if Margo couldn't make it to Japan in life, maybe it would be a fitting place for her to rest. There were plots available, still many little LED Buddhas for purchase. They're crazy expensive (3,250,000 yen, that's like $40,000) but I've come across a lot of money recently (nothing illegal, just immoral) so I went for it. Usually someone's ashes are stored in a small locker behind the Buddha, but as you know, Margo was buried. So in place of an urn, I placed the iPod you gave me — the one with all of Margo's recordings, all the stories she'd ever recorded (as far as we know). I know it's not Margo's physical presence that I'm storing here, but in a way, it feels like her spiritual presence (I guess most people would call that a soul).

Anyway, I don't expect you to respond to this email. I know no one wants to receive a long-winded email from an ex (if I am technically an ex). Mostly I wanted to apologize for how things ended (sorry) and also to tell you that you're not getting your iPod back (sorry).

Lucas

It took me a week of wandering around Shinjuku, in and out of bars where I stuck out. I wanted to drink alone, and though Japanese people tended to leave me be, oftentimes the bars would be rowdy or there'd be karaoke. I couldn't imagine anything worse than singing in front of strangers, except being in the audience while it was happening, wishing that everything could just be quiet and peaceful for a goddamn second.

But eventually, I stumbled into Crawlspace. Up a flight of stairs, I was stunned to discover that the bar was just a counter and four stools. The name was fitting. There was no room for anything else — the entire place maybe a hundred square feet tops, smaller than the bedroom I'd had back in Queens.

No one else was at the bar except the bartender, a tall, wiry Japanese man who looked like he was in his early sixties. He had long gray hair and a neatly groomed matching gray mustache. He wore a bright yellow Hawaiian shirt that featured a print of intricately illustrated pineapples.

I asked for a whiskey.

"You are American?" he asked.

"Is it that obvious?"

"Ah yes, very obvious." His English was strong, though he carefully overenunciated each syllable, the way a language-learning program might. "What is your name?"

"I'm Lucas."

"It's very nice to meet you, Lucas." He bowed. "You can call me Joe."

"I can call you by your Japanese name."

"But I would like you to call me Joe."

So I called him Joe.

The only thing behind the bar besides booze was a small record player, the kind with a footprint that was smaller than the record itself. The LPs and the needle arm extended over the body of the player, which also meant Joe was often accidentally bumping into it.

"Ha-ha fuck," he'd say, amused, seemingly thrilled to use an English curse in front of an American.

I asked him what record was playing. He told me, but I didn't recognize it. I couldn't even tell if he'd named a person or a band.

"Would you like to listen to the Beatles instead?"

"No, this is great. I want to listen to Japanese music."

This pleased Joe. He pulled out a milk crate from below the bar and set it on the counter, presenting it like a gift.

"Please pick the next record." He bowed again.

I thumbed through Joe's small vinyl library while he poured me another whiskey. I was by no means an expert on Japanese music, but I thought I might find something familiar from my PORK days. No dice. Most of the music was Japanese, but nothing I could identify by the text or shape or design of a record. Even if it was an album I'd heard before, it was unlikely I would know since I couldn't read the Japanese titles.

Eventually, I pulled out something at random.

"You know this?" Joe asked.

"I don't."

"Let us listen together."

Joe put the record on. It was heavy metal — not what I had been expecting. The little record player filled the even littler room with the sound of shredding guitars oscillating from high-pitched shriek to muddy growl, the relentless pounding of the bass drum, a singer shrieking something in Japanese. Joe began air drumming to the beat, thrashing violently. I was concerned he was going to knock over a bottle behind the bar, or accidentally punch me in the face. He was having fun, and I realized I was too.

I went to Crawlspace every night. Usually I was the only patron, and I wondered how the hell Joe stayed in business. Why was I always drawn to bars that no one else went to? We'd talk, and I would check my phone to see if Jill had written me back. She hadn't.

Each night, Joe wore a different Hawaiian shirt and brought a different crate of records. He explained that he had a massive collection at home, but since the bar was so small, he had to bring a rotating selection every day. It was a joy to drink whiskey and browse the new arrivals each day.

When Joe had asked if I wanted to listen to the Beatles, I had assumed he'd said so because the music would be familiar to me. But it turned out Joe genuinely loved the Beatles. In each crate there was at least one Beatles record, or at the very least a Wings album (Joe argued repeatedly that Paul was the best of the bunch, even though I never disagreed). He would always put it on before closing, which was usually when I finally left.

Joe and I talked a lot. He had an endless number of subjects to discuss with me, a stranger, which I deeply appreciated. Since I'd landed in Tokyo, I spent most of my days talking to no one because I had no one to talk to.

Maybe it was because he was talking to a foreigner, but Joe liked to tell me about Japan. He had philosophical ideas about the country's place in the world, its fate. He asked me if people in America liked Japanese people.

My gut immediately went cynical. "Well, during World War II, Japanese people were sent to internment camps in twenty-two different states."

Joe did not recognize the word "internment." I had to look up a translation on my phone for him.

"Ha-ha fuck," he said, as if he'd just bumped the record player.

I'm not sure why, but I didn't want Joe to feel like he belonged in the U.S. I wanted him to understand why I was here, in Japan.

"Let's not forget: Asians are the only people who've ever been nuked," I said.

He paused for a moment, having taken a slight affront to my phrasing. "Japanese are the only people who have been bombed by an atomic weapon," he said.

I nodded and felt the need to apologize, so I did. I wasn't sure if I was apologizing for how I'd said it or for saying it at all, or if I was apologizing on behalf of America.

"We Japanese all fear" — he spent a moment searching for the word — "annihilation."

He went on: "But it is not just the atomic bomb. We fear earthquakes and tsunami. People forget, but more Japanese died during the earthquake in 1923 than from the bombs in Nagasaki and Hiroshima."

Joe couldn't remember how to say large numbers in English, so he took a pen from his breast pocket and wrote it on a napkin: *50,000.*

"That's how many died in the earthquake?"

"No, Nagasaki."

He wrote another number: *80,000.*

"Hiroshima, with radiation poisoning," he explained.

He wrote a third number. It was astronomical.

"142,000 people died in the earthquake?"

"Yes, the Great Kantō earthquake."

Japan, Joe explained, had always been doomed. Because of the way the island was situated, the tectonic plates far beneath the surface would cause small earthquakes frequently, and large, human-erasing devastations every so often. Joe referred to it as a kind of reset. It almost sounded like he was welcoming it — oblivion, for the people he knew and loved and cared about. It was an inevitability. Nothing could stop it. Everyone was just waiting for it to happen, for extinction to come.

It was five or six days before I finally recognized something Japanese in Joe's record crate. I leapt out of my seat when I saw it — just at the recognition of something familiar. It was that song Jill knew. Or, it was the song she thought she knew, but had been sampled by a newer, American artist. Joe could see how excited I was, so he interrupted the current record to put it on.

The music played. Crawlspace was suddenly taken by the sound of melancholy synths, the notes dancing slowly.

It was a rare occasion, when there were other patrons at the bar — two company men, still dressed in their suits. I tried to make conversation, but they didn't speak a lick of English. Not that it mattered. Even though the two knew each other, they were barely speaking. Mostly they just wanted to get shit-faced, exhausted from what must have been a very long day at the office.

They were also going through cigarettes like crazy. The two were splitting a pack and it was finished almost immediately. The bar was smoky to the point that I was rubbing my eyes and clearing my throat. But Joe didn't seem to notice, and if he did notice, he certainly didn't seem to mind. When the first pack was done, they pulled out another.

One of the men said something to Joe in Japanese. I couldn't understand it, but I could tell from his body language that it was a complaint.

Joe translated for me. "He says the music is too sad."

Joe responded to the man, gesturing toward me, indicating that the music had been my selection. The other man said something to Joe. He translated again.

"He says you must be a very sad man if you listen to this music."

I raised my glass at the man, then downed the whiskey in a single gulp. Joe and the two men started laughing. Then there was another round of drinks. And then another.

THE BARBARIANS OF TOKYO

It's Japan, the year 3009. We live in a society ruled by technology. Everyone is connected through vast digital networks; organic flesh and bone have been improved upon through cybernetic implants. For enough money, you can replace your weak, feeble human arm with a stronger, more durable mechanical one. For a price, your beating heart can be improved by a small generator, one that will never fail, never be susceptible to disease and illness. Everything can be upgraded except the brain, the last bastion of humanity.

Technology has improved human life in every capacity — if you are a person of certain means. And from the rise of enhanced human beings emerges a new kind of caste system, one that favors, if not reinforces, the wealthy and the elite. Neo-Tokyo's empress is M4V15, a woman who had her entire organic body replaced with a robotic one. The only thing left of her humanity is her mind, and it is a brilliant one.

Though the full embrace of technology may sound cold and inhumane, the country of Japan has never flourished more. There are no wars, no hunger, no greed. M4V15's mechanical body strips her of any identity, and, no longer tied to any physical human attributes, she is able to rule without prejudice.

M4V15 believes that the world would be a better place if everyone could free themselves of their physical form, if everyone could just be like her. She makes that her mission, the imposition of progress. At first, people will resist, but eventually they will see the long-term good it will do for everyone: the end of bias and bigotry.

M4V15 is surprised when her subjects oppose the mandate of technological upgrade, even when her regime generously offers it for free. Can't they see that this is the future? No matter, she concludes, logically. Progress is inevitable.

The Great Uprising of Neo-Tokyo occurs in 3054. M4V15 is not surprised. (She is too coolly rational to ever be surprised.) The common people storm the castle of the ruling regime, ripping apart everything and everyone in their path. And though the enhanced humans of M4V15's ruling class are stronger, smarter, eventually they succumb to the rebels in their numbers. She observes that they are violent and brutal in ways that only lesser humans can be. The force with which she ruled was more benevolent. Sure, it could be vicious at times. Those who resisted upgrade had to be punished — there couldn't be exceptions to progress. But M4V15 was sacrificing short-term discomfort for long-term benefits. These common people couldn't see that. They can only think of themselves, only consider right now.

When the rebels eventually reach the throne room, M4V15 is waiting for them. The people demand to know why she has been such a cruel ruler, and she explains that sovereignty is simply defined by a monopoly on violence. They don't understand what that means. They tear her limb from limb, like barbarians.

Failure was always a possibility, and knowing that meant M4V15 always had a backup plan. For more than a decade, she'd dedicated resources in her government to funding a small, secret lab of the country's best scientists in pursuit of a single mission: to duplicate the mind.

M4V15 knew that every great leader had a single vision, but could find many paths to it. The Great Uprising was a foreseeable outcome, and it would not stop her from completing her life's work. Progress could only be rolled back if M4V15 was mortal.

In the moment just before that horde of angry fools can reach her, M4V15's consciousness is sent to another body, perfectly replicated and immediately awakened. The transition is instant, flawless. Hundreds of miles away, on a small island off the coast of northern Japan, a second version of M4V15 comes to life.

To maintain absolute secrecy, M4V15 had entrusted the entire operation to a samurai. He was a young boy who had always served her with blind loyalty, a kind of devotion that was so pure that it could only come from the naivete of a human with no technological enhancements. M4V15's advisors and officers thought it strange that she kept such a creature like the boy in her court. Organic humans were irrational, the sort of pollution that M4V15 had vowed to clean up. And yet here was one at the empress's side, day and night. M4V15 was always able to explain away the boy's presence: How would she understand the weaknesses of organics if she didn't keep one near?

The first thing M4V15 sees when she wakes up in her new body is the samurai boy. He is weeping, thankful that the transition worked, grateful that his master has not left this world. M4V15 tells the boy to stop crying, and commands him to put himself in a rational emotional state — at least as rational as an organic can be. She needs him to be useful because there is so much work to do.

On this small island, M4V15 is starting from nothing. She has no supporters, no resources; what she needs is an army to reclaim her throne. But M4V15's greatest advantage is

434

that no one thinks she's alive. No one will see her coming. This isn't revenge, though. That would imply malevolence and bitterness, neither of which are things M4V15 can feel. No, this is logical, a means of plotting to do the right thing.

The samurai helps M4V15 disguise herself by dressing her in the uniform of a peasant. Most of the island's denizens are farmers, poor and completely organic. M4V15 thinks about how much more efficiently this land could be exploited if the people were all enhanced, rather than trapped in traditional forms and tools of agriculture handed down through generations.

But despite the abundance of farmland, the island remains largely under the control of the American military. It is both a base of operations for the U.S. to control the Pacific theater in case of war, and also a reminder to the nation of Japan that it has defeated the country twice and is capable of committing atrocities like those of the Third World War again. The locals resent the presence of the U.S. military. M4V15 views this discontent as illogical, but recognizes how it can be harnessed.

The samurai humbles himself by working as a farmhand, saving what little he can and bringing it to M4V15 to begin funding her insurgency. Years pass, but M4V15 is patient, as all great leaders are. She spends her days gathering information about the American base, studying its defenses, attempting to identify its weaknesses. As M4V15 becomes more comfortable in the community, she begins making allies by spreading dissidence about the U.S. presence on the island. More years go by, and M4V15 has established herself as a central pillar among the island- ers. She understands the plight of farmers, the common people. She vows to rectify the situation.

Eventually, M4V15 is able to assemble a small force of young men and women. In secret, she trains them how to fight. They don't have advanced weaponry like the Amer- icans, so they must learn to be resourceful, savage. Finally the day comes and M4V15 leads her militia in a covert operation to sabotage the American base from the inside. Many die in the ensuing fight, but eventually M4V15 and her forces claim the base. Years of planning come to fruition at once.

The Americans are furious to have lost a military stronghold, but they are even more terrified of what the base contains. The strength of the U.S. for a near millennium has been defined by its nuclear power. But now that a small Japanese island possesses its own nuclear weapons, the Americans are at a standstill and withdraw entirely from the Pacific.

U.S. military strategy is based on assuming that its enemies think like the U.S. does. The only thing America fears is the idea that someone else might be as aggressive as they are. But M4V15 knows that nuclear weapons have no place in war. That kind of violence and destruction doesn't result in a victory. It's a form of moral surrender.

Now, M4V15 is not just in possession of nukes, but also a small fleet of ships and fighter jets. It's not enough to take back the mainland of Japan, but it is enough for M4V15's island to declare independence. She becomes a hero not just among the islanders, but of the many surrounding Asian countries that would like to see a new regime in Japan. Since M4V15 lost power, the economy — now subject to the whims of emotion — has declined steadily for decades, causing widespread poverty and hunger. With the organics in power, the country has been riddled with corruption and fraud. Leaders have come and gone, betrayed by their own staff in the selfish pursuit of power.

You know, human stuff.

People have a short memory, especially when times are tough. No one seems to remember the grievances they'd had with

M4V15's authoritarian government, or how she'd constructed a regime that favored wealthy elites. All that matters now is that she is different. M4V15 promises her followers that she will return Japan to an era of prosperity, a time when progress was all but inevitable. Organics and enhanced humans alike flock to her cause. Hope and change are powerful ideals. M4V15 ruled once before and she will rule again.

The war is swift — the bloodiest, most brutal war the world has seen in centuries. M4V15 is on the frontlines, an army behind her, moving through the north of Japan with ruthless efficiency. Even with the U.S. covertly supporting the current Japanese government with weapons and resources, the war M4V15 started will be won quickly, and she will have reclaimed what she'd once lost.

It doesn't take long for the fighting to reach Neo-Tokyo. M4V15's forces easily overwhelm the current regime's, and the conflict takes to the streets. M4V15 walks among them. She observes that some blocks have been battered and ruined by the violence, while others have remained pristine, seemingly untouched. She wanders the city, basking in her victory. It took half a century to return, and finally all of this is hers again.

The city is largely abandoned. All the noncombatants have fled to the countryside to escape the fighting. But down one quiet alley, M4V15 discovers a small restaurant with its lights on. She enters.

It is a diner, just half a dozen seats situated around a counter.

"I was wondering when you'd arrive."

M4V15 recognizes the woman behind the counter immediately. It is herself.

"You are me," M4V15 says.

"Yes, I am you," the other M4V15 replies, wiping her hands on her apron.

M4V15 demands an explanation. How is there another M4V15? The situation defies all logic. But the other M4V15 appears to be in no hurry. She is in the middle of preparing an order. She removes a basket of noodles from a pot of boiling water and places them in a bowl. A ladle of broth is added, the dish carefully finished with a garnish of green onions. The steaming bowl is served in front of an old woman at the counter.

The cook begins, "During the Great Uprising of Neo-Tokyo in 3054, the organics rebelled against their empress and stormed her castle. Knowing that her life would be in jeopardy, the empress had an escape plan. In that moment before the barbarians reached the throne, her consciousness was secretly duplicated and sent into a new body on a remote island off the northern coast of Japan.

"But the empress made one critical assumption: that the organics would destroy her original form. And yet she was not destroyed. She was spared. Stripped of her power and her rule, but spared nonetheless, thanks to the compassion of a young woman," she says.

The cook points to the woman eating at the counter. Now, fifty years later, she is not a young woman. Her hair is white, her back hunched. M4V15 can tell that her eyesight is poor, if not entirely gone, by the way she feels around the counter in search of her chopsticks. But she looks content, enjoying the aroma of her steaming bowl of noodles, before taking a big slurp of them.

"So you're the original M4V15 then?" M4V15 asks.

The cook nods, and begins preparing another bowl of noodles.

"And in the fifty years since you were in power, instead of plotting your return to the throne, you have merely been here, cooking at this diner?"

"That is correct."

In the half century that M4V15 has spent reestablishing her rule, making careful moves toward reclaiming Japan, the original M4V15 has settled into a simple life as a cook in a small restaurant. It is confusing. With all the computing power in her head, M4V15 cannot make sense of it.

Someone enters the restaurant. It is the samurai boy, his face covered in soot, a rifle slung over his shoulder. He has just come from the battle. He bows at the M4V15 behind the counter, and finds a seat next to the old woman. He orders a warm sake.

Though M4V15 understands the concept of time, the passage of it is not something she feels. What year is it now? 3109, exactly a century since M4V15 first took power in Japan. She looks around the table. The boy is there, as he always is. But he is no longer a boy. He is an old man, graying and wrinkled. He has scars from years of working farmland to raise money for M4V15's cause; wounds from years of fighting at her side. His unwavering loyalty has led him to this moment, quietly drinking sake at a small diner. The old man pours a glass for the old woman. She bows, thanking him for his politeness, and they both drink together.

A bowl of noodles materializes in front of M4V15.

"You know it is not necessary for us to eat. We are not organic, and therefore do not require food for sustenance," she says.

"Not everything is necessary. Some things

are meant to be enjoyed," the original M4V15 says.

M4V15 still cannot make sense of the situation, but she concedes that there is a distinct possibility that it may be beyond comprehension for her.

The battle is raging outside. Every few minutes, the muffled sound of gunfire can be heard in the distance. Occasionally, a nearby explosion rattles the foundation of the diner, causing the lights to flicker and small bits of debris to fall from the ceiling.

And yet, in a moment of illogical thinking, M4V15 decides to eat the noodles, to enjoy them.

RE: The Barbarians of Tokyo
Lucas, some notes:

1. Largely thoughtful work here, though a bit rough in places. My overall criticism is the way you've constructed your universe: it fits too conveniently with how you want the world to operate. Science fiction attempts to do the opposite — create an oppressive world that is incongruous with the humans that move through it. Though I will say that this is my general issue with all of

442

Margo's stories too. You two certainly share that.

2. Where you diverge from Margo is the ending. Her work is so much more . . . cynical? The only thing her characters ever come to realize is that humanity is doomed or irredeemable. I like that your central character learns something. There's an optimism here that you don't see from Margo, the idea that people can become more than who they are.

3. Margo's work was always pretty on the nose, but naming the empress M4V15 might give her a run for her money.

4. I did get your first email, and after I read it, I didn't feel the need to respond. I have a policy about not answering messages from exes, especially when I can tell they've been drinking. (I've decided recently that while we were never officially dating, we were together long enough to now qualify as exes.) But I did want to say that I appreciated your apology, even if it was kind of a non-apology. I hope you are well,

and that everything is as it should be on the other side of the world.

RE:RE: The Barbarians of Tokyo
Thank you for the notes. I am well and things are good here. I've started a weird, new life, even if I can't stop thinking about the old one. During the day, I wander the streets of Tokyo, feeling like a stranger in a strange land. Everyone looks like me, but I'm still a foreigner. The only places that feel comfortable are bars, because at least there, I know what everyone is there to do.

I'm sorry I said that I'm glad Margo never met you. I have no idea why I did that. I'd take it back if I could. And since I can't, all I can do is ask for your forgiveness.

RE:RE:RE: The Barbarians of Tokyo
The apology isn't necessary, really. I've thought a lot about this — and you, and us — and I've realized that it is a very human thing to try and solve things, even when we know they can't be solved. We try so hard to fix things, to do everything in our power to make things better, when in reality, all we need to do

444

is trust that time and space sort every-thing out.

So, Lucas, I guess that's what I'm ask-ing you for: time and space.

RE:RE:RE:RE: The Barbarians of Tokyo
Right, but how much time and space does it take?

At Crawlspace, the music was loud, the air suffocated by cigarette smoke, courtesy of two patrons who had smoked an entire pack in just under an hour. They'd picked the music, too, and they righteously head-banged in unison at the guitar solo's every squeal. Though it had been empty earlier, it turned into a surprisingly busy evening — Friday night, I supposed, though I'd lost any sense of the week. People were packed into every square inch, so tightly that it felt less like a bar and more like the subway at rush hour, everyone headed to the same destination.

I'd secured one of the few seats at the bar, where I'd been camping out since it opened that day. I was putting back whiskeys and looking at my phone. Given that Tokyo was thirteen hours ahead of New York, Jill was likely asleep right now. Did I expect her to write me in the middle of the night? She might not respond at all — we might not speak for a long time, or maybe never again. These were all reasonable possibilities, and I wouldn't blame her. But that didn't stop me from refreshing my inbox for the millionth time, awaiting her reply.

ACKNOWLEDGMENTS

There are a few things included in this book that I did not write myself: the parts of the FAQ on death come from actual Facebook copy; the Achievable Threats of Violence slides are pulled from internal Facebook policies, leaked and published in a report by *The Guardian;* the Craigslist casual encounters are real posts — the first three I found (so shout-out to the guys with the fetish for Asian women), and the blacklist comes from a freely available text file put together by a Christian group, so thanks to them for summoning all the racial slurs they could think of.

I am so grateful to the three editors on this book — Chris Jackson, Victory Matsui, and Emi Ikkanda — for all their smart and careful work, and thanks to the team at One World. Without them, this would be a bunch of weird ideas in a Google Doc. Now it's a bunch of weird ideas in a book.

Thanks to Vivian Lee and Morgan Parker, who read the first semblance of this novel before it was anything. I'm also grateful to Chloé Cooper Jones and Brendan Klinkenberg for early reads. And special thanks to Soleil Ho for the Japanese at the end of the book. (Only I would entrust this responsibility to a Viet.)

I wouldn't be anywhere without my family — Mom, Dad, Jon, Pilar, and Olivia. Big thanks to my colleagues past and present at *GQ* and *The Verge.* Also, shout-out to all my strange, intimate friends in Dark Social.

And to Naomi, who makes everything feel possible.

ABOUT THE AUTHOR

Kevin Nguyen is the features editor at *The Verge* and was previously a senior editor at *GQ.* He lives in Brooklyn, New York.

The employees of Thorndike Press hope you have enjoyed this Large Print book. All our Thorndike, Wheeler, and Kennebec Large Print titles are designed for easy reading, and all our books are made to last. Other Thorndike Press Large Print books are available at your library, through selected bookstores, or directly from us.

For information about titles, please call:
(800) 223-1244

or visit our website at:
gale.com/thorndike

To share your comments, please write:
Publisher
Thorndike Press
10 Water St., Suite 310
Waterville, ME 04901